THE
GIRL
IN THE
WINDOW

BOOKS BY A J MCDINE

THE
GIRL
IN THE
WINDOW

A J MCDINE

bookouture

Published by Bookouture in 2025

An imprint of Storyfire Ltd.
Carmelite House
50 Victoria Embankment
London EC4Y 0DZ

www.bookouture.com

The authorised representative in the EEA is Hachette Ireland
8 Castlecourt Centre
Dublin 15 D15 XTP3
Ireland
(email: info@hbgi.ie)

ISBN: 978-1-80550-294-4
eBook ISBN: 978-1-80550-293-7

PROLOGUE

If I'd known what would happen when I first glimpsed her through the window, would I have still done what I did?

Maybe.

Probably.

I was transfixed, because it was like gazing into a mirror. She had my wide-spaced, dark-brown eyes. My wavy chestnut hair. My scattering of freckles across the bridge of her nose.

I told myself I just wanted to meet her. To see if the resemblance was real. But I was lying to myself, to us both. I wanted her life. I sure as hell wanted out of mine.

Throw a stone in a pond and the ripples will reach far and wide. Who could have predicted that our meeting would have such far-reaching consequences?

Such *deadly* consequences.

PART ONE

1

LAURA

It was supposed to be the perfect holiday. Two weeks in a cosy cottage in a ridiculously pretty Cornish fishing village with the man I love. A holiday I've looked forward to for months. Me and Vinnie. No work, no responsibilities, just long walks, pub lunches, open fires and early nights.

Instead, I am alone as I drive along the tiny lanes towards Porthmerryn with an almost reckless abandon, each bend in the road a game of Russian roulette. Will I meet a cyclist? A tractor? A cliff edge? It is a game, one I don't care if I win or lose, because nothing matters. Not any more. Not since I found out my fiancé was cheating on me.

As the countryside flashes past, my tears finally dry, though my throat still aches like a bad case of tonsillitis. Beatrice, my elderly VW Beetle, judders as I clip a pothole, and the jolt is enough to pull my thoughts away from Vinnie to more pressing matters: the need to find Gull Cottage so I can lick my wounds in private.

Porthmerryn's streets are narrow and there's no parking at the cottage, so I find a space in the car park at the edge of the village. Once I've bought a ticket, I lug my case from the back seat and set off down the hill, glad to stretch my legs after the six-hour journey from Kent.

My gaze switches from left to right as I march down the ever-narrowing cobbled lanes towards the harbour, pulling my case behind me. Little seems to have changed since I was last here, twenty-five years ago. Whitewashed cottages with brightly painted front doors are tucked neatly into the narrow valley that cuts through jagged cliffs to the sea. Above, seagulls ride the thermals, screeching blue murder. I fill my lungs with briny air and quicken my pace.

When Vinnie suggested we book a cottage in Cornwall, the lure of Porthmerryn was too strong to resist. I haven't been back since I was eleven, our last family holiday before Dad left. Mum wanted a fortnight in Spain, but the budget only stretched to a mobile home at Porthmerryn's one and only caravan park. Her face had fallen when she clapped eyes on our accommodation's faded candlewick bedspreads, tacky teak furniture and cheap aluminium windows, but even she was won over by Porthmerryn's quaint, winding streets and the stunning coves dotted along the coastal path in each direction.

We spent our holiday crabbing on the harbour arm and bodyboarding in the finger-numbing cold of the Atlantic. Days measured in Cornish pasties and ice creams, sandy sandwiches and sandcastles.

It's easy to look back with rose-tinted nostalgia, to forget it wasn't all flip-flops and fun. It rained. I got bored. Mum and Dad bickered, little things sparking the same old rows – Dad leaving a used teabag on the draining board or the loo seat up – and before you knew it, old slights and resentments bubbled to the surface, the arguments going round and round, only to end up back where they started.

That holiday was the defining moment of my childhood: the beginning of the end of my safe and familiar little life. Before my parents' marriage crashed and burned and my unshakeable faith in my father was left in tatters. Not that I knew it then, of course, though the clues were there if you looked hard enough.

I pass a small boutique and a fancy-looking café whose glossy black fascia looks newly painted. They are both closed and shuttered, hardly surprising since it's gone half five on a chilly October evening, and dusk is just around the corner.

Out of the corner of one eye, I catch my reflection in a mirror in a gift shop window. I pause, curious to see just how blotchy and crumpled I look. With a start, I realise it's not a mirror at all, but a black and white photo of a woman in side profile on a windswept beach.

I stop, cursing roundly as the edge of my case clips my shin. I study the photo for a moment, then carry on my way. The woman and I might share a passing resemblance, but that's as far as it goes.

Which is why I'm surprised by the shiver that runs down my spine, as if someone has just walked over my grave.

* * *

Gull Cottage is just as pretty as the pictures on the cottage rental website. With plants in wicker baskets scattered around and driftwood mirrors and old nautical maps on the white-washed walls, it's the epitome of seaside chic. It's an upside-down house with the bedroom and bathroom on street level and the open-plan living area upstairs to make the most of the harbour views.

The bedroom has a king-size bed on which cushions and throws in soft greys and ocean blues have been artfully arranged. The furniture is mismatched and quirky, the accessories – wooden lantern table lamps, gingham bunting, a beach hut doorstop – on the tasteful side of cutesy. I dump my suitcase at the end of the bed, poke my head around the bathroom door

– walk-in rainfall shower, his and hers basins and Neal's Yard toiletries – then explore upstairs.

The open-plan living area on the first floor comprises a small kitchen, a round dining table with two chairs and an L-shaped sofa facing a small wood-burning stove and a flat-screen television. The place has everything I could possibly need for a perfect romantic getaway.

Everything except Vinnie.

My eyes fill with tears as the shock of his betrayal hits me afresh. I dash them away with the back of my hand and run myself a glass of water from the tap, drinking it in snotty, hiccupping gulps. I picture him as I stormed out of the flat, guilt written all over his face, each excuse sounding lamer than the last. Apologies falling like autumn leaves. Half-hearted attempts to talk me into staying.

It's not what you think.

I'm sorry.

I love you.

All pointless, because by then it was already too late.

The chime of a clock on the mantel above the wood-burner is a welcome distraction and I turn my thoughts to my immediate priority: food and drink. I haven't eaten since grabbing a service station sandwich just before noon, and although there's a pint of milk in the fridge and home-made shortbread, a jar of honey and some tea and coffee in the welcome basket, I need something for dinner. And wine. Lots of wine.

I grab my purse and the house keys and clatter down the wooden stairs to the front door, glad I checked that the little corner shop on the harbour is open till seven on a Saturday.

The quayside is as deserted as the rest of the village, the buttery light from the shop like the glow of a lighthouse in the gloom. I pick up eggs, mushrooms, a crusty loaf, a slab of cheese and a bottle of Pinot. The teenage girl behind the counter, who wasn't even born when I used to spend my pocket money here on pear drops and aniseed balls, barely looks up from her phone as she rings up the items.

She's handing me a receipt when the door clicks open and a slight woman walks in, bringing a blast of cold air with her. She's wrapped up in a padded coat, a hand-knitted scarf wound round her neck. A matching woollen hat is pulled down so low over her forehead it's hard to tell her age. She catches my eye and does a double-take.

'Marcus let you out, has he?'

Her Irish accent takes me by surprise. I stare at her, perplexed, wondering who the hell Marcus is, but before I can say anything, she slaps a couple of twenty-pound notes on the counter, making the teenage girl jump.

'You can tell Reg we're square, so he can stop hassling me.' She pulls another note from her pocket. 'And I'll have a packet of Marlboro Red while you're at it.' She's unwrapped the cellophane before the girl has handed over her change.

Patting her pockets for a lighter, the woman turns to leave, then stops beside me and touches my arm, her voice softening. 'You watch yourself, won't you, lovely?' and before I can reply, she's gone.

2

LAURA

The woman's words ring in my ears as I leave the shop and wander down to the harbour. *You watch yourself, won't you?* It sounded uncannily like a warning. And what did she mean about Marcus letting me out? The only Marcus I can think of is a skinny kid from primary school whose prominent front teeth and geeky glasses made him a target for the class bullies, but he moved schools in Year 3 and I haven't seen him since.

Even though I tell myself the woman has clearly mistaken me for someone else, the encounter has still unsettled me, and the thought of going back to an empty cottage, no matter how cosy, holds little appeal.

I gaze around the small harbour. The tide is in and a handful of fishing and pleasure boats bob about in the choppy water. A solitary angler perches in a fold-up chair on the harbour arm, a rod in his hands, in the exact same spot Dad and I used to spend many a happy hour crabbing. The lifeboat station's still here, but the old chandlery is now an upmarket seafood restaurant called Harbour Lights. Across the way is The Ship Inn. Dad took me there once. I had a Coke and a packet of dry-roasted peanuts, which I'd considered the height of sophistication. As I watch, the door of the pub opens and a couple spill out. Behind them, I catch the sound of chatter and the smell of vinegar. My stomach clenches in hunger and my mind is made up. Moments later I'm in the pub ordering plaice and chips and a pint of lager from a ruddy-faced man with a broad Cornish accent.

I carry my pint to a table in the snug and check out my surroundings. The pub has had a facelift. Gone are the swirly carpets and nicotine-stained Anaglypta wallpaper I remember. The original flagstone floor has been restored and the walls are painted a tasteful deep blue above the oak panelling. There are tealights on the tables and fairy lights strung along the low beams. A fire crackles in the inglenook fireplace and pewter mugs swing on hooks behind the bar. But my attention is caught by a series of framed black and white photos that line the walls. The one behind my table is a dramatic view of Merryn Cove, the nearest beach to Porthmerryn. In the photo, waves hurl themselves against the rocks, white foam exploding into the darkening sky. Another picture shows a circle of wild swimmers in the sea, each hugging a buoyancy aid. There's a portrait of a farmer, his face as rumpled as the hessian sack in his hand, and another landscape: this one, the ruins of an old tin mine, stark against a stormy sky. They have the same vibe as the picture I saw through the gift shop window, the one of the woman who looked a bit like me.

My reverie is broken by the ping of my phone and I'm checking the screen before I can stop myself. It's a text from Vinnie.

Babe, please don't let this misunderstanding be the end of us. I love you. V xx

Misunderstanding? I snort so loudly the couple at the next table glance up from their moules marinière.

The phone pings again.

At least let me know you arrived OK. I've been going out of my mind xx

My disbelief turns to anger. How dare he play the concerned fiancé after what he did? Perhaps I shouldn't be surprised. It's yet more evidence he's a consummate liar, as if I needed it.

Alongside the anger there's a degree of vindication. I always knew the four-year age gap between us would be a problem. I was thirty-one and Vinnie twenty-seven when he took over as practice manager at the vet surgery where I work as a vet nurse. All the nurses harboured a secret crush on him except me. Loud and outgoing, he was like a Labrador puppy, exuberant and eager to please. The first time he asked me out, I thought it was a wind-up. The third time he asked, I relented. He took me to the zoo, then, as we walked back to his car, he asked me back to his flat.

'Is that a good idea?'

He'd frowned. 'Why wouldn't it be?'

'The fact that we work together, for starters. What happens when it all goes pear-shaped? It'll be so awkward.'

'You say it like it's inevitable. I didn't have you down as a pessimist.'

'Realist,' I countered. 'And you're so much younger than me. You should be playing the field, not settling down with an older woman.'

'I asked you in for a drink, not to move in with me,' he said mildly, a mischievous glint in his eye. 'And you're not *that* old.'

I rolled my eyes in despair.

'Anyway, it won't go pear-shaped,' he said with authority, as he opened the car door for me. 'I have a good feeling about this.

Once you get to know me better, you'll come to understand that where love is concerned, I'm always right.'

'If you say so,' I huffed, but conceded that a quick drink would be a nice way to round off the day. The rest, as they say, is history. I gave notice on my house share and moved in with him a month later.

Five years on, memories slam into each other like cars in a motorway pile-up. The time Vinnie whisked me to Amsterdam because he knew I'd always wanted to visit the Anne Frank House. The surprise party he organised for my thirty-fifth birthday. The way he always set his alarm ten minutes early on frosty mornings so he could scrape the ice off Beatrice's windscreen. Foot rubs after a manic day at work. Cups of tea in bed, hot-water bottles and painkillers when I was sick.

It's impossible to reconcile this Vinnie, *my* Vinnie, with the stranger who has betrayed me. But that's the thing about liars, isn't it? By definition, you can't trust a word they say.

* * *

My fish and chips arrive, and even though my appetite has deserted me, I eat them anyway, mindlessly chewing until the plate is empty. I push my chair back and go in search of the toilets, which are down a long corridor at the back of the pub. Normally, the sign – men to the left because women are always right – would make me chuckle. Not today.

In the ladies, I stare at my woebegone reflection. My face is pale and my hair needs a wash. Dark shadows circle my eyes, which are puffy and red-rimmed, and my forehead appears set in a permanent frown. When I was little my nan always used to warn me my face would stick if the wind changed. She was right, because I can't imagine ever smiling again.

There are more black and white photos on the back wall of the pub, and I examine each one, hoping they'll take my mind off Vinnie. These are all portraits, but they are so much more than that: each is a story, a window into other people's lives. A trio of fishermen at sea, hauling a net of shimmering fish onto the deck of their boat. A craggy farmer leaning on a shepherd's crook, his Border collie panting at his feet. A cherubic-faced toddler peering into a rock pool. A woman standing on top of the cliffs above Merryn Cove...

I stop in my tracks. It's the same brown-haired woman whose side profile I saw in the photo in the gift shop window. This time she is staring straight at the camera, her hands in her pockets and her expression inscrutable. Fear floods my body, first hot, then icy cold. The face I am staring into is my own. But how can it be? The last time I set foot in Cornwall, I was a child. I reach out, my fingers trembling as they touch the glass. My head spins.

No. This isn't possible.

3

LAURA

I stare at the photo until my vision blurs, examining every centimetre as if my life depends on it. The woman – because it can't be me, it *can't* be – is slim with an oval face, high cheekbones and dark, almond-shaped eyes. Like me, she has wavy, dark hair, though mine is long and hers falls to just below her shoulders. She is wearing white, wide-legged linen trousers, a floaty blouse over a simple vest top and leather thong sandals, a delicate chain around her neck. Behind her, cliffs plunge down to the cove below. To her left, the coastal path threads through a tunnel of gorse towards Porthmerryn. I know the spot; have, in fact, stood just where she is standing, wiry grass tickling my bare feet and Mum urging me to stay away from the edge. But that was twenty-five years ago, when I was eleven.

I close my eyes and give my head a little shake, because a simple explanation would be that I'm dreaming, and any minute now the alarm will go off and I'll wake up in bed with Vinnie, relieved that the last twenty-four hours were nothing more than a nightmare.

Even before I open my eyes, I realise that's not going to happen, because this is no dream. Vinnie and I are over, I'm in

Porthmerryn alone, and I'm staring at my own face in a photo I know has never been taken.

'Talented guy, isn't he?' someone says, and my heart leaps into my mouth as I spin round to see the blonde woman who was eating moules marinière on the table next to mine. She stands beside me, admiring the photo, then frowns, her gaze tracking from the woman on the cliffs to me. Her mouth falls open. 'OMG, it's you, isn't it?'

I stare at her in silence, unsure what to say, because she has just crushed any hopes I'd had that the likeness was in my head. Clearly, she can see it too.

'My husband wants to buy the one of the harbour, but they're not cheap, are they? Five hundred quid, and they're not even colour!'

I click my tongue because I seem to have lost the power of speech.

'He says it'd be an investment because it's a limited print, and this Marcus Adams guy' – she stabs at some initials on the corner of the mount with a scarlet fingernail – 'is the Banksy of the photographic world. But I said no way. I'd rather put the money towards a new kitchen.'

I peer at the initials. MA. Marcus Adams. My stomach somersaults as I remember the woman in the corner shop and her look of recognition. *Marcus let you out, has he?*

The walls of the narrow corridor seem to close in on me, making it impossible to breathe.

'Sorry,' I say, pushing past the blonde woman, desperate to grab my coat and bag and get out of the pub, trying to ignore the heat of her gaze as I scurry away.

The landlord has disappeared when I go up to the bar to pay, and I'm served by a lanky boy who asks if I enjoyed my meal. I tell him it was delicious, then pause.

'I was admiring the black and white photos. Is the photographer local?'

'You're asking the wrong person. I only started here last week.' The boy hands me the card reader and I press my bank card against it till it beeps.

'Would the landlord know?'

'He's captain of the pub darts team and they've got a match in Penzance tonight. He won't be back till closing time, I'm afraid.'

'Don't worry.' I slip the card back into my purse and am about to thank him and leave when an elderly man nursing a pint of stout at the bar looks up from his drink.

'That Marcus Adams you're asking 'bout?'

I nod.

'I've known him since he was this big.' The man touches his knee.

'Where would I find him?'

The old man takes a long draught of his pint, then wipes his top lip on his sleeve. 'There's a gallery in St Ives that shows his work. The Seaforth. They'll be able to point you in the right direction.' He stares at me through narrowed eyes. 'If that's what you want.'

He looks as if he's about to say something else, and I hold my breath. Instead, he grunts and turns back to his pint.

Clearly having been dismissed, I swallow a sigh and head back out into the night.

* * *

Gull Cottage feels chilly and I light the wood-burner before pouring myself a large glass of Pinot and settling on the sofa with my phone to google Marcus Adams. My fingers tap impatiently on my thigh as I wait for the results to load. I'm expecting the search engine to spit out a deluge of links, so I'm surprised when it returns just a single page. Adams, it appears, doesn't have a website, nor does he have social media profiles.

I click on a news article from the *Guardian*'s culture section from five years ago. The only photos accompanying the piece are three of his distinctive landscapes. Intrigued, I start to read.

Few figures in the world of photography are as elusive as Marcus Adams. For two decades, his work has captured the raw beauty of Cornwall's people and landscapes, earning him a reputation as one of the UK's most gifted photographers. But unlike his peers, he shuns social media and avoids the art glitterati.

Jasper Trelawney, close friend and owner of The Seaforth Gallery in St Ives, said: 'Marcus believes true art doesn't need a sales pitch or likes on an Instagram post. It doesn't chase algorithms or airtime. It simply exists to be seen – or not seen.'

Adams's stance has only deepened his mystique and the appetite for his introspective, haunting style has never been greater.

Despite the demand for his work, exhibitions are rare, often announced without fanfare and held in low-key venues near his Cornish home.

Does he keep such a low profile to protect his creativity or to snub the industry that made him famous?

We may never know. He hasn't given an interview since his 2005 debut.

I growl with frustration, no closer to finding out anything useful about Marcus Adams, let alone discovering who the woman in the photo is. I scroll through the half a dozen other entries, gleaning little fresh information until I find a Q&A published by Glasgow School of Art in 2004 – the only interview he seems to have given.

Today we're in conversation with Cornish photographer and

former student Marcus Adams, whose black and white photos are taking the art world by storm.

The world has gone digital, yet you still use film. Why?

I sold all my digital equipment the day a model asked me to edit out her butterfly tattoo. I refused and she burst into tears. These days it's just me, my Canon SLR camera, a roll of film and a darkroom. I'm old-school.

Where is your darkroom?

In the cellar at home. When I walk down the stairs and close the door it's as though I'm escaping from the world. For me, developing film, the chemical process of it, is a mindful experience.

Why do you think film has the edge over digital?

Shooting on film demands maximum focus. You have to think about every single frame. To excel, you need to be technically proficient in the whole process. A darkroom print has a depth that doesn't exist in digital prints.

You are best known for your black and white portrait and landscape photography. Why don't you shoot in colour?

I see in black and white. I shoot in black and white. I have no interest in colour nor shades of grey.

I refill my glass and consider what I have learnt. There's no getting away from it. Marcus Adams may be a talented photographer but he also sounds like a pretentious arse with an ego the size of Australia.

I try to picture the woman in the photo, but the memory of her is already fading, the image as slippery as a fish, refusing to take shape in my mind. All I'm left with is an impression, like a negative image on one of Marcus Adams's rolls of film.

I tell myself I must have been mistaken, that after staring at my own reflection in the bathroom mirror I was simply projecting my face onto hers. But even as I think this, I remember the woman in the corner shop and the blonde woman with the scarlet nails. Two strangers who also mistook me for the mystery woman.

It's too much of a coincidence. The woman in the photo may not be me, but the resemblance is uncanny. The need to know who she is gnaws at my insides, like an itch that won't go away. I make up my mind. I will find her while I am here in Porthmerryn, whatever it takes.

4

LAURA

I wake just after seven and once I've showered and had breakfast, I plug the address of The Seaforth Gallery into my phone. It's just over sixteen miles to St Ives, and Google Maps says the journey will take close to forty minutes.

I drain the last of my coffee and head out of the cottage and up the hill to the car park. Beatrice has caught the eye of a man parked a couple of spaces along, and as I unlock the driver's door, he beams at me.

'Just been admiring your wheels. Me mam had one back in the day. Brings back memories, it does. Let me guess: is it the seventy-six model?'

'Close,' I tell him. 'Seventy-eight.'

'Not for sale, is it?' he asks, running his hand along the Beetle's postbox-red paintwork almost reverentially.

''Fraid not.' Vinnie was always on at me to flog Beatrice and buy what he called a 'decent set of wheels' but she is so much more to me than a way of getting from A to B. Yes, she's a money pit, and keeping her running is virtually a full-time job, but she's worth the trouble. She gives me joy, and how many cars do that?

The man pats the bonnet. 'Ah, well, worth a try. You drive safe now.'

I let myself into the car and give the man a wave as I pull away. I'm surprised to find the roads to St Ives comfortingly familiar, even though I haven't been this way for twenty-five years. The route cuts across Cornwall from south coast to north, through rolling countryside, fields dotted with sheep and sleepy villages. Every now and then, the view opens up to reveal glimpses of the turquoise sea. I stop to refuel at the same garage Dad always did and, as a nod to the old days, buy a tin of the travel sweets he always kept in the glove compartment of the family saloon. I pass the farm shop Mum loved to linger in and the lay-by we pulled into that time I was carsick. There are memories around every corner.

I park at St Erth Station and catch the train to St Ives, sitting opposite a woman about my age with twins in a double buggy, one dressed in blue dungarees, the other in pink. They must be about eighteen months old.

The woman hands the toddlers a packet of chocolate buttons each and scrolls through her phone while I stare out of the window, trying to ignore the sharp tug of longing deep inside me. I'd always been ambivalent about having children until my thirty-fifth birthday, when my biological clock started ticking, right on cue. Suddenly, seeing friends with babies or kids at the park filled me with an almost visceral yearning to be a mum.

Vinnie had taken some persuasion, finally agreeing we would start trying for a family when we got back from Cornwall.

'Let's have one last holiday together, just the two of us,' he said.

Buoyed by the promise of motherhood, I happily agreed. But as the train chugs into St Ives Station, it hits me that I might not get another chance. Not just at motherhood, but at the life I always imagined we'd have. The rough and tumble of a chaotic but happy home filled with kids. Saturday-morning swimming lessons and picnics at the beach. Playdates and parents' evenings. Teasing and laughter.

The kind of childhood I missed out on, but one I'd always imagined for my own family.

I lean my forehead against the train window as the countryside speeds by. Did Vinnie not realise that by cheating on me, he hasn't just rewritten my past, he's destroyed my future too?

* * *

At just before ten o'clock on a Sunday morning in mid-October, St Ives is probably as quiet as it ever gets. Even so, I still have to weave through knots of tourists to reach the seafront. The tide is out, exposing a wide, sandy beach. People amble along, ice creams in their hands, seemingly oblivious to the beady-eyed seagulls waiting for an opportunity to dive. The Seaforth Gallery sits between a pasty shop and a wine bar, a closed sign hanging inside the door. I rattle the handle anyway, then peer through the window, my pulse quickening when I spot a black and white print on the wall. It's a shot of a sinewy guy in a wetsuit, a surfboard under one arm and waves crashing on the beach behind him. A classic Marcus Adams portrait. I double-check the opening hours – ten till four Monday to Sunday – then pop into the pasty shop and order a takeaway flat white while I wait for the place to open.

'Come far?' the woman behind the counter asks.

'Kent, though I'm staying in Porthmerryn. I was hoping to look round the gallery next door, but it's closed.'

She tuts. 'That'll be Jasper's new girl. Her timekeeping's terrible. Give her half an hour and she should be there.'

I thank the woman, head across the road and sit on one of

the benches overlooking the harbour. My phone chirrups with another text from Vinnie, begging me to call.

My fingers fly over the keypad.

Stop contacting me, Vinnie. I mean it. I never want to hear from you again.

I press send before I change my mind.

I close my eyes, my hands wrapped around the takeaway cup, Marcus Adams and the woman in the photo temporarily forgotten as I replay the moment I found out Vinnie was cheating on me.

It was my last appointment before lunch on Friday and I was carrying out a health check on Princess Tallulah, an overweight Pomeranian with borderline diabetes.

I coaxed Tallulah onto the scales, watched closely by her owner, Kiara Newson-Price, an overprotective dog mum who wasn't helping the situation because she insisted on carrying the Pomeranian everywhere.

'She's four and a half kilograms, which is' – I checked Tallulah's records and stifled a grimace – 'actually eight hundred grams more than she weighed last time. We need to get her weight under control if we can, Kiara, because diabetes is something we really want to avoid. How's the diet going?'

'I did try that food you recommended but Tally doesn't like it, so we've gone back to her favourite.'

'And the new exercise regime?' I asked, not holding out much hope. Tallulah eyed me balefully. I summoned a smile. 'Let's try again, shall we? Clean slate? You know what they say: "Insanity is doing the same thing over and over again and expecting different results." The power to make a change is in your hands.' I paused for dramatic effect. 'I'd like Tallulah to have lost five hundred grams when I next see you.'

Pleased with my pep talk, I handed the Pomeranian's lead

back to Kiara. She was halfway out of the door when she stopped and turned.

'Oh, I forgot to say! I bumped into Vinnie outside Casa Rossa on my way over. He was meeting his sister for lunch.'

It took a second for her words to sink in. 'Sorry,' I checked. 'You just saw Vinnie at Casa Rossa?'

'With his sister,' Kiara agreed. 'Pretty little thing, isn't she?'

I closed down my expression to hide my shock, because Vinnie doesn't have a sister. He's an only child. And as far as I knew, he'd taken the day off to pack for our holiday.

'He didn't look too pleased to see me, actually,' Kiara said with a frown. 'Probably thought I was going to chase him about Tally's insurance claim.'

'Probably,' I managed. 'He introduced you to his sister, did he?'

'Actually, Tammy introduced herself.' Kiara's perfectly symmetrical nose wrinkled. 'There's not much of a family resemblance, is there?'

'She takes after their mum's side of the family. Vinnie's the spit of his dad,' I'd said, wracking my brains. The only Tammy I knew was one of the pharmaceutical sales reps who was always popping into the surgery trying to sell new drugs and medical equipment. Blonde and bubbly, she flirted outrageously with the vets. Vinnie too, come to think of it.

Aware that Kiara was watching me, I summoned a smile.

'Now, don't forget, the power to make a change is in your hands. I'll see you in a couple of months, OK?'

I left the surgery on the dot of one, telling myself there was nothing to worry about as I scurried up the high street towards Casa Rossa, a chichi wine bar at the top end of town where a glass of red set you back twelve quid. There would be a simple explanation. Tammy probably took clients out to lunch all the time, a perk of the job.

Before I knew it, I was outside the restaurant. Feeling a bit foolish, I pressed my face against the window and looked inside. It took a moment to locate my fiancé because he was sitting in the far corner with his back to me. Opposite him, Tammy was talking, her hands waving expansively. She would be extolling the virtues of the latest wonder drug for diabetic cats or arthritic dogs, I thought, relief making my legs weak. I would go in and say hello, maybe even join them for a quick drink if there was time.

I was reaching for the door when Tammy took Vinnie's hand and kissed it, and the action was so familiar, so *intimate*, it was as if someone had forced their fist through my ribcage and yanked out my still-beating heart.

At that moment, Tammy looked up and we locked eyes. She must have said something to Vinnie because he spun round and saw me staring at them in horror. He pushed his chair back and jumped to his feet and that's when I knew we were over.

A seagull lands in front of me in a flurry of feathers and pecks at a sweet wrapper by my feet. Momentarily, I forget where I am. Then it comes back to me in a rush. I have come to St Ives to find out about the elusive photographer who took a photo of a woman who looks just like me.

I glance over my shoulder. A girl is setting up an A-board on the pavement outside the gallery. I stand stiffly and drop my coffee cup into the nearest bin, then cross the road in search of answers. Anything to stop me stewing about Vinnie and his new flame.

5

LAURA

The girl looks up from the A-board as I hover on the pavement outside the gallery.

'Please, come in,' she says, holding the door open for me, and I step inside. 'Were you looking for anything in particular?'

I clear my throat. 'Someone said you sometimes have Marcus Adams's work on show. I'm a bit of a fan.'

I search her face for even the smallest flicker of recognition, but her smile is guileless. 'We do. In fact, there's one right behind you.' She points to the surfer guy, who is even more ripped up close. Vinnie joined a gym back in the summer, claiming he was training for Hyrox, and I'd believed him, because why wouldn't I? Of course he wasn't training for bloody Hyrox. He wanted to look buff for Tammy.

'This one's already been sold, unfortunately,' the girl says, waving a hand at the red sticker on the bottom right-hand corner of the frame.

'Do you have any more?' I ask, trying to hide my frustration. The possibility that I've come all this way to see one measly picture of a beach bum with dreadlocks and a six-pack is hard to swallow. Perhaps I was naive to assume the entire gallery would be given over to the work of the infamous Marcus Adams.

'Not on show, though Jasper usually keeps a few out the back.'

My ears prick. 'The owner of the gallery?'

The girl nods.

'He and Adams are old friends, I believe?'

'That's right.'

'What's Adams like?'

'I've never actually met him. He hardly ever comes here. He's a bit of a recluse.' Her smile fades and her hand flutters to her neck. 'You're not a journalist, are you?'

'Me?' I laugh. 'No. Why?'

'Jasper will have my guts for garters if he thinks I've been talking to the press about Marcus and I really, *really* need this job.'

'Don't worry, you're safe with me,' I say, though she doesn't seem very reassured. In fact, her hands tremble as she flicks through a catalogue on the counter between us. I change tack. 'Will Jasper be in at all today?'

She glances at a clock on the wall behind her. 'He promised to be here at one so I can go for lunch.'

I pick up one of the business cards from the counter and slip it into my pocket. 'I'll pop back then.'

I kill time wandering aimlessly through the narrow streets of St Ives and at five to one I head back to the gallery, my heart skipping a beat when I see Jasper's assistant hurrying out of the door, her head tucked into her chest. I wait until she's halfway down the street, then let myself in.

The place is empty, and I feel a dart of frustration. Surely the girl wouldn't leave it unlocked and unattended, even if she was only nipping out for a sandwich? As I weigh up whether to wait or come back in half an hour, the sound of shattering glass cuts through the silence, swiftly followed by a volley of expletives.

Moments later, a man appears from a door at the back of the gallery, clutching a dustpan and brush. He is bald, with a neat beard and a short, waxed handlebar moustache. In his sixties, he's wearing a silk cravat over a tweed three-piece suit. I'm in no doubt this man is Jasper Trelawney, the owner of The Seaforth Gallery and a close friend of Marcus Adams.

'For heaven's sake!' he grouses in a plummy voice. 'What on earth possessed the foolish girl to leave a Kit Penhallow original on the cistern? Three hundred pounds – quite literally down the pan!'

He finally looks up and the frown on his face turns into a wide smile.

'Alana!' he cries. 'I wasn't expecting to see you today.'

His greeting sends a shockwave through me. My double has a name. Alana. She isn't a figment of my imagination. She exists. And this man knows her. The realisation rattles me to my core. A dozen questions ping around in my head, but I can't form a single one.

'Alana?' he asks, his face wreathed in concern. 'Are you all right? You've gone white as a sheet. You're not about to faint, are you? Here, let me find you a chair.' He hurries round to the other side of the counter and wheels out an office chair. I flop into it gratefully, because I seem to have lost all strength in my legs. 'That's right. You take the weight off. I'll fetch you a glass of water.' He peers at me. 'Or something stronger?' I shake my head weakly and a look of understanding crosses his features. 'Don't tell me, you're up the duff and the old boy's finally getting a son and heir? How jolly marvellous!'

I shake my head again, trying to process everything.

'Then what is it, m'dear?' He pales too. 'Please tell me you're not sick. Everyone I know seems to be shuffling off this mortal coil. I'm beginning to wonder if I should put my own affairs in order in case I'm next.'

'It's not that,' I mumble.

'Then what in heaven's name is the matter?'

I look him in the eye. 'I'm not Alana.'

6

LAURA

Jasper Trelawney throws his head back and guffaws.

'Of course you're Alana,' he says when he finally stops laughing.

'I'm really not,' I assure him.

'Then who are you?'

'My name's Laura Jarvis. I'm staying in Porthmerryn, but I'm actually from Kent.'

'Kent,' he repeats with pursed lips, as if the very idea is disdainful to him.

'Margate,' I add. 'It's no St Ives, but it's very arty these days.'

'I'll take your word for it,' he says archly. 'Though I hear the Turner Contemporary is worth a visit.' He frowns. 'But that's not the point. The point is, why should I believe you? What's to say you haven't been practising an estuary twang for one of those dreadful TikTok pranks? How do I know some ghastly television C-lister isn't about to jump out and yell "Gotcha!" at me? I have no desire to go viral, darling. No desire at all.'

I glance around the room, wondering how to convince him I'm not Alana. Then I remember – I never took my passport out of my bag after a day trip to France in the summer.

'Here,' I say, pulling it out and handing it to him.

He fishes a pair of reading glasses from the top pocket of his tweed waistcoat and slips them on, mouthing silently to himself as he scans my details. He lingers over my passport photo. It was taken a couple of years ago. My hair is tied back and I'm trying not to laugh at Vinnie, who was clowning around outside the photo booth, much to the amusement of a small boy and his mum waiting to have their pictures taken.

'Do you believe me now?'

He frowns, then looks up. 'I suppose I do.' He studies my face and I try hard not to fidget under his gaze. 'Well, I never,' he says, almost to himself. 'The likeness is uncanny.' He hands me my passport and crosses the gallery, locking the door and turning the open sign to closed.

'Come with,' he commands, disappearing into a room at the back of the gallery. A small voice in my head whispers, *Is this a good idea? The man could be a serial killer for all you know.* But I dismiss the thought immediately. I may have only just met Jasper Trelawney, but instinct tells me he's about as dangerous as a cheese sandwich. Besides, I'm desperate to find out more about my double.

I follow Jasper into a small, square, windowless room. Canvases wrapped in brown paper lean haphazardly against the walls, crates are filled with bubble-wrapped ceramics and stacks of unframed prints are piled high on an old pine table. He beckons me over to a large wooden print rack.

'You know the work of Marcus Adams?'

'I saw some of his photos at The Ship in Porthmerryn last night,' I admit.

Understanding dawns on his face. 'Which is why you're here.'

I nod. 'I saw a photo of a woman who looked like me. I was curious, you know? And an old boy in the pub said you had more of his work.'

'I do indeed.' Jasper flicks through the unframed prints in the rack. By now, Marcus Adams's moody coastlines and intimate portraits are instantly recognisable, even to my untrained eye. 'Ah, here it is,' Jasper says, pulling out a print almost reverentially.

He holds it towards me, and I gasp. The woman is standing in a cobbled street, looking back towards the camera lens. Her hair swings around her face as if she turned at the precise moment Adams clicked the shutter.

'Alana,' Jasper says with more than a hint of pride. 'One of Marcus's finest portraits, I would say. The way he's captured the fluidity of movement. The play of light and shade. The attention to detail.' He studies my face. 'You could be identical twins. The likeness is quite remarkable. I know they say everyone has a doppelgänger somewhere, but to see one with one's own eyes is rather extraordinary.'

I can't tear my eyes away from the photograph. This Alana and I are mirror images of each other, from our high foreheads to the shape of our chins. Jasper is right. The likeness is extraordinary. It is also as freaky as hell.

Jasper pulls a phone from his pocket and taps away. For an awful moment I worry he's calling up Marcus to tell him some blow-in from Kent has waltzed into the gallery pretending to be his favourite model, and I cringe at the thought. But Jasper quickly puts my fears to rest.

'There's a photographer, isn't there, who takes photos of doppelgängers?' He taps some more, then looks up triumphantly, waving his phone in my face. 'That's him. François Brunelle. Canadian chap. Says here he's been photographing identical twins from around the world since 1999. Only – spoiler alert – none of them are actually related.'

He shows me a series of black and white photos of people who look remarkably alike. Some even share identical features despite being of the opposite sex.

'No need to look quite so stricken, old love. It's obviously more common than you think. Though if I came face to face with my double, I dare say I'd need a stiff drink. I'm not sure the world's ready for two of us.' He guffaws again, then pats me on the back. 'I was about to make myself a cup of tea. Care to join me?'

I pull myself together and smile at him. The people in François Brunelle's photos all had a chance to meet each other at their photoshoot. They could ask questions, swap stories, see if they shared the same quirks, the same laugh, the same way of seeing the world. In short, they could satisfy their curiosity. Whereas mine burns like a fever, intense and suffocating. I need to know everything about Alana. Not just because she looks like me, but because thinking about her stops me obsessing about Vinnie, and right now, I'll take any distraction I can get.

'That would be great, thank you.'

'Earl Grey all right? Not sure why I'm asking. It's all I have.'

'Mmm, lovely,' I say, even though Earl Grey tastes like dishwater in my humble opinion. But I'll force down a cup of the stuff if it means I can keep Jasper talking.

We return to the main gallery and he offers me the chair while he perches on the edge of the desk.

'You have such beautiful artwork here,' I say, banking on the fact that the way to his heart is through flattery, pure and simple.

'You're too kind. My artists must take the credit, though I do admit to having a knack for discovering new talent.'

'Did you discover Marcus Adams?'

His chest puffs out. 'Indeed, I did. Of course, I've known him since he was a boy. His father, Alastair, was a well-known landscape artist. I used to show his work too.' Jasper sips his tea thoughtfully. 'Marcus is a chip off the old block, though he would never admit it.'

'He didn't take up painting, like his dad?'

Jasper shakes his head vigorously. 'Marcus and Alastair were estranged. Marcus only moved back to Merryn's Reach when the old man died fifteen years ago.'

I file this away, keeping my expression a study in indifference because I have the distinct feeling Jasper would clam up if he thought I was pumping him for information.

'I make it a point to visit as many graduate exhibitions as I can so I can find the brightest new stars before anyone else does. The trick, you see, is to spot the talent before they know their own worth. And if that sounds rather grubby, then so be it. But I am running a business. A rather successful one, even if I do say so myself.' He pats his stomach expansively.

'Is that how you discovered Marcus, at a graduate exhibition?'

Jasper nods. 'The Glasgow School of Art. As soon as I saw his work I knew the drive had been worth it.'

I raise an eyebrow and Jasper steeples his fingers.

'True talent can't be taught, my dear. Anyone can learn the mechanics of photography, but only the lucky few have that instinctive eye for a shot, a natural feel for light and composition, a way of seeing the world differently. And Marcus had it in spades. Six months after I staged his first exhibition he was featured in a Sunday supplement as one to watch. Not that he ever gave any interviews.' Jasper chuckles. 'Not one for the limelight is our Marcus. But that's all right. It just adds to the air of mystery. I'm happy to handle the media.' He stops himself, then claps his hands together. 'Hark at me, wittering on. I'm sure you have better things to do than listen to the ramblings of an old man.'

'Not at all,' I reassure him. 'It's fascinating. And such a thrill to see my double. I'd buy the print if I could but it's out of my price range. I don't suppose Marcus does greetings cards?'

'Most definitely not.' Jasper grimaces as if I've hurled the worst kind of insult at him, then his face softens. 'You're interested in your doppelgänger, aren't you?'

I don't tell him I'm being eaten alive by my desire to find out everything I can about Alana. I'd sound like a demented stalker. Instead, I shrug carelessly, place my cup and saucer on the counter and wander over to the photo of the ripped surfer guy. 'The people Marcus photographs, they're all from Cornwall, aren't they?'

'They are. It's part of his USP.' Jasper watches me closely. 'You're wondering if your doppelgänger is local?'

'I guess.'

'She is.' He lets a few seconds of silence hang in the air. 'Not originally, mind you, but she is now.'

'Oh?' I will him to elaborate. Eventually, he drops a bombshell that leaves me reeling.

'You didn't realise? But then, why would you? Alana is Marcus's wife.'

7

LAURA

Jasper's revelation that Alana is married to Marcus Adams is my cue to leave. I mutter a goodbye to the gallery owner, making up an excuse about my parking ticket running out, and hurry into the street.

My stomach churns with a heady mix of nerves and excitement. Alana Adams, wife of renowned photographer Marcus Adams and my double, lives here in Cornwall. Normally, I'm not a superstitious person, but this feels like fate. I know it.

I head along the seafront until I'm out of sight of the gallery, find an empty bench and sink onto it. I can't shake the feeling that by coming to St Ives I've set in motion a chain of events in which everything leads to Alana. Breaking up with Vinnie, seeing Alana's photo through the gift shop window, her portrait in the pub. Like a ball gathering momentum as it rolls downhill, the way forwards feels inevitable. Unstoppable. All I can do is hang on and see where it takes me.

At least it stops me thinking about the mess I left behind.

Meeting my doppelgänger might be my destiny, but I have to find her first. Fortunately, the garrulous Jasper Trelawney dropped a golden nugget into our conversation. *Marcus only moved back to Merryn's Reach when the old man died fifteen years ago.* Could Merryn's Reach be the name of a house?

I'm fishing my phone from my pocket when it starts to ring.

Vinnie, I think, my heart lurching, but when I check the screen it's a number I don't recognise. I'm about to ignore it, then curiosity gets the better of me. I answer with a breathless, 'Hello?'

'Laura, it's Sam. Can we talk?'

Sam. My half-sister and the reason my parents' marriage imploded.

I grip the arm of the bench, glancing over my shoulder, as if she might be watching me from a nearby doorway. But the only people behind me are a couple of teenagers eating chips as they amble along the narrow street.

I force air into my lungs.

'When will you get the message? I don't want you contacting me.' My voice rises, grows shaky. 'So take the bloody hint and leave me alone!' I end the call and slump back, my legs like jelly. When my heart rate finally slows, I smooth down my jeans, tuck my hair behind my ears and pick up my phone again, full of resolve. Whatever Sam wants, I don't have the time or the headspace for her right now. I have bigger fish to fry.

With trembling fingers, I type Merryn's Reach into Google and wait for the results to load.

There are a handful of entries for Porthmerryn from Visit Cornwall, Wikipedia and Tripadvisor and I scroll through them impatiently. And then I find what I'm looking for, an article on a house called Merryn's Reach published in the local paper twelve years ago.

> *A fire has destroyed the clifftop home of the late Cornish water-colour artist, Alastair Adams.*
>
> *Merryn's Reach, a grade one listed Edwardian house near Porthmerryn, was being renovated when the blaze broke out in*

*an upstairs bedroom. Firefighters from Penzance and Helston
spent four hours at the scene tackling the fire but were unable
to save the property.*

*A spokesman for Cornwall Fire and Rescue said no one
was in the house when the fire started.*

*'Initial investigations show that the fire began in a first-
floor bedroom and spread to the rest of the house through the
roof beams,' the spokesman said.*

*Gerard Butterworth, chairman of Porthmerryn Historical
Society, said the destruction of the property was a huge loss to
the village.*

*'Alastair Adams bought Merryn's Reach in 1970 and
painted some of his best-known works in his studio in the attic
which overlooked Merryn Cove. The house was a fine example
of turn-of-the-century architecture and will be sadly missed.'*

*A planning application to demolish the building and build
an ultra-modern home in its place was refused by the district
council last year.*

*No one from Alastair Adams's family was available for
comment.*

I rock back in the seat, a grin spreading across my face. I
know – *knew* – the house. We used to pass it when we walked
from our holiday home to Merryn Cove. Set back from the
coastal path, it was almost hidden by tall fence panels and gorse
bushes ten feet deep. But if you were small – and twenty-five
years ago I was – you could creep under the gorse to the fence
and, if you happened upon a gap in the wooden slats, you could
see right into the garden.

I search my memories, picturing the house in my mind's
eye. Aged eleven, I'd been struck by the sheer size of it. It
seemed as big as any of the National Trust properties my
parents used to drag me round. Ivy crept up the red-brick walls
like a marching army of ants and the garden was an overgrown

tumble of wild roses and honeysuckle. But what I remember most is the turret on the right of the house, closest to the sea. It was the kind of turret you read about in fairy tales, and my over-active imagination had been quick to add a spiral staircase, a trapped princess and a wicked stepmother into the mix.

I find myself agreeing with Gerard Butterworth, that losing such a beautiful, historic home was a tragedy. At least no one died. And when Marcus Adams rebuilt the place he would surely have recreated it in its former glory, because a house like that was too beautiful to be simply erased from the coastline.

The sun has disappeared behind clouds and the wind has whipped up, blowing sand across the beach below me. I check the time and jump to my feet. If I catch the next train back to St Erth I'll be able to call by Merryn's Reach before dark.

* * *

It starts to rain as the train pulls into St Erth, the kind of driving rain that soaks you to the skin in seconds. Head down, I bolt across the station car park to Beatrice, yank the door open and slip in behind the steering wheel, averting my gaze from the yellow gerbera on the dashboard because it reminds me of the day Vinnie proposed.

We'd parked up by Joss Bay, a sandy beach backed by chalk cliffs three miles east of Margate, and we were about to set off on a walk when, out of the blue, Vinnie whipped the gerbera from its little vase, popped it between his teeth and dropped to one knee.

'Marry me.'

'What?' I'd said, laughing.

He fumbled in his pocket and produced a black velvet ring box. I took it and flipped it open. A platinum ring sparkled in the weak winter sun. A diamond flanked by two rubies.

'It's beautiful,' I breathed. 'But, Vinnie—'

'I know,' he said, taking the plastic gerbera out of his mouth. 'Marriage is an outdated social construct introduced by misogynists.'

It was true that, especially after a couple of glasses of wine, I would knock the institution passionately and vociferously to anyone who would listen.

'Why would any woman want to walk down the aisle in a frilly white dress, just to be handed from one man to another, like they're a bag of bloody sugar?'

Marriage wasn't a glue; it didn't hold you together. It might offer a tax break or two, but it wasn't a magic bullet or a ticket to happiness. No one knew that better than me. But, as Vinnie gazed at me with love in his eyes, my resolve fell away.

'Come on,' he said, thrusting the ring box under my nose. 'You know you want to.'

And, just like that, I found myself laughing and nodding and saying, 'Yes, yes, I do.'

Vinnie slipped the ring on my finger and as I held up my hand to admire it, he picked me up, whirled me around and told me he loved me with all his heart. Giddy with happiness, I couldn't quite remember why I'd ever been opposed to marriage, social construct or not.

I close the memory down and turn the key in the ignition, my breath fogging the windscreen. The engine misfires once, twice.

'Not now, Bea,' I plead with the car. 'Please, not today.' I wait a few minutes in case I've flooded the engine, but when I try again the Beetle still refuses to start. Exhaling loudly, I grab the latch for the boot and step back out into the rain.

Water runs in rivulets down my neck as I contemplate the engine. Having owned Beatrice for almost twenty years, I know most of her quirks, and if I haven't flooded the engine with the choke, a wet distributor cap seems the likely cause. I yank the cap off, dry it with the hem of my top, blow on it for good measure, then clip it back on.

'Need a hand?'

I look round to see a man in walking gear watching me from under a large umbrella.

'I'm good.' I ease the boot closed. 'Thanks anyway.'

I climb back into the car, the man's eyes on me as I turn the ignition. 'Come on, you old rust bucket,' I mutter. The engine splutters, then grumbles into life. I thrust the gearstick into first, wave at the walker and splash out of the car park towards Porth-merryn and the home of Marcus and Alana Adams.

8

LAURA

Dusk is falling when I reach the outskirts of Porthmerryn. I ignore the signs for the car park and instead follow the narrow lane that leads to the caravan park that was our home for the summer all those years ago. I always thought the lane was a dead end, but when I checked Google Earth on the train, I noticed a fork off it that leads to two more houses. By my reckoning, one of them must be Merryn's Reach.

Beatrice's old springs protest loudly as she bumps down the potholed lane, little more than a dirt track. I slow down as we pass the caravan park, suddenly hit by a wave of nostalgia for those happy, sun-filled days before our family disintegrated.

The place has clearly had a makeover and, curious, I stop to get a better look. Sure enough, the scruffy caravans and mobile homes have been replaced by assorted yurts and shepherds' huts and, according to the tasteful sign outside, there's a well-ness centre and an on-site restaurant serving Mediterranean food. Mum would definitely approve.

I continue along the lane, passing a small, shabby chalet bungalow that sits forlornly behind a broken fence. I'd have assumed the place was abandoned if it wasn't for the powerful-looking motorbike parked on the drive outside. Just past the bungalow there's a lay-by and I pull over, deciding that as it's stopped raining I'll walk the last hundred yards to Merryn's Reach.

I grab my bag and set off along the track, fizzing with anticipation. I'm about to meet my double, and how many people can say they've done that? There were identical twins in my year at secondary school. Daisy and Rosie Thornbury looked the same and dressed the same. They finished each other's sentences. Sometimes even their parents couldn't tell them apart. As an only child, it blew my mind that someone could have such a close connection with another human being and I longed for a sister.

It was only later, when I discovered I wasn't an only child after all, that I realised you should be careful what you wish for.

The track twists right, a panoramic view of the cliff edge and the sea opening up before me. I stop for a moment, trying to still the buzzing in my head. Marcus is a notoriously private man. It's no good turning up on his doorstep overwrought and antsy. He might dismiss me as a wacko and tell me to bugger off. No, I need to play it just right. Friendly yet unassuming. I need to charm the pants off them both. I set off again, practising what to say when Alana opens the door.

I hope you don't mind me dropping by, only I saw the photo of you in the pub and couldn't help but notice we look similar. I thought it would be interesting to meet...

I cringe inwardly because there's no getting away from it – it does sound weird. Briefly, I consider turning round and heading back to the cottage, but then I stop myself. Chances are, this is the only shot I'll ever get to meet my doppelgänger, and I'll always regret it if I don't grab the opportunity with both hands.

Even though I know the rambling Edwardian house was razed to the ground, it's still a shock to see that the thickets of gorse I remember have been grubbed out and the wooden fence panels replaced with a ten-foot-high, white-rendered wall. I stand on tiptoes, but I can't catch even a glimpse of a roof, let alone the top of the turret I admired so much when I was eleven. Perhaps Marcus didn't recreate a faithful facsimile of his childhood home after all.

When I round the corner and reach a pair of imposing wrought-iron gates, it quickly becomes apparent that the new house looks nothing like the original. This Merryn's Reach is a behemoth of a building with floor-to-ceiling windows, a sedum roof and white-rendered walls to match the ones that surround it. A cantilevered terrace the width of the house looks out over the Atlantic and sleek steel balconies jut from the upper floors, defying gravity. It is impressive, imposing and unashamedly ostentatious. A strange choice for someone who shuns the limelight.

The sheer size of the place is intimidating, and I have to force myself to walk the few steps to a keypad on the wall to the right of the gates. I make a split-second decision as I press the call button. I'm not sure my doppelgänger story will cut it.

'Parcel for Marcus Adams,' I chirp.

While I wait for someone to answer, I turn and look back up at the house. It has a shuttered feel to it, like a holiday home locked up for the winter. Perhaps they're away. They probably have a second home somewhere hot like the Canaries, maybe even the Caribbean. Disappointment courses through me. If Alana and her husband spend their winters abroad, I might never get the chance to meet her.

Anxiously, I press the call button a second time, cocking my head towards the intercom. Though it's hard to make anything out above the roar of the waves I'm sure I hear someone breathing.

'Is anyone home?' I say a little desperately.

Nothing.

I throw one final look at the blank-eyed building and that's when I see her. A figure in an upstairs window, silhouetted in the fading light. I lean forwards, squinting. It's definitely a woman; I can tell by the slender taper of her shoulders. She stands completely still, watching me. My heart skitters in my chest. It can only be her. Alana.

But before I can react, she's gone.

I hover by the gate in case she appears at the front door, but after ten minutes and no sign of her, I give up. Shoulders drooping, I tramp back to the car.

For once, Beatrice starts first time, and I execute a clumsy five-point turn on the track and set off for Porthmerryn. As I approach the shabby bungalow I throw caution to the wind and pull into the driveway behind the motorbike. Nothing ventured...

I march up to the peeling front door and rap the knocker, my hand curling around the phone in my pocket like a toddler clutching a comfort blanket. The place screams neglect, and I'm questioning my decision to rock up on the doorstep when the door swings open with a creak.

A woman about Mum's age is framed in the doorway. She is thin, her face gaunt and her collarbones visible through the thin material of her blouse. Over the blouse, she's wearing a navy apron dusted with flour. She wipes her hands, sending another puff of flour into the air. It is then that I realise I recognise her. She's the woman in the corner shop, the one who told me to watch myself.

'You all right, lovely?' she asks in that lilting Irish accent, her forehead creased as she looks nervously over my shoulder.

She thinks I'm Alana. A jolt of pleasure shoots through me. It's another confirmation that my lookalike and I are indistinguishable. For a moment I consider pretending to be her, then change my mind. I want this woman to tell me where Alana is and that's not going to happen if she thinks I am her.

'I'm not Alana. My name's Laura Jarvis,' I begin. 'I've come to see her. I called at the house but she's not in. D'you happen to know where I can find her?'

The woman is staring at me in fascinated horror, her hands clasped to her chest.

'Do you know where Alana is?' I say again, slowly and precisely, in case she's hard of hearing.

'You need to leave!' the woman hisses. 'Go, now, before she sees you.' She crosses herself, leaving floury imprints like police fingerprints on her apron and mutters, 'Sweet Jesus, save us...'

'Save us?' I frown. 'From what?' But she is already stepping back into the house.

'Please!' I cry, and my throat is thick with tears, because suddenly, meeting Alana is the one thing I want more than anything else in the world, and there's a chance this woman knows where she is. 'Don't shut the door in my face. I need your help.'

She falters, and I press harder. 'I'm not a crazy stalker or anything, I promise. I'm just someone who looks like Alana. That's all.'

The woman's gaze darts over my shoulder almost furtively. Satisfied no one's watching, she beckons me into the house. I hesitate for a moment then follow, desperately hoping I'm not making a terrible mistake.

9

LAURA

The woman leads me through a dark and dingy hallway into a kitchen at the back of the house and indicates I take a seat at a small Formica table. She slides a tray of scones into the oven, then fiddles with a kitchen timer shaped like an avocado. Finally, she sits opposite me, her bony hands clasped together once again.

'Who are you?' she asks in a tremulous voice.

'My name's Laura Jarvis. I'm in Porthmerryn on holiday. I saw some of Marcus Adams's photographs when I had fish and chips at the pub last night and there was a girl – a woman – in one who looked like me. I was curious, so I went to St Ives today and spoke to Jasper Trelawney at The Seaforth Gallery—'

'That pompous gobshite,' the woman says dismissively.

'—and he said the woman, my double, was Marcus's wife and they lived at Merryn's Reach. I wanted to come and say hello.'

She looks at me with deep distrust. 'Why would you want to do that?'

For a moment I'm stumped, because even I have to admit that at best it sounds odd, at worst downright sinister. I glance at the ceiling, then back at her. 'Wouldn't you be curious if you found out you had a double? Wouldn't you want to meet her?'

'No, I feckin' wouldn't! Saints preserve us. What kind of eejit would want to meet their fetch?'

'Their what?'

'Fetch,' she replies impatiently. 'In Irish folklore a fetch is a supernatural doppelgänger. To meet your fetch is an omen of death.'

I swallow a smile, because surely the woman can't be serious. Who believes in nonsense like that in this day and age? She has to be winding me up. But her expression is resolute, as if she knows I'm sceptical but doesn't care.

'The poet Shelley saw his fetch swimming towards him just before he drowned off the Italian coast,' she continues. 'And President Abraham Lincoln met his fetch at the stage door of a Washington theatre just before he was assassinated.'

'Oh,' I manage. I want to ask how anyone knows the two men saw their doppelgängers before they died, because the dead don't talk, but there seems little point. I have a feeling I won't change her mind.

'I'm not a fetch. I give you my word,' I say instead, my hand on my heart.

She regards me for a moment, then nods.

'So you'll tell me where Alana is?'

'She'll be in the house where she always is.'

'But I rang the buzzer. No one answered.' I don't add that I saw Alana at the window. What if I conjured her up through sheer willpower, seeing only what I wanted to see?

The woman shifts in her chair. 'Perhaps she didn't hear.'

'Perhaps,' I say uncertainly. 'Could they be away?'

'I don't think so.'

'I guess I can try again in the morning.'

The woman looks as if she's about to say something but is

interrupted by the timer. She pushes herself to her feet with a weary sigh and crosses the room to check on her scones.

'I'll leave you in peace,' I say, suddenly keen to get out of the claustrophobic kitchen.

'As you wish.'

'I'll see myself out. It was nice to meet you...'

'Mairead,' she says, setting the tray of perfectly cooked scones on a trivet. She turns to me. 'I know you think I'm a superstitious old fool, and maybe I am, but please ask yourself this: do you really need to meet Alana?' She holds my gaze, her eyes huge in her thin face. 'Because if I were you, I'd walk away now, while you still can.'

LAURA

Mairead's words haunt me as I close the front door softly and unlock Beatrice. What did she mean, 'walk away now, while you still can'? And what was she about to tell me just before the timer went off? I picture the concerned expression on her face when she opened the door to me, thinking I was Alana. Alana Adams is clearly a pampered, privileged woman, married to a renowned photographer and living in an amazing home on one of the most beautiful stretches of coastline in the country. Why would Mairead be worried about her?

One thing's for sure. I hold no truck with the Irish woman's mystical fetch. Harbingers of death? I don't think so. They're no more real than leprechauns or wailing banshees. She might mean well, but if she thinks she's changed my mind about meeting my double, she's mistaken. Every obstacle, every dead end thrown my way, just makes me even more determined to find Alana.

Mum's always saying I'm a contrary bugger.

Back at Gull Cottage, I make myself a mushroom omelette for dinner, washed down with the rest of the Pinot, and find a film to watch on the small TV in the corner of the room.

Outside, the wind has whipped up, but in front of the wood-burner it's toasty, and my eyes soon grow heavy. The film is barely halfway through before I'm asleep.

I wake with a start sometime later, stiff-necked and disorien-tated, and it takes a moment to remember where I am. The logs have almost burned to ash and a draught is whistling through the small wooden window at the front of the cottage. At first, I assume it's what's woken me, until the screen of my phone lights up with the fifth of five voice notes from Vinnie. I know why he's sent them: so he can speak, uninterrupted, without me cutting him off or talking over him. But he's wasting his time. I'm not interested in his excuses. I've heard them all already.

It seems a lifetime ago that I saw Tammy fawning over him in Casa Rossa, yet it was only the day before yesterday. I fled back to the surgery, safe in the knowledge that there was no way he'd want to have a showdown in front of our colleagues. The afternoon passed in a blur. I dressed wounds and sent off samples. I discharged day patients and carried out post-op checks. I smiled and I chatted to owners and my colleagues. But I was going through the motions, images of Vinnie and Tammy consuming my thoughts. I left for home just after five with the enthusiasm of a condemned man heading to the gallows.

Stomach churning, I let myself into the flat, dropping my bag onto the floor and heeling off my shoes. The hallway was in darkness and I flicked on the light. The sight of our two suit-cases lined up and ready for our fortnight in Cornwall had been another kick in the gut.

'Laura?'

I'd stiffened at the sound of my name. Part of me wanted to slip out of the flat unseen. The other part – the side that refused to take this lying down – wasn't so easily cowed. I shrugged off my coat, straightened my shoulders and marched into the living room.

Vinnie was slumped on one end of the sofa, a huge bouquet

of creamy-white roses on the coffee table. He only ever bought flowers when he was feeling guilty. Up till now, his transgressions involved forgetting an anniversary or not pulling his weight around the flat. Not infidelity.

'You think a bunch of roses is going to fix this?' I said, sinking into the armchair opposite him and shaking my head. 'Honestly, Vinnie, you're a walking cliché.'

'It's... it's not what you think,' he began lamely.

'So said every lying, cheating bastard ever.'

'I mean it, Laura, baby. Tammy wanted to talk about a drugs trial. I said she was better off speaking to Barney, but she insisted.'

'And don't tell me, you couldn't say no?' I laughed without mirth.

Vinnie slumped further into the sofa. 'It was just lunch.'

'I don't believe you. If it was "just lunch", why did Tammy tell Kiara Newson-Price she was your sister?'

'I think she meant it as a joke.'

'I don't find it very funny.' I eased my engagement ring over the knuckle of my ring finger. Vinnie's eyes grew round.

'What are you doing?'

'What do you think?' I said, slamming it on the coffee table next to the roses.

'But I haven't done anything wrong!'

'OK, then.' I held out my hand. 'Give me your phone.'

'What?'

'Give me your phone and let me check your messages. If it's all as innocent as you say, there'll be nothing incriminating on there, will there?'

Vinnie's phone was face down on the arm of the sofa. His hand slid over it protectively.

'I'll take that as a no.' I stood, my eyes smarting with tears. 'I think it's best if you leave.'

'Leave?' He sat up. 'But it's my name on the lease.'

I stared at him in disbelief. 'You... you *bastard!*'

He rubbed his face, dark with five o'clock shadow. 'Laura, please, calm down.'

'Calm down? How dare you tell me to calm down? You're the one who's screwing around behind my back. We were going to start trying for a family, Vinnie. We were going to have a *baby.*'

The tears were streaming down my face and I brushed them away with the back of my hand.

'Having kids was your bag, not mine.'

My head jerked towards him and he shrugged.

'I'm only telling it like it is. You were the one who suddenly decided you wanted children.'

'You said you did too!'

'Because it's what you wanted.'

'Is this what this is?' I said, waving my hand at Vinnie's phone. 'You and Tammy? A pathetic last-ditch fuck-fest before you're tied down with a family?'

'I'm not your dad, Laura. Don't tar me with the same brush.'

'That's why you joined the gym, isn't it? Not because you wanted to train for Hyrox but because you wanted to look buff for *her.* And that boys' weekend in Bournemouth. Were you really playing golf and paintballing, or were you having a cosy tête-à-tête with Tammy?'

'Of course I wasn't.' He dragged his hands down his cheeks. 'It was just a few texts and lunch, if you must know, OK?'

I glared at him mutinously. 'And if I hadn't seen you, what would it have been then? Back here for a quickie while I was at work?'

'No!'

I folded my arms across my chest. 'I'm sorry, I don't believe you.'

Vinnie held up his hands. 'Maybe I crossed a line, but I wasn't unfaithful, I promise. Look, let's treat Cornwall as a reset. We can talk properly about the future. Kids, our wedding, the whole shebang. It'll be good to take some time out just for us.'

'Are you kidding me?' I'd exploded. 'I'm not going to Cornwall with you now.'

'What about the cottage? It's too late to cancel. We'll never get our money back.' He tried a smile. 'You're overreacting, babe. You'll feel differently in the morning.'

'What, a good night's sleep is going to make this all better, is it? I don't think so.' Couldn't he see he'd ruined everything? 'How could you?' I said, my voice wobbling. 'You of all people should know how this makes me feel.'

He'd looked up at me with hangdog eyes.

'I'm sorry.'

I hardened my heart. 'You don't get it, do you? It doesn't matter if you slept with Tammy or not, the fact is I trusted you, Vinnie. And you've betrayed that trust. We're over. I'll go to Cornwall on my own and you... you can do what you like. I don't care.'

And now, here I am, alone but unbroken. I pick up my phone and hit delete again and again until all the voice notes have gone. I'm not interested in anything Vinnie has to say. He can go screw himself.

I have two weeks before I must face the reality of my situation. Two weeks on borrowed time. If I were sensible, I'd spend them working out what happens next. Where I'm going to live. What I'm going to do with the rest of my life. But why would I do that when I have the perfect distraction? Finding Alana may only be a temporary break from my troubles, but I don't care. It's helping me forget the car crash I've left behind.

11

LAURA

Over breakfast the next morning I google doppelgängers and am soon dropping down a dozen internet rabbit holes. I discover they're more common than you think, though that's probably more to do with how our world is shrinking thanks to the internet than an actual increase in the number of lookalikes. It's just easier for people to find their doubles online these days. There are even apps for it, using face recognition software to compare someone's picture to millions of others in their database.

I read about the wave of competitions to find lookalikes for A-listers like singer Harry Styles and actor Timothée Chalamet. But these competitions are nothing new. According to his son, Charlie Chaplin came third in a contest to find his own lookalike in the 1920s, and Dolly Parton once entered one of her lookalike competitions, getting the least applause but finding the whole experience uproariously funny.

I scroll through pictures of famous lookalikes, like the Lancashire model who's the spit of Kate Moss and a David Beckham double who runs a lookalike agency with over three thousand people on his books. Curious, I click through to the website. Sure enough, they're all there, from Agatha Christie's famous detective Poirot to Angelina Jolie.

These days there seems to be a definite kudos attached to finding your double but it hasn't always been the case. The doppelgänger was, I learn, once something to be feared. People really believed they were portents of death or wanted to steal your identity. Think body-snatchers in sci-fi movies. Now, only the deeply superstitious like Mairead view lookalikes with alarm. Everyone else finds them fascinating and a great excuse for an Instagram post.

I switch off my phone and drain the last of my coffee. All this research has made me even more determined to meet Alana. It's a beautiful morning, clouds scudding across a sky the colour of forget-me-nots, and instead of driving I decide to follow the coastal path up to her house. I rinse my breakfast things and leave the cottage, intrigue churning in my stomach.

* * *

My thighs are burning and I'm puffing by the time I reach the top of the cliff, so I stop for a moment to catch my breath and admire the view. Porthmerryn looks so pretty from here. Stone cottages hug the valley and boats sway in the harbour. How wonderful it must be to live in such a postcard-perfect village.

With a lurch, I remember once again that I have nowhere to go when my fortnight in Cornwall is over. I can hardly stay with Vinnie. As he so kindly reminded me on Friday night, it's his flat. Renting a place of my own, even a poky one-bedroom apartment, is out of reach on a vet nurse's salary in Margate. The thought of renting a room in a shared house at the age of thirty-six fills me with despair.

I set off towards Merryn's Reach. Approaching the house from this direction, I don't pass Mairead's scruffy bungalow, and I'm glad. I could do without another dose of her superstitious mumbo-jumbo this morning.

I'm nearly at the house when the sound of clanking metal rings out over the cries of the seagulls wheeling overhead. I stop in my tracks and watch the gates swing slowly open. Moments later, a silver Aston Martin roars out of the driveway then flies down the track towards the village, spitting gravel in its wake. It disappears so quickly I catch only a fleeting glimpse of the driver. Even so, I know in my gut it's Marcus Adams. My pulse quickens, because I'm pretty sure he was on his own, which means there's a good chance Alana is home alone.

The gates make a grinding noise as they start to close. Without stopping to question whether it's a good idea or not, I slip between them and scurry up to the house.

I pause on the slate doorstep, then rap a jaunty rat-tat-tat-tat... tat-tat – the universal code for visitors who come in peace – rock back on my heels and wait.

And wait. And wait.

After five minutes, I admit defeat. I'd been sure Marcus was alone in the car, but maybe I was mistaken and Alana was with him. It's clear no one's at home. And if no one's at home... Once again, curiosity gets the better of me and I wander round to the side of the house looking for a window to peek into. As I make a beeline for a set of floor-to-ceiling bifold doors, another of Nan's sayings comes to me. *You know what they say about curiosity, Laura.*

'I know, Nan,' I say, glancing skywards. 'But when opportunity knocks...' With a quick look over my shoulder, I step up to the glass and peer in.

The first thing that hits me about Marcus and Alana's home is the sheer size of it. The whole downstairs is one vast, open-plan space. It's so minimalist it's hard to imagine anyone actually living in it. There's no clutter, no knick-knacks, no sign of life, just sleek, expensive-looking furniture in shades of black, white and charcoal. It is masculine, uncompromising and clinical.

The floor is polished concrete, the stark white walls bare except for a series of Marcus's photographs. Each at least two metres tall, they dominate the space. A craggy-faced fisherman staring out to sea. A skeletal tree against a granite sky. A grey-haired woman, her head thrown back in a silent scream.

I shiver, remembering the interview Marcus gave to his old art college. *I see in black and white. I shoot in black and white. I have no interest in colour nor shades of grey.*

I can't help but wonder what this says about his personality. Is he someone who only deals in absolutes? Someone who thinks people are either right or wrong? Guilty or not guilty? Good or bad? But people aren't like that, and nor is life. It's complicated and messy, full of ups and downs that we can't always predict, let alone control. I know that more than anyone.

I turn and walk away, my head buzzing. What must it be like to live in this monochrome behemoth of a house? More to the point, what must it be like to live with a man like Marcus? Maybe I've got it wrong and Alana's the one with the mini-malist tastes. But then I picture the photo of her on top of the cliffs above Merryn's Cove. The wavy hair, the floaty blouse, the leather sandals, the delicate chain around her neck. Everything about her is soft, feminine. No. I'd bet my last pound the design of this place is all Marcus.

Reaching the gates, I scan the walls for a release button. But there's nothing. Just a discreet keypad which needs a code I don't have.

My stomach tightens. The walls are too tall to climb. The voice in my head whispers *I told you so*, but I ignore it and set off around the perimeter, hunting for a side gate, because there must be one somewhere.

There isn't.

I stare at the screen of my phone, wondering who I can call.

But there isn't anyone. All I can do is wait for Marcus and Alana to come home and slip through the gates before they close. It's a terrible plan. What if they see me? What if they don't come home at all? But it's the only plan I have.

I pull my coat tightly around me and crouch down to wait. And then, a miracle. With a metallic groan, the gates start to open. I tense like a runner on the starting blocks, ready to bolt when Marcus's Aston Martin sweeps past. But no one comes, not Marcus, or Alana, or anyone. The gates have opened as if of their own accord.

I stare at the house, looking for my saviour, but the house stares back at me, expressionless and empty.

Heart pounding, I tuck my chin into my chest and run.

12

LAURA

It's lunchtime when I arrive back in Porthmerryn, and before I head back to the cottage I call in at the corner shop to stock up on supplies. As I wait in the queue to pay, I check my phone. There are no new voice notes from Vinnie, but there is a text from Sam.

Please reconsider, Laura. I'm begging you.

The same tired old message, though the begging element is new. A familiar wave of frustration rises in me, not just at her persistence, but at the guilt that invariably follows.

Perhaps I should be the bigger person. Perhaps I should stop shutting her out. But my half-sister's constant attempts to make contact have the opposite effect. They make me feel contrary, even bullish. I don't want her in my life. How many times do I have to say no before she gets the message?

'That's nineteen pounds fifty, please,' the man on the till says, and I press my card to the card reader and shuffle outside, only to stop in my tracks, jaw dropping to the floor. Marcus Adams's Aston Martin is parked outside Harbour Lights, the seafood restaurant on the harbour arm. My breath catches in my throat. If Marcus is here, perhaps Alana is too. Could this be the opportunity I've been waiting for?

I hotfoot it over to the restaurant, barely registering the carrier bags bouncing off my shins, so focused am I on meeting my double in the flesh. I'm ten steps away when I see them through the window, their heads bent towards each other, deep in conversation. I slow, then stop, realising that walking into a restaurant and striking up a conversation without invitation or warning isn't such a good idea. I want to make a meaningful connection with Alana. I'm not sure why, but it matters. The last thing I need is to upset her. As I dither, a waiter arrives at the table with a pad in his hand, ready to take their order. Alana breaks eye contact with her husband to look up at him with a smile, but Marcus waves him away with a dismissive hand. The waiter nods obligingly and retreats.

I bristle. In my experience, the way people act towards those who work in bars, restaurants and shops is a reliable barometer of their personality. Kind people are kind to everyone, but the opposite is true for the arrogant or entitled, who treat service workers like dirt. It's easy to see which camp Marcus falls into.

I drop the two shopping bags at my feet, pull my hood up and pretend I'm enjoying the harbour views, my face turned to one side so Marcus and Alana will only catch my profile if they notice me watching. I hold up my phone as if I'm taking a picture, instead angling it just enough to use the selfie camera as a makeshift periscope.

Alana twiddles with her wedding ring, her gaze back on her husband now the waiter has disappeared. Once again, she is dressed in white – this time a fitted, ivory wool dress – and wears her hair in a loose chignon at the nape of her neck. It's the kind of outfit I might have chosen, had I been filthy rich and shopped in designer stores. Marcus looks debonair in a charcoal cashmere roll-neck sweater and black tailored trousers. Sitting at the table with its starched white linen tablecloth and napkins, they look like the subjects of one of his carefully curated monochrome photos and the absurdity of it makes me snort with laughter.

I keep watching. I can't help myself. This glimpse into someone else's marriage is as intoxicating as a class A drug. They finally order their food. When it arrives, Marcus attacks his with gusto but Alana picks at hers, her movements small and precise, as if she's afraid of drawing attention to herself. He dominates the conversation. She nods demurely, always in agreement with him.

I think back to meals out with Vinnie. We'd never go to a place like Harbour Lights. Couldn't afford it, for a start. Pizza Express and Bella Italia were more our style. We'd share a bottle of red and try each other's dishes, finishing each other's sentences and attempting to outdo each other with stories from work. Meals out were loud and boisterous and *fun*.

All of a sudden, my eyes glaze with tears as Vinnie's betrayal hits me anew. I wipe them away with an impatient hand, because wallowing in self-pity won't change anything. Instead, I focus on Marcus and Alana, hoping that studying their body language will take my mind off my faithless fiancé.

Marcus regards Alana over steepled fingers, looking more like a teacher lecturing a wayward student than a loving husband chatting to his wife. The waiter refills their wine glasses and clears their plates. Marcus's is empty; Alana's barely touched. The waiter brings a dessert menu. Once again Marcus waves him away. As far as I can tell, he's still holding court. I hate men who think they're the only ones with anything interesting to say and my dislike towards him curdles into something deeper.

I lean forwards, stretching my back, then risk another glance at the restaurant. Marcus is standing and shrugging on a black overcoat. The waiter holds Alana's coat for her. It's the same shade of ivory as her dress. Marcus follows his wife out of the restaurant. My heart flutters in my chest. If I was going to approach Alana, now would be the time to do it. Make it low-key and casual, as if we're old friends who've bumped into each other after a gap of years. But I stay where I am. Subconsciously, I know it would be a mistake to meet Alana today, with Marcus breathing down our necks. No, better to wait for the right moment, when she is alone.

Instead, I watch out of the corner of my eye as Marcus grips Alana's elbow and walks her to the Aston. He unlocks the car and holds open the passenger door for her, the epitome of the perfect gentleman. She smiles her thanks and climbs in, gracefully folding herself into the leather seat. They make an elegant, beautiful couple. On the surface, everything seems perfect. So why do I sense something darker hiding just out of view?

13

LAURA

That evening, I settle in front of the fire with a thriller I found on the bookshelf in my bedroom but it's impossible to concentrate, so I pick up my phone instead and look for mentions of Marcus and Alana on social media. I know this fixation isn't healthy, but I can't switch it off. Not when there's still so much to discover about the woman I glimpsed through the window.

Marcus's work gets a few shout-outs, but there are no pictures of the man himself, nor his wife. It's hard to believe that in this day and age someone can have such a light digital footprint. Next, morbid curiosity prompts me to check out Vinnie's Instagram. I don't know what I'm looking for – photos of candlelit tables and sketchy references to cosy nights in? – but the last picture he posted is of Smoky, a little black kitten that was brought into the surgery after being found on a building site a week ago and is now looking for a home.

I fling my phone onto the coffee table and turn on the TV, channel-hopping until I find a new episode of my favourite true crime show. I pour myself a second glass of wine and try to focus on the story, which is about a woman who stole the identity of a missing person so she could wreak revenge on an old lover, but I can't concentrate. I feel antsy and uptight, like tiny insects are burrowing under my skin. When the wine is finished, I admit defeat and head downstairs to bed, even though I know I'll never sleep.

I'm on the bottom step, one hand on the newel post, when there's a tap at the door. It's so quiet that at first I think I must have imagined it, but then it happens again. I glance at my watch. It's almost ten o'clock. Who in their right mind knocks on the door of a holiday cottage at this time of night?

I scoot into the bedroom and peek through the curtains. A man is standing on the doorstep, illuminated by the security light. I'm about to slip away before he sees me, because there's no way I'm opening the door to a strange man this late, when he looks up and our eyes meet.

Damn.

He motions me to open the door. I open the window a crack.

'I think you must have the wrong house. This is a holiday cottage,' I tell him.

He thrusts his hands deep into his pockets. 'I'm Rory, Mairead's son. Me mam says you want to meet Mrs Adams. Says you're her double.'

'Perhaps we can talk about this in the morning? It's late, and I was heading to bed.'

He frowns. 'You want to meet her or not?'

'I do, but...'

'You might not have another chance.'

'Why? Is she going away?'

He doesn't answer, just stands there, watching me. It's unnerving. I weigh up the risks. Let a man I've never met into the cottage and face the consequences if he turns out to be a knife-wielding maniac, or pass up the opportunity to finally meet Alana? I open the window wider.

'I suppose you'd better come in.'

Rory kicks off his boots and follows me up the stairs to the sitting room, his footsteps heavy on the wooden slats. He's wearing workman's trousers and a check shirt under a green gilet and he smells of wet grass and sweat. He's a big man, at least six foot two, and the room seems to shrink in his looming presence. I offer him a cup of tea, but he shakes his head.

'I don't drink tea.'

He speaks slowly and deliberately, as if he's choosing each word with care. I gesture for him to take a seat and I perch opposite, my hands on my knees, ready to run if he tries any funny business.

'Mam was right. You do look like her. A *lot* like her.'

He is gawking openly at me, like a child who's never been told it's rude to stare. I squirm under his gaze and jump up and stick the kettle on anyway.

'That's why I thought it would be nice to meet her,' I say over my shoulder. 'I went up to Merryn's Reach yesterday, but she and Marcus were out.'

'And today,' he says. 'I saw you there today.'

I freeze, the mug in my hand suspended in mid-air. He must have seen me walk past the bungalow this morning. Warmth floods my cheeks.

'I happened to be passing,' I say defensively.

'If you say so.' His mouth twitches as he reaches into his pocket. Fear turns my stomach to ice. What the hell is he getting? A knife? Cable ties? A roll of duct tape? I watch, a rabbit caught in the headlights, as he dangles something from his little finger. A key fob. 'I'm the one who let you out,' he says with a sly smile.

'Who gave you that?'

'Mr Adams.' Rory shrugs. 'I need it. I'm his gardener.'

'Oh.' My shoulders sag with relief. 'Thank you.'

'That's all right. We used to have keys to the house, too, when Mam cleaned for them, but we've had to give them back.'

'Right.' I finish making my tea and carry it over to the sofa. 'You must know Alana well.'

'I do.'

'What's she like?'

He hesitates. 'She's always very kind to me.'

'And Mr Adams?'

His gaze drops to the key fob palmed in his hand and he shrugs. 'He's my boss.'

'Is he kind to you too?' The question slips out.

His expression darkens. 'He's my boss,' he repeats.

It's obvious I'm not going to extract any more information about Alana and Marcus so I clear my throat and ask, 'You said you could help me meet Alana. Will you take me to the house?'

'Not the house. You need to go to Merryn's Cove.'

'Why there?'

'She swims there most mornings.'

I gape. 'Even this time of year? It must be freezing!'

'Mr Adams has a meeting with his agent in his London club at one o'clock tomorrow,' he says, almost as if he is reading by rote. 'High tide is at eight o'clock. If you're at the cove then, you will meet Mrs Adams.'

I eye him with suspicion. 'Why are you telling me this?'

'High tide is at eight o'clock.' He pushes himself to his feet and slips the key fob back into his pocket. 'I'll see myself out,' he adds, before clumping down the stairs.

The whole cottage shivers as the front door slams. I sit for a while, hands cupping my tea, my emotions shifting between intrigue and apprehension. I have lit the match. Now I must sit back and watch it burn.

14

LAURA

I lock the door of the cottage and set off through the cobbled streets towards the coastal path, brimming with anticipation. Today is the day I'm finally going to meet Alana.

It's another beautiful morning; warm for October with not a breath of wind in the air, and I've stripped off my coat and tied it round my waist before I'm even halfway up the valley. It's too early for ramblers but I pass a couple of dog walkers who wave a cheery greeting as they march past.

I cross the grassy headland, looking left and right for the narrow path down to the cove. It's steeper than I remember and I stumble a couple of times when my feet hit loose rocks.

Halfway down, the view of the small sandy beach opens up and I stop for a moment to drink it in. The water is turquoise and as calm as a millpond, the white sand pristine. I shade my eyes and scan the shoreline, spotting a bright orange tow float bobbing about in the sea ten or so metres from the shore. Next to it, a swimmer carves through the water like a knife through butter.

Alana.

I stay where I am, frozen to the rocks, watching her from my vantage point. Every three strokes she turns her head to breathe, her movements economical and assured. We may look alike but she is a far better swimmer than I could ever hope to be, and this discord reminds me that we are two very different people.

I shift my weight, my legs suddenly weak. I don't know where the nerves have come from. It's what I wanted, isn't it, to meet my double?

'Get a grip, Laura,' I mutter, setting off again. It's a relief to finally reach the beach and I step onto the sand gratefully as Alana emerges from the waves, water streaming from her wetsuit. She pulls off her goggles, peels off her swim cap and flicks back her hair. I feel a jolt of triumph, because even at this distance it's like staring straight into a mirror. Same cheekbones, same jawline, same wide-spaced eyes. She is me and I am her.

I step forwards, confident now.

'Alana.'

Her eyes widen and she looks around wildly, as if she's the butt of a prank and the joker is watching from a hiding place behind the rocks. Too late, I realise my mistake. While I've spent the last three days getting used to the idea that I have a doppelgänger, for Alana it's a complete shock to see me and has clearly knocked her sideways.

'Who are you?' she stutters.

She is American. I give a small start of surprise. In all the scenarios I've imagined since I saw her photo, I hadn't once considered she was anything other than British.

'My name is Laura. Laura Jarvis. I know you're probably a little freaked out right now, but please don't be. I saw a photo of you in the pub in Porthmerryn. The Ship?'

She gives a little nod.

'I saw how alike we looked and, well, I thought it would be fun to say hello.'

Alana's expression says it's anything but fun. In fact, it's no exaggeration to say she looks utterly horrified.

'Are you from round here?' she finally manages.

'God, no, I could never afford to live in Porthmerryn. I'm on vacation, as you would say.' I laugh a little self-consciously. This is not going how I hoped. 'I'm from Kent. You can't get much further east without dipping your toe in the North Sea. Though we came here once on holiday when I was little and stayed in the holiday park down the road from your place. Mind you, it was caravans and mobile homes in those days. None of your posh yurts and fire pits.' I am gabbling, but I can't stop myself. Nerves are making me garrulous.

She frowns. 'You know where I live?'

'Someone at the pub mentioned it,' I lie.

'Right.' Her eyes narrow. 'And how did you know I'd be here this morning?'

I hesitate, not wanting to drop Rory in it. 'Oh, I didn't. I was on a walk. I only realised it was you when you came out.' I force another chuckle. 'Small world, eh?'

She grunts, then shivers. 'I should get out of this,' she says, plucking at her wetsuit. She sets off towards the rock pools on the edge of the cove, where a bundle of clothes is piled neatly on some rocks, and pulls on a navy, fleece-lined dry robe. I turn and stare out to sea while she changes.

'I know this is all a bit weird, but don't you think it's uncanny that we look so alike?' I say, addressing the sea. 'I mean, what are the chances of having a double, let alone bumping into them? They must be infinitesimal.'

'I guess.'

I turn back to her and smile. 'And now we have, I thought we could, I don't know...'

She raises an eyebrow. 'Hang out together?'

'Yes!' I cry, glad she's coming round to my way of thinking. 'Hang out. Exactly.'

'I'm not sure that's a good idea.'

'Why not?'

She doesn't answer, bending down to pull a watch from her rucksack instead. After checking the time, she turns to me abruptly. 'I'm sorry, but I need to go.'

'Already?' I feel myself deflate. Perhaps she realises, because her voice softens.

'I'll be here again at the same time tomorrow. Bring a flask and a blanket.'

She scoops up her clothes and smiles at me. It lights up her whole face and I smile back instinctively, a mirror image.

'Tomorrow,' I agree, plunging my hands into my pockets as I watch her walk away until all that's left is a line of neat footprints in the sand.

15

LAURA

Sleep is elusive. I'm too wired, like a kid on Christmas Eve, my brain refusing to power down. Eventually, I must drift off, because when the alarm on my phone buzzes in the silent bedroom it takes a moment for me to remember where I am and what's so special about today.

A burst of adrenaline soon kicks my exhaustion into touch and, after a quick shower, I fill a flask with coffee and pack it, along with one of the throws from the sofa, into my rucksack and head out of the cottage with a spring in my step. At the corner shop, I'm about to ask for two cinnamon swirls – my go-to Danish pastry – when I hesitate. Just because I like them doesn't mean Alana will. I order two cinnamon swirls, a pain au chocolat and a couple of croissants to cover all bases.

It's windy today, and the sea is so choppy I worry Alana might have decided to forego her morning swim, but as I negotiate the path down to the cove I spot her orange tow float and my face splits into a grin.

I was like a kid before Christmas last night. Even another message from Sam – *Laura, please. Just hear me out. It's important* – couldn't put a damper on my mood. I barely slept, waking on the hour every hour, worried I'd miss my alarm. And now here I am, clutching a bag of pastries as I wait for Alana to emerge from the waves.

'I brought breakfast,' I say as she steps onto the beach, her float tucked under her arm and her wetsuit glistening like the skin of a seal. I follow her over to the rocks, where she's left her dry robe, and unpack the pastries while she changes. 'D'you swim every morning?'

She takes a flask from her bag and joins me. 'When I can. You should come tomorrow.'

'God, no. I'm more of a sauna and jacuzzi kinda gal.'

'So we may look similar—'

'Identical,' I interject.

'But that's as far as the likeness goes,' she finishes.

'We don't know, do we?' I'm feeling emboldened now. 'That's why I wanted to meet. To see if we had more in common than our looks.'

She pours herself a black coffee and regards me. 'How do I know you're not here to steal my identity?'

Her question throws me off balance and I search her face to see if she's joking, but she seems deadly serious.

'Only I was reading up on lookalikes last night,' she continues. 'I found a story about a woman in Germany who tracked down her doppelgänger so she could kill her to fake her own death. And one about a Russian woman who poisoned her lookalike with a cheesecake laced with tranquillisers then stole her passport.'

'Hand on heart, I promise I'm not here to murder or poison you. Look,' I say earnestly, pointing at the pastries. 'Not a cheesecake in sight.'

To my relief Alana laughs, and I grin back at her, glad the ice is broken.

She takes a sip of her coffee. 'So, Laura Jarvis, according to your Instagram, you're a thirty-six-year-old veterinary nurse from someplace called Margate with a fiancé named Vinnie and a cute VW Beetle called Beatrice.'

'Someone's done their homework.' I smile to show her I'm fine with it because I don't blame her. I could be anybody. Besides, didn't I trawl the internet looking for mentions of her and Marcus?

'You're right about everything apart from the fiancé bit. Vinnie and I split up on Friday. That's why I'm down here on my own.'

Her brow creases in concern. 'I'm sorry to hear that. What happened?'

I take a cinnamon swirl and push the pastries towards her. 'You really want to know?'

'Of course.'

'I saw him having lunch with one of the sales reps at work.'

'That's it?'

'You didn't see them. They were all over each other.'

'O-kaay. And what did he have to say about it?'

I pull a face. 'That it wasn't how it looked. That she was talking to him about a work thing. That it was "just lunch". The usual.'

'You don't believe him?'

'I don't.' I sigh. 'I've had my fingers burned before.'

'With Vinnie?'

'Not Vinnie.'

'Another boyfriend,' she guesses, and I don't bother to correct her.

'What about you?' I ask.

She hesitates. 'What about me?'

'How did you end up living over here?'

'Well,' she says, 'that's a long story. The short version is, I was studying at the London College of Fashion when Marcus came to do a shoot. It was love at first sight.' She fiddles with the platinum band on her ring finger. 'Three months later, we were married.'

'I moved in with Vinnie after a month,' I admit.

Alana's eyes widen. 'No way!'

'Crazy, eh? Serves me right.' I break off a piece of cinnamon swirl and look sidelong at her, curious about her relationship with Marcus. 'You know what they say about marrying in haste.'

'Oh, I think when you know, you know. Besides, Marcus swept me off my feet. I couldn't resist. That was ten years ago. I was twenty-two.'

I try to hide my surprise. If I'd been asked to guess I'd have said Alana was older than me. She seems so much more poised and together than I'll ever be. 'Where are you from originally?'

'New England, though my father's British.'

My ears prick up at this.

'It's why I came to London for my master's, though he's not in our lives any more.'

Not in our lives any more.

It's a strange choice of words and I'm about to ask her why when I stop myself. There'll be plenty of other opportunities to have a heart-to-heart. My mind drifts off, imagining the two of us enjoying girlie nights in with Prosecco and pizzas, shopping trips followed by lunch in trendy wine bars, trips to the cinema to see the latest romcom. The sister I didn't think I wanted.

She cocks her head. 'Penny for them, as you Brits would say?'

I flush, glad she can't read my mind. My flights of fantasy are much too eager. 'Oh, I was just remembering the picnics we used to have at Merryn's Cove. Jam and Marmite sandwiches covered in sand. Warm bottles of Fanta and Coke and an ice cream from the van in the car park if I was lucky.'

'Sounds dreamy,' she says, sipping her coffee.

'It was, when I remember to wear my rose-tinted spectacles.' I push the pastries towards her. 'Aren't you having one?'

'They look lovely, and it was so thoughtful of you to bring them, but I shouldn't.'

'You've been for a swim. You've earned it.'

'No, I really shouldn't.' She sets her cup on a flattish rock. 'I should make a move.'

'So soon?' I say, not bothering to hide my disappointment.

'I have things I need to see to.' She pauses. 'But Marcus is in London for the next couple of days. We could have dinner tonight?'

My heart soars. 'That would be amazing.'

'I'd offer to host but our place is a mess.'

I'm about to argue that it looked fine when I peered through the patio doors on Monday when I stop myself. It'd come across as too creepy for words. Instead, I say, 'Come to mine. I make a mean chilli. I'm staying at Gull Cottage. It's number five, Harbour Terrace. The white one with a slate roof. You know it?'

'No.' She smiles. 'But I'm sure I can find it.'

16

LAURA

After lunch, I go for a walk to pass the time. According to a guidebook in the cottage there's an old tin mine a mile or so along the coast that's worth a visit.

On the quayside a girl in leggings and a faded black baggy T-shirt is tying her laces, her dark-blonde hair scraped back in a high ponytail. As she looks up, a jolt of recognition passes through me.

'You're the girl from the corner shop.'

She tucks a strand of hair behind her ear and nods.

'You're Pinot lady.'

I pull a face. 'You paint such an attractive picture of me.'

She grins sheepishly. 'Sorry. I just play this game to pass the time when I'm working. Like the tray game you play at kids' parties? I have to remember every item that goes through the till. For example, you bought cheddar, bread, eggs and mush-rooms as well as the wine.'

'Impressive.'

She smiles again, pretty dimples forming in her cheeks. She's younger than I remember. Only fifteen or sixteen.

'Going for a run?' I ask.

Colour creeps up her neck and she plucks at her T-shirt. 'I'm doing Couch to 5K. I'm only on week two.'

We stand aside to let a grimy black van pass. The girl produces AirPods from a pocket, slots them in her ears and fiddles with her phone, then does a few half-hearted stretches.

'Have a good one.'

She nods and sets off at a brisk walk along the road that skirts the harbour. It's the way I need to go too, but I give her a couple of minutes' head start before I follow more slowly, not wanting her to feel obliged to talk to me. I'd have hated having to make conversation with a stranger at her age.

I've reached the far end of the harbour when I become aware of the drone of a diesel engine behind me. I glance over my shoulder and frown. It's the same black van that passed us a moment ago. The driver accelerates as he passes me, then slows down as he approaches the girl from the shop. I watch, eyes narrowed, as he leans across the passenger seat and says something to her. At first, I assume he's asking for directions, but when her head drops and she quickens her pace, her gaze on the ground, it becomes clear he's after something else entirely and I break into a jog.

He's still crawling alongside her when I catch up, too intent on his prey to notice me.

'...aw, come on, give a man a break. I'm a nice guy. Ask anyone,' he is wheedling.

She shakes her head. 'I don't... I mean I'm not...'

'Don't tell me you've had a better offer?' His voice hardens. 'Cos most men wouldn't touch you with a bargepole with an arse that size. I'd be doing you a favour, love.'

'Oi!' I yell, banging on the side of the van without stopping to think. 'What the hell d'you think you're doing?'

He slams on his brakes, yanks up the handbrake and turns to me, his face puce.

'What the fuck has it got to do with you?'

Fury rises inside me like steam in a pressure cooker. How dare this overweight, unshaven, ignorant prick think he has the right to intimidate a teenage girl? I step between her and the van, one hand reaching for my phone.

'It has everything to do with me.' I lift the phone and start recording.

'Gimme that, bitch!' he yells, lunging out of the window, but I step smartly away.

'Not a flipping chance.' I direct the camera at his registration plate. 'So why don't you and your incel brain piss off before I call the police and report you for harassment?'

His face is so red now he looks like he could explode at any minute. He's a big guy with broad shoulders and hands the size of plates. Briefly, I wonder if I should have been more circumspect, but the flicker of doubt is groundless. He slams the gearstick into first and, with a 'Fuck you, ugly bitch!' roars off down the street.

The girl hugs herself, her gaze flitting between me and the disappearing van. I give her a reassuring smile.

'You OK?'

She nods.

'He's just a coward. Most of them are. You don't have to take it, you know.'

'I guess.'

I glance down at my jeans and Converse. I'm hardly dressed for a run but who cares? Besides, she's only on week two. I should be able to keep up.

'Want some company? I could use the exercise after all that Pinot and cheese.'

When I look back up, there's the faintest glimmer of a smile on her face.

'Thanks,' she says. 'That would be cool.'

17

LAURA

I give Alana's wine glass a final polish and step back to survey the room. Candles flicker on the coffee table and mantelpiece. The wine glasses sparkle, the cutlery gleams. The small dining table is set with a wine-red tablecloth and matching napkins I found in a drawer in the oak sideboard and a bottle of Chilean Merlot breathes on the worktop. The wood-burner is lit, the cushions are plumped. It looks like the stage for a seduction, and in a way, I suppose it is. I'm wooing Alana. I don't just want to be the woman who looks like her. I want to be her friend.

I've felt rootless since Vinnie and I split up. Cast adrift, like one of the boats in Porthmerryn Harbour, going wherever the current takes me. A week ago I knew exactly who I was and my place in the world. I was Laura Jarvis, vet nurse, daughter and one half of Laura and Vinnie. Home was a takeaway and a boxset in a cosy garden flat five minutes from Margate seafront. I had so much to look forward to. A wedding, a baby, a house big enough for our growing family. But the future I pictured was a mirage, because now I am alone. Untethered, homeless, with no idea what happens next.

That's why tonight is so important. Not just because

finding Alana has been a distraction from the heartache, but because I crave connection. Friendship. And I think she does too.

Pleased with my efforts, I check the chilli and measure out some rice. I've bought an eye-wateringly expensive sourdough loaf too, to cover all bases. I want this to be perfect.

There's a knock at the door and I run down the stairs to answer it. Alana is on the doorstep, her face hidden by a huge bunch of pink stargazer lilies.

'My favourites!' I lie, taking them from her and breathing in the heady, sweet smell. I loathe lilies – I've seen too many cats at the surgery with kidney failure after coming into contact with them – but I don't want to appear ungrateful.

'Mine too,' Alana says, nudging me with her elbow. 'At last, we have something in common!'

I peer out of the door before locking it. 'Where's your car? Did you leave it in the car park at the top of the village?'

'I don't actually have one. That's to say we're a one-car family and Marcus took it to the station this morning. I walked.'

'Along the cliffs?' I gape. 'But it's pitch-black out there.'

She pulls something out of her pocket and waves it at me. 'I have a torch. It's all good.'

'I can call you a taxi to save you walking home. It's no trouble.'

She laughs. 'I'll be fine. I often walk along the coastal path at night. There's something magical about watching the moon over the water. Reminds me of home.'

'Your mum lives near the sea?'

'Camden. Not the London one. Maine. Ours is more lobster boats and lighthouses than music and markets. If you like Porthmerryn, you'd love it.'

I make a mental note to google the place once Alana has gone, keen to see where she grew up, then wave at the stairs. 'It's an upside-down house. The living room is upstairs.'

'Oh my gosh, this place is just adorable,' Alana exclaims as she follows me into the living room.

'I can't really take the credit.' I chuck another couple of logs on the fire. 'Would you like a glass of wine?'

'I wasn't going to, but why the heck not?'

'How did your mum end up marrying a Brit?' I ask as I pour us each a glass of Merlot and give the chilli a stir.

Alana gives me a wry look. 'They weren't actually married. Mom's a lawyer and used to work for a big international firm with offices in Boston and London. She was sent to the London office on a three-year secondment and that's where she met my father.'

'Did he work at the same company?'

She shakes her head. 'They met at a conference. Anyway, enough about me. Tell me why you wanted to be a vet nurse.'

She listens intently as I describe how we never had pets at home because of Mum's allergies, and I made up my mind aged ten that I wanted to work with animals.

'I wasn't brainy enough to be a vet, so I went to college and studied to be a vet nurse instead.'

'You're very single-minded,' Alana remarks.

'Bloody-minded, more like.' I grin. 'Vinnie always used to say I was as tenacious as a terrier.' I shrug. 'He was probably right.'

'Marcus is the same. I've never met a man more driven. His work consumes him.'

'He's very talented.'

'He is.' Alana goes quiet and I take advantage of the lull in the conversation to serve up.

'This looks delicious. Thank you,' Alana says, when I set her plate in front of her. 'Beats the bowl of cereal I was going to have.'

'Does Marcus work away often?'

'Only when he has to. Merryn's Reach is his happy place. He grew up there, you see.'

I frown, feigning ignorance. 'But the house looks new.'

'The old one burned down before we met. Marcus wanted to replace it with something contemporary because he can't bear pastiche, so he commissioned Patrick Leveson to design it.' When I look blank she adds, 'He's one of the most influential architects of the twenty-first century.' She gives me a conspiratorial grin. 'I hadn't heard of him either.'

'It must be amazing to live in a place like that. Vinnie and I had a one-bedroom flat in a Victorian conversion. The landlord threw in the damp for free. Though to be technically correct, Vinnie still has the flat and the damp,' I add gloomily. 'I'll have to look for somewhere else to live when I get back.'

Alana's eyebrows rise in concern. 'What will you do in the meantime, move back in with your folks?'

'My mum lives in Hampshire. It would be a hell of a commute to Margate. My dad died a few years ago.'

'Oh, I'm sorry.'

'It's fine. He was doing something he loved.' That's what the headline in the local paper said, anyway. *Farnborough dad-of-two dies doing what he loved.* Falling twenty feet from a ladder while fixing the guttering might not be everyone's idea of a 'good death', but a neighbour told the reporter Dad was a keen DIY enthusiast, so there it was in black and white. It's true. He did enjoy DIY. But given the choice I doubt he wanted to die while he was doing it.

'I'll find something,' I say, sounding more optimistic than I feel. 'How's the chilli? I added a bit of dark chocolate to make it richer.'

'Delicious,' Alana says, though she's barely made a dent in hers. Surely she can't be watching her weight? She's as slim as a reed. She's halfway down her wine glass though, and I top it up.

'Has Porthmerryn changed much since you were here as a kid?' she asks.

'It's much posher these days. There weren't any Michelin-starred seafood restaurants, for a start. It was fish and chips from the pub or nothing.'

'Marcus loves Harbour Lights. You should go. See if they can squeeze you in before you head home.'

I had a look at the menu online last night and gawked at the prices. What must it be like to be rich enough to splurge so much money on a single meal? Still, it's not something I need worry about since it's never likely to happen. But I smile at Alana anyway and say I'll phone the restaurant to see if they have a table.

The wood-burner is kicking out more heat than I expected and the room is starting to resemble a sauna.

'Christ, it's hot in here.' I fan my face with my side plate. 'Sorry. I think I overdid the logs.'

'That's all right.' Alana's cheeks are as rosy as mine feel. She peels off her cardigan and drapes it over the back of her chair, reaching for her glass of water. As she does, her sleeve rides up just enough to reveal an area of puckered skin on the back of her right hand, the kind of scar left by a bad burn.

I open my mouth to say something, but Alana catches me looking and shifts her arm away, her other hand curling over the mark. She flashes me quick smile, but it's too bright, too practised.

So,' she says, her voice light. 'Silly question time. If you could be an animal, what animal would you be?'

When I don't answer straight away, her smile falters.

'I told you, I'm a terrier,' I say eventually. I meet her gaze. 'Once I set my mind to something, I never give up.'

18

LAURA

What are those marks on your wrist?

The words I'm desperate to ask Alana are on the tip of my tongue when my phone jumps into life, vibrating on the table by my wine glass.

I'm about to ignore it when Alana says, 'Shouldn't you get that?'

I glance at the screen. 'It's only my mum. I'll phone her later.'

'You should speak to her now. She'll only worry otherwise. You know what moms are like.' Before I can react, she picks up my phone, accepts the call and hands it to me.

'Hi, Mum,' I say, rolling my eyes at Alana, who smiles and starts clearing the table.

Mum doesn't beat around the bush. 'Why are you ignoring Sam's calls?'

I bristle. 'Why d'you think?'

She exhales so loudly it's like there's a fault on the line. 'Don't you think you should let bygones be bygones? It's all water under the bridge.'

'It might be for you.' I watch Alana tip most of her chilli in the food waste then open a couple of cupboards looking for the dishwasher. 'But it isn't for me. And can you please stop talking in clichés?'

'I understand it's hard for you, sweetie, but you're not the only one who's hurting here. And if anyone knows how you feel, it's Sam. Besides, carrying around all that resentment isn't good for you. Look what happened to your Uncle Phil.'

I snort. 'Uncle' Phil, technically not an uncle but a long-time friend of my parents, died from a stroke after spending a decade seething about a neighbour's extension which he claimed overlooked his conservatory.

'Uncle Phil was four stone overweight and had dangerously high blood pressure,' I scoff.

Mum tuts. 'They might as well have written "Died from a grudge" on his death certificate. Don't be that person, Laura. Don't be Uncle Phil.'

'Now you sound like a terrible meme. Will you stop with the Instagram homilies, Mum, please. It's embarrassing.'

'For the love of God.' She whistles through her teeth. 'Mark my words, one day you'll realise you're the one missing out.'

I close my eyes and take a deep breath. 'Is that all?'

'Of course not. I want to know how you're getting on. How's the cottage? Did Vinnie sign up for surfing lessons like he said?'

My stomach clenches. Mum has an uncanny ability to sniff out a lie, but I keep my voice breezy. 'He did. He's completely hooked. And the cottage is great, thanks. Really dinky, but it has everything we need.'

'I'm glad. You looked washed out the last time I saw you. I hope you're taking it easy.'

'I am. In fact, we were just about to settle down in front of the fire with a film and a bottle of wine, so...'

'It's OK, I can take a hint. Give my love to Vinnie, and remember what I said, Laura. What happened is ancient history. It's time we all moved on. And when I say we, I mean you. Don't be Uncle Phil.'

'Sorry, you're breaking up. I can't hear—' I end the call and toss the phone onto the table with a harrumph.

Alana is watching me, her expression curious.

'She thinks Vinnie is here with you. Why haven't you told her you've left him?'

'Technically, I didn't leave. Well, technically, I did, but only because he's having an affair.'

'You *think* he's having an affair.'

'I *know* he's having an affair.' I drag my hands down my face. 'I'll pop in on my way home and tell her face to face. There's no point worrying her. She already thinks I look washed out.'

'All moms think their daughters look washed out, like, all the time. It's the law.'

'Unless you're tanned, in which case they worry about skin cancer,' I say.

'Or if you're flushed, they assume you're running a fever,' Alana finishes, and as we laugh, pleasure ripples through me.

This is what I'd hoped for when we met. That Alana would be that someone who really gets me. That person I can laugh and cry with, who'll fight my corner and be my biggest cheer-leader. Someone I can spill my secrets to and know they are safe. Someone who never judges me or finds me wanting. Someone who'll celebrate the good stuff and commiserate when things go wrong. Someone who sees my flaws and loves me anyway. Someone just like me.

A best friend.

'I should go,' Alana says, pulling me from my reverie.

'Already?' I glance at my phone. 'It's not even nine.'

She hesitates. 'I know. But Marcus always calls before I go to bed if he's away, and if I'm not back he'll worry.'

Warning signs flash like neon lights in my peripheral vision. 'Can't you text him to let him know you're here?'

She shakes her head. 'I don't have a cell. He phones the landline.'

'You don't have a mobile phone?' I say, incredulous.

'Not for years. I know I'm in the minority but it's freeing, not having to constantly check social media and emails. You should try it.'

I tighten my grip on my treasured iPhone. 'Maybe. Listen, are you sure you don't want me to call you a cab?'

'Honestly, I'm fine.'

'At least let me walk with you some of the way.'

'Do you have a torch?'

'I'll use my phone.'

She acquiesces, and we grab our coats and leave the cottage. The breeze has dropped, taking the temperature with it, and our breath curls as we walk through Porthmerryn's narrow streets. Lights twinkle in the harbour and, above, the sky is a navy blanket studded with a million stars. It's so beautiful I would bottle it if I could so I could enjoy it forever. Instead, I follow the beam of Alana's torch as it dances like a firefly along the coastal path. We walk in silence, lost in our thoughts, until we reach the headland.

Alana stops. 'Thank you, Laura. It's been such a fun evening.'

The words have an air of finality about them and a sense of panic rises in my chest. Is this where we part ways, two acquaintances who happen to share the same facial features? I push the panic down and make my voice light.

'How about lunch tomorrow? I could see if there are any cancellations at Harbour Lights.' I'll have to go into my overdraft, but it'll be worth it.

'Marcus isn't due back till the evening so I guess it could work. But not Harbour Lights. Tell you what, come to me.'

'Sounds perfect.' I smile, even though it's too dark for her to see.

'Come over about one,' she says, and walks away.

It's only then that I remember I never asked her about the scar on the back of her hand. I want to shout after her, to find out who did it to her, even though I suspect I already know, but she has gone.

All that's left is the flicker of her torchlight, which is soon swallowed by the dark.

19

LAURA

I'm too keyed up to go straight back to the cottage, so I decide to walk along the harbour wall instead, hoping a blast of sea air will help me sleep. Porthmerryn is as pretty as a picture at night. The pastel-coloured cottages gleam in the streetlights like the glow-in-the-dark stars I used to have on my bedroom ceiling when I was a kid. In the harbour, boats bob in the water, their hulls creaking as waves slap against them. The Ship is quieter tonight, and I debate going in for a nightcap, then decide against it. Better to save my money for a deposit on a flat.

As I walk, I replay the evening, from the moment Alana arrived to the second she disappeared into the darkness on top of the cliffs. A smile creeps across my face. It was everything I'd hoped for and more. I'd wanted us to click, but knew it wasn't guaranteed. I needn't have worried. The rapport between us felt real. A balm for my soul after Vinnie's betrayal.

Even after just one evening, I feel like I've known her for years. She's warm and funny, with a wry sense of humour that's never at someone else's expense. She lives in an amazing house with a famous husband. She could be entitled, privileged – totally insufferable, actually – but she isn't. Far from it.

I sensed a vulnerability about her the first time we met. No, I think, shaking my head. Before that. When I saw her photo for the first time. Much as I might dislike the man, I'll give Marcus this: he captured the fragile essence of her, like the soft centre of a chocolate.

She stirs something in me, I know that much. An instinctive urge to protect her, to fight her corner, because if I don't, who will? I remember the scar on the back of her hand. Not her husband, that's for sure.

I pass the old telephone box on the quay. It's been turned into a little library and I pull open the door, about to see if there's anything that takes my fancy, when a memory slams into me, knocking the wind from my lungs.

I'm eleven, sitting on the harbour wall with my crab line in my hands and a bucket of seawater beside me. The bucket is empty, because the crabs aren't biting today, and I'm getting bored and hungry. Mum's back at the campsite with a headache, leaving Dad in charge, only Dad is nowhere to be seen.

I'm not unduly concerned: he's always wandering off somewhere. He's a haulage contractor and works away from home so often I'm quite used to it being just me and Mum. That's why holidays are such a treat. I get to hang out with him all the time.

I wind up the crab line, tip the bucket of water into the sea and stand up stiffly. My bum's gone completely numb and the tops of my thighs are pink because Dad forgot to bring any sunscreen. He also forgot to bring a drink and I'm so thirsty my tongue feels swollen in my throat. I picture the refrigerated display cabinet in the corner shop, the cans of Fanta, Sprite and Coke so cold condensation bubbles on the logos like sweat on a long-distance runner's brow. I'd run straight there and buy one, but I don't have a penny to my name.

I stretch my legs and scan the harbour, hoping to see Dad talking to one of the fishermen or maybe even – fingers crossed

– queuing at the ice-cream van. Then I spot him in the telephone box by the public toilets.

I don't think anything of it. He has a work mobile, but Mum made him leave it at home 'because you're always on the damn thing, and this is supposed to be a holiday'. But he finds it hard to switch off. He's probably checking in with his stand-in, Andy.

I drop the crab line into the bucket and amble over, already imagining the fizz of bubbles on my tongue from the ice-cold can of Fanta I've set my heart on. I ease the door of the phone box open just enough to hear.

Dad's back is to me, the handset pressed to his ear. He's running a hand through his hair like he does when he and Mum are having one of their 'discussions', which is shorthand for 'stand-up row'.

I open my mouth, about to ask him for fifty pence, when—

'Debbie, please don't be like that. You know why I can't. I'm in Cornwall with Val and Laura.'

My skin prickles, and it's not the sunburn.

'I know she will. But tell her I'm sorry and that I'll make it up to her when I'm home.' Dad massages the bridge of his nose and I hold my breath. 'Of course I miss you, Debs. Both of you. And I know it's hard on you. But we've got our week in Great Yarmouth to look forward to, haven't we?'

Both of you? I hide a gasp of shock.

'Look, I need to go. I've left Laura on her own. I'll call tomorrow, OK?'

My gaze is drawn to his right hand. He's wound the phone cord around it so tightly that his skin has gone completely white. 'Tell her Daddy loves her and if she's a good girl I'll get her one of those shell necklaces she loves—'

I don't hang around to hear more. I edge away before he sees me, my thirst forgotten. I duck around a family watching a fishing boat chug slowly into the harbour, and sprint back to my crabbing spot, my heart pounding, the shell necklace he bought *me* like a noose around my neck.

The conversation doesn't make sense.

And yet, somehow, it explains everything.

20

LAURA

I never told Dad what I'd heard. I didn't tell Mum, either. I packed it into a little box in my brain and threw away the key. As an exercise in self-preservation, it worked a treat. Until the following February, when Dad's lies unravelled and everyone found out that Pete Jarvis, haulage contractor, proud father and all-round great guy, had a secret family.

He met Debbie through work. She was his boss's secretary. They started their affair when I was six months old. Debbie fell pregnant a fortnight before my first birthday. My father, who loved kids and had been gutted when complications meant Mum couldn't have any more children, decided to have his cake and eat it.

Two homes. Two families. It's no wonder he was always so dog-tired. He could fall asleep at the drop of a hat, my dad. On the bus, at the cinema, at the dinner table. Once, he even fell asleep while sitting in the front row at a carol concert in which I was performing a solo of 'Away in a Manger' on my recorder. Mum put it down to his long hours at work and was always on at him to hand in his notice and find something with more family-friendly hours. In truth, it was because he was burnt out by his double life. He was, put simply, completely knackered.

Debbie and her baby lived in a council flat in Aldershot, three miles down the road from our two-bed terrace in Farnborough. Dad used to juggle his time trying to keep both families happy. He never missed a birthday or a parents' evening. He always had time to help me with my homework or listen to my problems. I was, he told me, his best girl.

I just didn't realise there were two of us.

Debbie knew from the start that he was married and had a daughter. Mum only found out about Debbie when he had an accident at work six months after our holiday in Porthmerryn. He was blue-lighted to hospital with a suspected broken back after falling from the cab of a lorry. A distraught Debbie went with him in the back of the ambulance. Mum arrived at A&E after a call from hospital staff as his official next of kin. I can only imagine how the conversation went when his two worlds collided. Mum would tell me if I asked, but the truth is, I don't want to know.

By a small miracle, Dad's back was bruised, not broken, but his marriage never recovered and he and Mum divorced when I was twelve and my half-sister, Sam, was ten.

The betrayal I felt was devastating. Dad, my hero, my rock, had ripped our family apart. I didn't think I'd ever be able to forgive him. Then he went and died before I had a chance to change my mind.

I learnt to live with the guilt, but my trust in men had been dealt a fatal blow. I treated every relationship as if it was doomed from the start, terrified history would repeat itself. I knew I was destined to fall for a cheat, just like Mum. My cynicism was so ingrained it was part of the very fibre of my being. The scars were too deep to ever heal.

When I met Vinnie, he made me feel that monogamy was not just possible, it was a given. When he told me he loved me and promised he would never betray me like my father had, I believed him. What a fool.

'And now Sam wants to make contact,' I tell Alana, as we sit at her vast kitchen island, picking over the cheeseboard she threw together after a surprise power cut scuppered her plans to make carbonara.

I turned up an hour ago with a box of chocolates from the corner shop and a burning desire to offload. She took one look at my wan face and asked me what was wrong as she ushered me through the front door. The words tumbled out of me before I could stop them. How I found out Dad had another family, and I had a sibling I neither knew nor wanted.

'Sam's your sister?' Alana checks, pouring me another glass of wine before taking a sip of her own glass of sparkling water. She doesn't drink at home, she explained, as she pulled the bottle of Rioja from a wine rack next to the fridge. I'm already on my second glass and the alcohol is making me loose-lipped.

'Half-sister. She's been texting me for a couple of weeks asking to meet.'

'You've never met your half-sister?'

'Nope.' I blow my hair out of my eyes. 'Never even seen a picture of her.'

Alana stares at me, open-mouthed. 'Wow.'

I glower and she holds her hands up. 'Sorry, I'm not judging. Honestly.'

'I don't care what she looks like, and I don't want to meet her. She tried when we were teenagers, too, but there's no way.'

Alana nudges a bowl of olives towards me. 'Why not?'

Now that's the sixty-four-million-dollar question. I can't pretend it's through loyalty to Mum. Fourteen years ago, when I was twenty-two and Sam was twenty and still at university, Debbie was diagnosed with a rare skin cancer. When she died eight months later, Mum swept in and picked up the pieces.

'I don't care what your father did or didn't do. That poor girl has lost both her parents and she needs me,' she said.

Friends and family were unanimous in telling her what a wonderful thing she was doing, but to me it felt like yet another betrayal. And every time she tried to get me to meet Sam, I shut her down.

'Laura?' Alana presses.

'Logically, I know it's not Sam's fault my parents split up. If anyone's to blame, it was Dad, and Mum's right: she probably is as much of a victim as me.' I stab an olive with a cocktail stick. 'But she's also a reminder of that terrible time and everything Dad did wrong. Two families! How could he? If she hadn't been born he and Mum would never have got divorced.'

'Are you sure about that?'

I sigh as I remember the arguments and asides, the pursed lips and petty griping that filled my childhood. 'No, not really,' I admit.

'Is it the only reason you refuse to see Sam?'

My cheeks redden under Alana's unwavering gaze. 'OK, maybe I'm jealous too. Dad was mine first.'

She nods to herself as if she'd guessed this all along. 'And you feel bad for feeling jealous, which makes you even more resentful towards her.'

'What's your name, Sigmund bloody Freud?' I ask grumpily.

'No.' She smiles. 'Just a friend who wants the best for you.'

I smile back. The knowledge that she cares about me and my feelings is as gratifying as slipping into a hot bath on a cold day. It makes my nerve-endings tingle and my pulse quicken. Alana and I are more than two people who simply look alike. We are *friends*.

Then she drops a bombshell.

'I understand how you feel because I have a half-sister too.'

21

LAURA

I understand how you feel because I have a half-sister too.

A piece of olive goes down the wrong way and my eyes fill with tears as I cough and splutter. Alana passes me a glass of water and I sip it slowly until my breathing's back under control.

'You *what?*'

'I told you my mom and dad never married. That's because he already had a wife and children.'

I sit up on the stool, my mind racing, but before I can say anything Alana shakes her head.

'I know what you're thinking, but my half-brother and sister are in their fifties. My dad's twenty years older than Mom, you see. We're not related, Laura.'

My shoulders slump and a little voice inside my head whispers bitchily, *Why are you disappointed Alana's not your sister when you already have a sister you refuse to see?*

I tell the voice to shut up and smile weakly. 'Stranger things have happened. Are you close?'

'Not since I moved to Cornwall. It's such a long way, and

they're busy people. George runs his own PR company and Hannah's the deputy head of a high school.'

'What about your dad?'

She gives a sad little smile. 'He's in a nursing home now. He has early-stage dementia.'

'Oh, I'm sorry.'

'That's OK. It's just one of those things.'

I think of Mum finding out about my own father's secret family in the middle of a busy A&E department.

'Does his wife know about you?' I ask.

'She did. Carol died just before Marcus and I were married. She and Dad were children of the seventies. They had a pretty relaxed attitude to monogamy.'

'Blimey.' I contemplate this for a moment, then something else occurs to me. London's not exactly on the other side of the world. It can't be a coincidence that she no longer sees her family now she's married to Marcus. I'm about to ask her when somewhere in the house a landline rings. She stiffens.

'That'll be Marcus,' she says, pushing back her stool. 'Won't be a moment.'

She disappears into the living room. Her voice drifts back, softly cadenced. Try as I might, I can't make out the words. A few minutes later she returns, her face impassive.

'Everything OK?' I check.

'He's staying in London till Saturday.' She closes her eyes for a moment, then slips off her stool and takes a wine glass from a cupboard. 'Which means I can join you in a glass of wine. Cheers,' she says, clinking glasses.

'Doesn't he let you drink?'

She laughs self-consciously. 'Oh, no, it's not that. We just have a no-booze rule Monday to Thursday. It seems disloyal to break it.'

I can't imagine someone like Marcus turning down a glass of Taittinger or a vintage cognac if he was offered one, and indignation on her behalf ruffles my feathers, but I bite my tongue. Instead, I tell her I met her neighbour the other day and almost gave the poor woman a heart attack.

'Mairead?'

I nod. 'At first she thought I was you, and when she realised I wasn't she went as white as a sheet and said I must be your fetch. It's a supernatural doppelgänger,' I add, seeing Alana's blank expression. 'They're supposed to be a portent of death if they rock up like I did. Irish folklore,' I explain. 'A load of old tosh if you ask me.'

'I'm with you, but I'm not surprised Mairead's feeling a bit superstitious. She's not been well. Lung cancer,' Alana says, miming smoking.

I picture Mairead walking out of the corner shop with a packet of Marlboro Red in her hand. She'd be better served putting her trust in proven health warnings than groundless folklore. Still, I wouldn't wish lung cancer on anyone.

'Is she going to be all right?'

'We hope so. She's in the middle of chemo. Marcus has been amazing, paying for a taxi to take her to her appointments in Truro.'

I make a non-committal noise. I know what men like Marcus are like. They don't do anything altruistic unless it benefits them. He'll have an ulterior motive, I have absolutely no doubt.

'You're not worried I'm your fetch, then?' I ask.

Alana laughs. 'Of course not. Though I do believe us meeting like this is fate. Don't you?'

I stab another olive and consider this. What if Mum and Dad had taken me to Newquay or Bude all those years ago? What if Vinnie and I had decided to go to Ibiza instead of Cornwall? I would never have seen the photo of Alana, would never have known of her existence, let alone tracked her down to Merryn's Reach. Yet here I am. So many decisions have led me to this cavernous clifftop house, to sit at a kitchen island drinking wine with a woman who looks just like me.

Meeting Alana wasn't a coincidence. It can't be. It feels too big, too strange, too significant. I don't know what it means yet, what I'm supposed to do, but I can feel it, thrumming under my skin. A purpose. A role I didn't ask for but can't ignore. Maybe it's fanciful, but I don't care. Alana already feels more of a sister to me than Sam ever will. I was meant to find her.

Sam is tied to everything I want to forget. Dad's betrayal, Mum's heartbreak, my splintered childhood. Every time I think about her, guilt, shame and anger settle over me like a heavy blanket. But Alana is untouched by all that. Our burgeoning friendship doesn't weigh me down. It buoys me up, makes me feel anything is possible. Like the first page in a brand-new notebook.

'I do think it's fate,' I say with feeling. A pause. Alana sips her wine and stares into the middle distance. She has pushed up the sleeves of her sweater, revealing the puckered scar on the back of her hand. The only dark cloud in an otherwise cloudless sky.

Alana's gaze slides to meet mine. 'You look worried. What's up?'

The question is there again, on the tip of my tongue. *What has Marcus done to you?* He is the key to understanding why I'm here. I push my empty glass away. The wine has given me courage.

'Come on,' I say. 'Let's go for a walk.'

22

LAURA

Alana blips a key fob and the gates slowly swing open. Was it only Monday that I was crouched in the garden wondering how the hell I'd ever get out? It feels like a month ago.

As if reading my thoughts, she nods at the keypad on this side of the wall. 'The code's two-four-zero-nine if you ever need it.'

'Your birthday?' I guess.

'Not mine. Marcus's. Mine's the first of March. What about yours?'

'The third of January. The dates are mirror images of each other too. That's weird.'

Alana laughs. 'Not really. Everyone's born on one day or another.'

I pretend to agree even though privately I see it as another sign that we are inextricably linked.

'Tell me about Marcus,' I say as we follow the coastal path west towards Penzance. 'I want to hear all about how you guys met.'

'I told you. He came to take some photos of our end-of-year fashion show.'

'You told me the short version. I want to hear it all. Go on,' I say, seeing her hesitate. 'I need my faith in men restored. There must be some decent guys out there, or humanity is doomed.'

She laughs again. 'OK, you win. So, I'd been in London studying for my master's for just over six months and I was loving every minute of it. When you grow up in New England the UK is your spiritual home. The fashion scene, the history, the culture, even the damn cute double-deckers and black cabs. I was a sucker for it all. And I loved the course. It was exciting, it pushed me and I was producing some of my best designs. You know how you said you knew you wanted to work with animals? I was the same with fashion. I was forever raiding the dressing-up box at school and always had a sketch pad in my hand. When I was in ninth grade, I cut up Mom's best linen tablecloth to make a dress for my freshman dance. Instead of hitting the roof, she bought me my own sewing machine and told me to follow my dreams. I never looked back. I was going to launch my own label, take the catwalks by storm, be the next Stella McCartney or Vera Wang. I had everything mapped out.'

'And then Marcus came along and swept you off your feet?'

'Like a modern-day Prince Charming,' Alana agrees. 'You can imagine how excited we all were. The famous Marcus Adams, who rarely left Cornwall, was coming up to London to shoot our little show. I have no idea how it came about. I think one of our lecturers was a friend of a friend. Anyways, we were all so excited.'

We stop to let a couple with a Border collie pass, then Alana continues. 'I'd been high on adrenaline all night. It was such a thrill to finally see my designs on the runway. Everyone was buzzing. And there was this stillness about Marcus. This intensity. We were kids playing at fashion and he was someone who'd been there, done that and bought the designer T-shirt. And he was so damn *handsome*. He made my insides turn to liquid honey.' She says this with a suggestive drawl and I can't help but laugh. 'That accent! Straight out of *Downton Abbey*. God, he was hot.' Alana pretends to fan herself. 'I knew he had a reputation for shunning the limelight, so I expected him to disappear right after the show. But he stayed. One of the lecturers called me over to introduce us, and Marcus and I, we just...' She blows hair out of her eyes. 'We just clicked. He asked about my designs and where I found my inspiration like he really gave a damn, you know?'

She glances at me and I nod. Vinnie had been enthralled by my every word in those heady few months when we first got together. For the first time in my life, I'd felt *heard*.

'We talked and talked, and suddenly it was midnight and the caretaker was chivvying us out of the hall. Marcus called me a cab and I went home, feeling a little like Cinderella leaving the ball. The next day two dozen red roses and tickets to the final night of London Fashion Week were delivered to my flat with a note from Marcus saying how much he'd enjoyed meeting me.'

'How did he know where you lived?'

'Oh, Marcus has a way of getting what he wants.' Alana laughs again, but this time it sounds hollow.

'So you went?'

'How could I say no? It's one of the most iconic shows in the world, and there I was, sitting in the front row next to this charming, gorgeous, talented man, sipping champagne and watching the designers I'd idolised since I was a teenager sending their collections down the runway. It was amazing.' Alana smiles at the memory. 'That night he told me he'd found the woman he wanted to spend the rest of his life with.'

'Wow. That's...' I search for the word. Cheesy? Excessive? Disturbing? I settle for, '...so sweet. Like, I dunno, something straight out of a romance novel.' I try hard not to grimace as I say this.

'I know, right?' Alana beams. 'It was a complete fairy tale.

The very next day he brought me to Cornwall and two weeks after that he proposed on the cliffs above Merryn's Cove. How could I refuse? I was infatuated.'

Infatuated, not in love. It's an odd thing to say and I glance at her, trying to read her expression, but it is curiously blank. I want to ask her how the endless red flags hadn't sent her running for the hills. Hadn't she realised that Marcus's behaviour was classic love-bombing? But this was ten years ago, I remind myself. Alana was only twenty-two and love-bombing wasn't on the radar like it is now. Would I have questioned the grand gestures, the flowers and the expensive restaurants if I'd been in her shoes at that age? Wined and dined by a handsome, famous man? I can't, hand on heart, say I would.

What intrigues me now is how their fairy tale really played out.

23

LAURA

'Follow me,' Alana says, veering off the path and onto a grassy promontory. 'There's a great view of St Michael's Mount from here.' She stops a few metres from the cliff edge and points out to sea. I follow her gaze, shielding my eyes from the sun until I spot the tiny island rising from the sea like one of those piles of rocks people leave on the top of mountains. The tide is out, exposing the centuries-old causeway that leads to the island.

We went to St Michael's Mount for the day during that fateful holiday to Porthmerryn all those years ago. It had been a happy day, I remember that. St Michael's Mount had reminded me of Kirrin Island from the *Famous Five* adventures I loved. Dad held my hand as we stepped carefully across the seaweed-covered granite setts to the tiny harbour, the tide lapping dangerously near our feet. Mum raved about the tropical plants in the castle's stunning gardens. The sun had been hot, the ice creams cold and delicious. When I caught Dad buying a shell necklace just like mine in the gift shop, I'd assumed it was for Mum, so we'd have one each. It was only later I learnt who it was really for. The secret sister I didn't know I had.

Alana takes another couple of steps towards the edge and

the contents of my stomach swoop like the seagulls riding the thermals below us. The urge to reach out and pull her back to a safe distance takes me by surprise. I stuff my hands in my pockets and tell myself to chill. She's not a child. She's perfectly capable of looking after herself. So why do I have this desire to protect her? Is my ticking biological clock to blame?

I spy a huge boulder that probably hasn't moved for millennia and settle down in front of it. The granite is warm against my back and its solid support is reassuring. My heart rate begins to slow.

'Come and sit down,' I call to Alana, patting the grass beside me. She lopes over and plonks down next to me, our shoulders touching. I pull out my phone and lean into her.

'We should do a selfie.'

She immediately stiffens and draws back.

'No selfies.'

'Why not?' I swallow my disappointment. I was going to pop it on Instagram and tag the doppelgänger photographer guy. With the right hashtags it'll get loads of likes.

'Marcus has a thing about social media. Says it's the scourge of modern-day society. All that personal data people are pumping straight into the hands of oligarchs and autocrats, never mind the fake news and toxicity. He'd lose his shit if I went against him.'

I glance away so she doesn't see my eyes widen. It's the first time she's even hinted that her life with Marcus is anything other than perfect.

'Understood.' I pick a long blade of grass and roll it between my thumb and forefinger. 'But how about if it was just for us? A memento of the two of us meeting?'

She rests her chin on her knees, her fingers laced around her shins.

'Please?' I wheedle. 'I promise I won't post it anywhere.'

A long sigh, then she relents. 'All right. But I'm serious, OK?'

'OK.' I hold the phone at arm's length and snap half a dozen photos. I scroll through them, deleting a couple in which I'm caught mid-blink. I zoom in, studying our faces. On camera we are even more alike than our three-dimensional selves. It's uncanny. Only our hairstyles are different: Alana has a fringe and shoulder-length hair. My hair is six inches longer with a side parting.

'Let's see,' Alana says, holding her hand out. I give her the phone and she squints at the screen. 'Look at us, two peas in a pod. If I narrow my eyes I can't tell us apart.' Her gaze slides to meet mine. 'Funny to think we could swap lives just like that.' She clicks her fingers, then smiles to show she's joking, but my heart is pounding in my chest.

Because the thing is, we could, couldn't we?

The thought lodges in my brain and won't budge. It should feel crazy, but it doesn't. Maybe it's the wine. Maybe I'm desperate for something good to come from my break-up with Vinnie. Maybe I'm just hardwired to rescue lost causes.

All I know for sure is that I am here for her and I will do whatever it takes to ensure she is happy. Safe. She only has to ask.

PART TWO

24

ALANA

I was infatuated.

I knew as soon as the words slipped out of my mouth that I'd made a mistake. I could see it in her eyes, clear as day. Doubt. Compassion. And something else. Something that looked very much like pity.

Poor, sweet Laura, who thinks the worst thing a man can do is have lunch with a blonde sales rep. She has no idea.

Of course, back then, neither did I.

It was 2015 and I'd been in the UK for almost a year. London was everything I hoped it would be and more. I was in love: not with the east London boys with their accents and swagger, or the posh City boys who chatted me up in the wine bars and nightclubs, but with the city itself. The dirty streets and graffiti, the history and glamour. It felt real and authentic and it seeped into my soul.

I spent my days at the London College of Fashion's imposing, brutalist campus in Marylebone, working my butt off perfecting my final collection, living off black coffees and meal deals from the Tesco Express in New Oxford Street. At weekends I scoured the shops in Brick Lane and Camden for vintage treasures and partied in Soho clubs and sticky-floored pubs in Kentish Town, loving every minute.

Being on the same continent as my father was the icing on the cake. I'd seen him a handful of times over the years when he'd flown to the States on business and we spoke on the phone every few weeks. Even though he wasn't exactly hands-on and had gone on to have several other affairs after the short-lived romance with my mother, he was still my dad and I called him up the day I arrived in London.

We arranged to meet for dinner at his swanky London club. He stood up when I arrived, and I had to hide my shock. He was in his mid-seventies by then, almost unrecognisable compared to the handsome, dark-haired man in Mom's photos back home. All the years of womanising had taken their toll. But his face lit up when he saw me, and he wrapped me in a cigar-scented bear hug that made me feel safer than I had for years.

'Look at you,' he said, holding me at arm's length, a huge smile on his face as he studied me. 'Even more beautiful than your mother. How is Kate?'

'She's good. Still working, though I keep telling her she should start taking it easy. She says hello.'

It always amazed me that Mom had never harboured a single shred of resentment that Dad was married when they met.

'Your father was upfront from the start, Alana. He loved Carol. He was never going to leave her. I knew we could never be together, but that was OK because I had you.'

'But you had to raise me on your own.'

'Your father helped out financially, and I did a pretty good job of bringing you up, didn't I?'

There was no arguing with that. Mom and I had been a tight-knit unit of two and I had nothing but happy memories of my childhood, but I'd read about fatherless daughters and how growing up without a dad left girls with self-esteem issues and problems forming lasting relationships. I didn't want to be the cliché who fell for an older man because I was desperate for a father figure.

I reassured myself that I didn't have to be, because Dad was back in my life. We used to meet up every couple of weeks, chatting non-stop over meals at his club as we filled each other in on our respective lives. He told me about his wife Carol and my half-brother and sister, George and Hannah. I told him about my childhood in New England and my burning passion to work in the fashion industry.

I can still remember how nervous I felt the first time I met my half-siblings. It was a week or so before Christmas, and Dad had invited us for a meal at a little French restaurant not far from Covent Garden. George and Hannah were well aware of their parents' unconventional marriage and, like Laura's sister Sam, had always known of my existence. Only a few years younger than Mom, they were friendly enough, if a little reserved.

'That's the British for you,' Mom said when I told her. 'Stiff upper lip and all that.'

'They'll come round,' Dad said, sensing my disappointment once they'd left. And he was right: they did. It took a few months, but by the time my course was coming to an end we were as close as I could hope for.

I'd been so proud to invite the three of them to my end-of-year show, and so devastated when Carol was rushed to hospital the day before after suffering a suspected stroke. Of course, I understood that their place was by her bedside, but it was an unwelcome reminder that although they had accepted me into their midst, I would always be on the outside looking in.

That's why the thrill of seeing my designs on the catwalk was tinged with sadness that Dad, George and Hannah weren't there to see them. I felt untethered, as though all ties to my family had been cut loose, like a Chinese lantern set free into the night sky. I had no idea if my future lay in the UK or back home. No idea what my future held at all, really.

That's why, when the celebrated photographer Marcus Adams gazed into my eyes and told me my designs had blown his mind, my heart raced. This supremely confident, talented enigma of a man thought *I* was the interesting one.

I fell for him hook, line and sinker.

25

ALANA

Ten years later, I can still remember exactly how I felt, sitting in the back of that black cab on the way home from my end-of-year show.

Giddy. Excited. *Alive.*

Marcus had walked me down to the street and summoned a taxi with an imperious click of his fingers. He opened the door, then took my hand and pressed it to his lips, making my already pounding heart miss several more beats. It was a ridiculously chivalrous thing to do, I thought, as I slipped into my seat in the back of the cab. And as the taxi rumbled through the empty streets towards my flatshare near St Pancras, I studied him out of the corner of my eye. Tall, dark and handsome, he was reserved but unfailingly gallant, and I was already a little in love with him.

I told myself not to let my imagination run wild. I'd googled Marcus when our tutor announced he was coming to our show and knew he was a notoriously private man who rarely appeared in public. His talent as a photographer was the stuff of legends. Word among the other students was that his patronage could make or break careers. And he'd positively raved about my designs. It was catnip for someone who was subconsciously seeking validation. Someone like me.

Pity I didn't see it at the time.

I wasn't lying when I told Laura I felt like Cinderella leaving the ball that night, my carriage about to turn into a pumpkin and my dress into rags. I'd trudged up the four flights of stairs to my flat with drooping shoulders and the sinking feeling that I would never see my Prince Charming again. I was still in my pyjamas and feeling sorry for myself when a delivery driver turned up on the doorstep the next morning with a hand-written envelope tucked into the biggest bunch of roses I'd ever seen. I ripped it open, my eyes widening when I saw the note from Marcus which said, in an elegant, sloping hand, that he hoped he wasn't being too forward, but he'd love to accompany me to London Fashion Week, but only if it was something I thought I might enjoy.

Was the guy for real? I'd have sold a kidney to go.

Marcus picked me up in a sleek silver Aston Martin, which turned heads in our shabby street. Dressed in a crisp white button-down shirt open at the collar, charcoal tailored trousers and polished brogues, he was the picture of sophistication.

'You look beautiful,' he said, taking my arm and leading me to his car. 'That dress, it's perfect for you. Valentino?'

My grin was in danger of splitting my face in two. 'Actually, it's one of mine.'

I was big into ethical fashion at the time, exclusively using remnant fabrics, swatch cards and offcuts for my designs. The dress, one I'd designed for a module on organic and recycled materials, had a floor-length dusky-pink satin skirt with a white organza top embroidered with orange and pink flowers, and cap sleeves.

'That is... remarkable,' Marcus said, his eyes not leaving my face. 'I'd like to photograph you in it one day, if that's not an imposition?'

I nodded, having temporarily lost the power of speech, and as I gazed back at him, a bolt of desire shot right through me, as powerful as an electric current.

Watching my favourite designers send their collections down the runway in the Georgian splendour of Somerset House with Marcus by my side, was a night I'll never forget. Afterwards, as drunk on excitement as I was on the vintage champagne, I accepted his offer of dinner. He took me to a two-Michelin-starred restaurant overlooking the Thames where the maitre d' discreetly found us a window table even though they were fully booked.

As my gaze darted around the room, taking in the elegant decor and a clientele so polished they all but shone, I thought about the women Marcus must usually date. Models and actresses, probably. Sophisticated women who moved in the same circles as him, not an unprepossessing Yank from Nowheresville. But it didn't seem to matter. He was the perfect companion, solicitous and interested in everything I had to say.

When the waiter came to take our order, Marcus smiled at him. 'We'll have the French onion soup to start, then the fillet of beef. Medium rare, but seared properly, not bleeding. And a bottle of the Barolo, please, Eduardo.'

I was about to tell him I'd stopped eating red meat the previous year but bit the words back. Pointing it out felt gauche. Ungrateful even. Because this was the kind of place where there were no prices on the menu and if you had to ask how much something cost, you almost certainly couldn't afford it.

'Tell me, Alana,' Marcus said, regarding me over steepled fingers. 'Do you like England?'

'No.'

For the briefest of moments his expression seemed to darken until I clarified, 'I *love* it. Everything about it. The architecture, the history, the roast potatoes, the beer. In fact, I'm considering joining AA.' The frown was back, and I quickly explained. 'Anglophiles Anonymous.'

'Ah, I see. Anglophiles Anonymous. Very good.' His face finally cleared as the waiter arrived with our soup. The melted Gruyère cheese on the crouton stuck in my throat like a ball of unshed tears. I should have known this meal was a mistake. I wasn't a part of this cosseted, elite world and Marcus was probably kicking himself for not dropping me back at my digs straight after the show.

I scratched around for something half intelligent to say, like a chook pecking about in the dirt for a kernel of corn.

'The catwalk is a big departure from the landscapes and people you usually photograph. Doesn't our world all seem a bit frivolous to you? A teeny bit trivial?'

Marcus took a slow sip of his wine, considering his answer, then he placed his glass carefully on the table. 'Beauty is never frivolous, Alana. Whether it's the hard-won lines on the face of a Cornish fisherman or the flawless skin of a dark-haired siren from Maine, it has meaning and power and deserves our admiration.'

Colour crept up my cheeks and I fiddled with my napkin. Under the table Marcus's knee brushed against mine. I dropped my gaze, suddenly self-conscious. I wanted to impress this handsome, sophisticated man so badly it hurt.

Marcus leaned back in his chair as if he was waiting for an answer. I fought a rising panic. Instinct told me I needed to play it just right.

'If that was a compliment, thank you,' I said graciously, and a lazy smile spread across his face. I had passed his test.

It was the first time I edited myself to fit the version of the woman he wanted me to be. What I didn't know then was that it wouldn't be the last.

26

ALANA

If I had hoped Marcus would take me back to his hotel that first night, I was sorely disappointed. Once again, he called me a cab. This time, instead of kissing my hand, he grazed my cheek with his lips.

'Don't be sad, little one,' he said, lifting my chin and gazing at me so intensely my legs went weak. 'We have all the time in the world to get to know each other.'

I was about to crack a joke about patience being a virtue but stopped myself just in time and simply nodded demurely and smiled back.

I was learning fast.

'God, you're beautiful,' he said, tracing the line of my jaw with his finger. 'You have bewitched me, Alana Harrington.' He dropped a kiss on my forehead, then tucked a strand of hair behind my ear. 'I think I've found the woman I want to spend the rest of my life with.'

I hid my shock. Men like Marcus didn't make proclamations like that over girls like me, especially on a first date. It was insane. This whole thing was insane. I wasn't Cinderella and

Marcus wasn't my Prince Charming. Real life didn't work like that.

I was saved from thinking of a suitable response by the taxi driver, who wound down his window and huffed, 'You want a bleedin' lift or not?'

'I'll call you tomorrow,' Marcus said, shooting the cabbie a dark look before holding open the passenger door and ushering me inside.

It was only as I was halfway home that I realised Marcus couldn't call me because he didn't have my number.

* * *

I was still asleep when my cell pinged with a text from a number I didn't recognise at half seven the following morning. I stared blearily at the screen.

Morning, gorgeous. Be ready for nine with an overnight bag packed. I have a surprise planned.

I pushed myself up on my elbows and frowned. The text could only be from Marcus, but how in heaven's name had he managed to find my number? The only people I'd given it to since I'd arrived in the UK were my college, a few friends on my course and Dad, George and Hannah. I felt a prick of unease but told myself not to overreact. He'd probably asked one of my lecturers. It was no biggie.

I was about to tap out a reply when I stopped myself. I assumed it was from Marcus, but what if I was wrong? Perhaps Dad's cell had run out of charge at the hospital and he'd borrowed someone else's? But no, that was silly. If he was still at the hospital he wouldn't be organising surprises. There was one way to find out. My fingers raced across the screen as I pinged off a text to him.

Hey, Dad, how's Carol doing? Ax

I chewed a nail as I waited for a reply.

Not good, honey. The doctors are talking about moving her to a hospice.

Oh, God, I'm so sorry. Is there anything I can do? I typed.

No, but thank you for offering, darling girl. I've got to go, the consultant's just arrived.

Sending you, George and Hannah all my love xxx

I sank back on the pillows, compassion for my father and half-siblings washing over me. Dad and Carol might have had an unconventional marriage, but it was clear they meant the world to each other. I pictured Dad, George and Hannah gathered around Carol's bed on a sterile hospital ward, watching over her like sentinels as her broken synapses tried to recover from the devastation caused by the stroke. My eyes brimmed with tears and, without thinking, I found Mom's number, about to call her when I remembered it was two thirty in the morning at home. Instead, I hit reply to the mystery text.

Marcus, is that you?

Why, do you have any other suitors I should know about?

Of course not. But please tell me where we're going. I hate surprises.

I watched the three ellipses as he typed out a reply, a fluttery feeling in the pit of my stomach.

You're going to have to get used to them if you're going to be the new Mrs Adams... I'll see you at nine. Don't make me wait.

I stared at the screen, my eyes bulging. The new Mrs Adams? But we'd only just met! It was true that I'd felt an instant attraction to Marcus. His confidence and worldliness were intoxicating. Until then, the guys I dated were my age but often seemed younger, their priorities firmly centred around having a good time. That's not to say I was particularly interested in settling down. I was having too much fun. But Marcus was a door to a world of expensive restaurants and fast cars, of art and privilege, a world I wanted to be a part of.

When his Aston Martin pulled up outside my flatshare on the dot of nine, I was ready and waiting for him. I'd spent an age ferreting through my wardrobe wondering what to wear, eventually settling on a vintage white floaty A-line dress and strappy gladiator sandals. My hair was newly washed and my face carefully made up to look like I wasn't wearing any make-up at all, a trick I'd learnt from one of the girls on my course.

He'd given a low whistle, then kissed me on the cheek.

'You look beautiful, darling. I'm so glad you're not one of those women who plasters themselves in make-up. It wouldn't suit you. Shall we?' He gave a little bow and opened the passenger door.

His car smelt of leather and expensive aftershave, a rich, heady mix that was at once thrilling and overwhelming. I smoothed down my dress with trembling fingers. It was ridiculous to be so nervous when he'd gone out of his way to put me at my ease.

'Where are we going?' I asked as he pulled away.

'Ever been to Cornwall?'

'That's where King Arthur and *Poldark* are from, right? I haven't, but I had a Cornish pasty once, if that counts?'

He smiled indulgently. 'It's a start, I suppose. Cornwall isn't just a place, it's a way of life, Alana. It seeps into your bones. It has it all: amazing light, a dramatic coast, resilient people. Did you know that Cornwall was a kingdom long before England even existed? We even have our own language.'

'We? Is that where you're from?'

'Cornish born and bred, as was my father and his father before him. I'm taking you to my house. Merryn's Reach.'

'Merryn's Reach,' I repeated, rolling the name around my tongue and liking the feel of it. 'It sounds so romantic, like something out of a Daphne du Maurier novel.'

Marcus glanced at me. 'You like du Maurier?'

'I've loved her ever since I read *Rebecca* at school. I forgot she came from Cornwall.'

'To be accurate, she didn't come from Cornwall, she moved there as a young woman and never left. So be careful.' Marcus looked sidelong at me, a smile playing on his lips. 'You might never escape.'

'Tell me about Merryn's Reach,' I begged, imagining a once-grand, gothic mansion perched on a hill like Manderley in *Rebecca*. Decaying, but beautiful. A house that was, as du Maurier wrote, 'ancient with stories'.

'Why don't you wait and see for yourself. Suffice to say, I think you'll like it.'

He was wrong on that score. I hated it on sight.

The first inkling I had that Merryn's Reach was no Manderley came when Marcus pulled up in front of a pair of wrought-iron gates set in what looked like the walls of a prison. He blipped his key fob and, as the gates slowly swung open, I let out a gasp. I couldn't help myself.

Mistaking my shock for pleasure, Marcus smiled. 'Pretty impressive, yes?'

I stared at the house with my mouth open, catching flies. Merryn's Reach wasn't a house, it was a vast concrete box. I was used to the clapboard houses of New England and London's Georgian and Victorian terraces. This place was an eyesore. There was no other word for it. There was a multistorey car park near my flatshare that had more soul.

Realising Marcus's male pride might never recover if I revealed what I really thought about the house, I smiled back.

'It's absolutely stunning, Marcus.'

'Better than those crumbling gothic nightmares du Maurier wrote about, don't you think?' he said, twinkling. 'And I can promise you one thing: there aren't any wives hidden in the attic.'

I forced a laugh, because I knew it was what he expected. But as he led me inside, a chill passed over me. He might not have a wife in the attic.

But that didn't mean he wasn't hiding something.

27

ALANA

Marcus was as excited as a child at Christmas as he gave me a tour of the house. His enthusiasm was infectious, and before long I found myself viewing the stark lines and uncompromising minimalism with a new perspective. He was right: the way the sunlight played through the huge windows into the cavernous living space *was* remarkable; the sleek, clutter-free surroundings *were* calming. And the views of the coastline were breathtaking.

Marcus's photographs adorned every wall, and I found myself drawn to them. The house was austere to the point of sterile, but his images were the opposite. They were alive with details. The pores on an old man's nose. Sprays of seawater suspended mid-air like ice crystals as waves slammed into rocky cliffs. Sand caked on the muscular torso of a dreadlocked bodyboarder. Each shot was so vivid I felt like a voyeur, staring at something I shouldn't be looking at.

As we moved from room to room, Marcus preened as I gushed.

'And, finally, the best room of all,' he said, a glint in his eye as we headed back down the wide, curving staircase.

I frowned. We'd already toured the four upstairs bedrooms, each with a luxurious en suite that would rival any five-star hotel, the fully equipped gym and the cinema room at the back of the house. What else could there be?

Marcus pressed his palm against a section of the wall under the stairs, and a hidden door clicked open. 'This is where the magic happens.' He smirked. 'Don't look so worried, Alana, darling. I'm not about to lead you into a chamber of horrors. It's my darkroom.'

'Oh, right.' My face cleared, a flush blooming on my cheeks as I peered past him down a flight of concrete steps. Marcus had told me on the journey down that he developed all his own film. Of course there must have been a darkroom somewhere. And it made sense for it to be in the cellar where there was no danger of natural light ruining his images.

'Want to see what I'm working on?' he asked.

'I... I'd love to.'

Marcus hit a switch and a red light flickered on.

'After you,' he said, giving a small bow.

I gave him a weak smile and headed down the stairs, taking care not to trip.

The room was rectangular, the left-hand wall fitted with a line of stainless-steel counters and a couple of sinks. Above them, images were pegged out on a length of wire, like shirts on a washing line. A tall projector-like machine was, Marcus explained, an enlarger, used to project negatives onto photographic paper. Gloves, goggles and tongs were arranged with military precision next to it. The air was heavy with the metallic scent of chemicals.

'I've always wondered why the light has to be red?' I asked, wandering over to the nearest counter, on which a series of thick plastic trays were lined up.

'Photographic paper is sensitive to blue and green light but red is safe because it doesn't expose the paper. Developing film is all about chemistry,' Marcus continued. 'You need a developer, a stop bath and a fixer. The developer converts the latent image on the film into a visible image. The stop bath neutralises the developer, and the fixer sets the image, making it permanent.'

'It sounds complicated.'

'Not at all. It's like anything. You put in the work, you get the results. Be careful!' he cried, as my elbow brushed against a plastic five-litre container. 'One drop of that would burn right through your skin.'

I shot my arm back, suddenly desperate to return from the darkroom to the light-filled house. The low ceiling was claustrophobic, the chemical smell so strong it made my eyes water. I muttered something about needing the bathroom and ran up the stairs, only to find the door was shut tight.

I reached for the door handle, but there wasn't one. Just smooth, cold metal. My stomach flipped. 'Where's the handle?' I called, forcing my voice to sound calm even though inside, my anxiety was rocketing. I ran my hand over the door again, pressing against it, expecting it to give. It didn't.

Behind me was the steady tread of Marcus's footsteps as he followed me up the stairs.

'Relax, darling,' he said, chuckling. 'It's just a magnetic lock. I keep the darkroom completely lightproof. Otherwise one accidental opening of the door would ruin hours of work.'

I stood back to let him pass and he reached out, pressed a keypad I hadn't noticed on the wall next to the light switch, and the door opened with a faint click. Suddenly, the stairs were flooded with light. He turned to me.

'Not that you'll ever need it, but the code's six-six-six-six. Just my little joke,' he added with an impish grin.

I rolled my eyes. 'Very funny.'

His expression turned serious. 'So. Do you like my house, Alana Harrington?'

I chose my words carefully. 'I love it. It's so... unique. Like your work. Like you.'

He clapped his hands in delight. 'You get it. I knew you would, the moment I met you. You and I, we are the same, Alana. We are meant to be together.'

* * *

In the space of a few short days, both Marcus and the house inveigled their way into my heart. I stayed at Merryn's Reach for the next two weeks, missing an important essay deadline and a seminar by a guest lecturer I'd been looking forward to for months. But suddenly, my master's felt trivial, a way of treading water till my real life began. And life with Marcus felt more real than anything I'd ever experienced in my twenty-two years.

He was an old-fashioned romantic with impeccable manners who made me feel as though I was the most interesting person he'd ever met. He cooked me exquisite meals and ran me candlelit baths. He filled the house with bouquets of my favourite stargazer lilies he had specially delivered from the same London florist who'd provided the flowers for William and Kate's wedding. He was rarely without his camera and took endless photos of me. At first, I was self-conscious, but I soon became used to the camera lens and found I enjoyed being the focus of his undivided attention. He was always telling me how beautiful I was; how much he adored me.

Sex with Marcus was like nothing I'd ever experienced before. Intense. Passionate. Exciting. There was no fumbling, no awkwardness. Foreplay to Marcus was as important as the act itself, and by the time we made love I was dizzy with desire. Once, he grabbed me as I walked past him and pressed me against the wall, his breath warm against my neck, his eyes almost black with longing. His fingers curled round my wrists as he held them above my head. 'Do you have any idea what you do to me?' he growled softly into my ear. 'You drive me crazy, Alana. Fucking crazy.'

I'd physically swooned.

The day before I was due to return to London, we went for a long walk along the cliffs. Marcus had seemed downcast from the moment I booked my train ticket but that morning his mood had brightened.

It was a windy day, clouds scudding across the washed-out sky in a race for the horizon. On the bluff above Merryn's Cove, Marcus stopped, took my hand in his and gazed lovingly into my eyes.

'Marry me,' he said.

I frowned, wondering if he was joking. It was true I had fallen head over heels in love with him, but we'd only known each other for just over a couple of weeks. It was too fast. Way too fast.

He must have sensed my hesitation, because he said urgently, 'We're meant to be together, Alana. Don't tell me you can't feel it too? This... what we have... only happens once in a lifetime. Don't let it slip through your fingers.'

Any doubts I might have had that we were rushing into things melted away as I gazed back at him.

'OK,' I said, half laughing, half crying. 'I will marry you, you crazy, crazy man.'

If only I'd known then just how true those words would turn out to be, I wouldn't have laughed.

I wouldn't have said yes.

I would have run like hell.

28

ALANA

Marcus and I married in a simple ceremony at Old Marylebone Town Hall, where Paul McCartney wed Heather Mills and Jude Law married Sadie Frost.

I was so in love that I refused to see the failure of both celebrity marriages as an omen.

I wore a dress I'd designed myself. An understated but elegant sheath of ivory satin that pooled at my feet and clung in all the right places. I wore my hair in loose waves down my back, the only adornment a simple headband of mother-of-pearl daisies. Marcus looked sexy as hell in a sharp black suit and white shirt, the top button undone. His old friend Jasper Trelawney, who owned a gallery in St Ives, was one witness. Dad was our second.

I'd been heartbroken when Mom couldn't make it, but she was in the middle of a complicated financial fraud case and couldn't get away at such short notice.

'Don't worry,' Marcus soothed, when I'd tearfully told him she wasn't coming. 'There'll be plenty of time for you to see each other after the wedding. We could even fly out. You can show me where you grew up.'

Dad seemed somehow diminished as he walked me down the aisle. Carol had passed away a month before, her husband and children by her bedside. I'd wanted to postpone the wedding till after her funeral, but Marcus had been adamant.

'Don't make me wait,' he'd said, the hint of a scowl darkening his handsome features. 'I'm sure your father won't mind.'

He was right. Dad had urged me to go ahead. 'It'll be nice to have something to celebrate. I know George and Hannah feel the same.'

The ceremony passed in a blur, and before I knew it, I was no longer Alana Harrington but Mrs Marcus Adams, admiring the diamond-studded platinum band on my ring finger and feeling so damn happy as my new husband picked me up and twirled me in his arms, announcing he was the luckiest man alive.

Afterwards, we had an early dinner at The Ivy. Marcus charmed the pants off my father and half-siblings. I was monopolised by Jasper, who regaled me with stories of Marcus when he was a boy.

I was all ears, as every time I asked Marcus about his childhood he shut me down, saying he didn't want to talk about it. From Jasper I learnt that Marcus's father, Alastair, was a respected landscape artist, though he'd never quite achieved the recognition he felt he deserved.

'That must have been tough. How did he deal with it?' I asked.

Jasper glanced at Marcus, who was deep in conversation with Dad. 'Badly,' he said with a pantomime grimace. 'He had a nasty temper, did Alastair.'

I let this digest, until another question occurred to me. 'What about Marcus's mom? What was she like?'

'Clarissa? Beautiful but fragile. I'm afraid she bore the brunt of Alastair's rages. I never understood why she didn't leave him, but I suppose women didn't in those days.'

'Marcus doesn't have a single picture of either of them,' I mused. 'Not that I've been able to find, anyway. Nor any of his dad's paintings.'

'I suppose they'd have been lost in the fire. Such a tragedy.'

Marcus had told me about the fire that had ripped through his childhood home two years previously. Blamed on faulty electrics in the loft, the fire had razed the old Edwardian mansion to the ground. Alastair and Clarissa were both long dead by then, and – fortunately – Marcus had been attending the opening night of an exhibition in London. The first he'd known about the blaze was when the police phoned to tell him his home had gone up in smoke.

'What are you two talking about?' Marcus said, snaking an arm around my shoulder, making me jump. I was about to tell him when I caught the look on Jasper's face.

'Jasper's been waxing lyrical about what a prodigious talent you are. I wasn't going to tell you in case your head got too big to squeeze through the door,' I said instead, batting him lightly on the arm.

Marcus grinned and I felt my shoulders relax. It wouldn't do to annoy him, today of all days.

* * *

For our honeymoon, Marcus booked a week at the art deco Burgh Island Hotel on Devon's south coast. I was enchanted when I discovered previous guests included not just The Beatles but Edward and Mrs Simpson, a couple who defied the odds to stay together.

Marcus couldn't have picked a more romantic place if he'd tried. The hotel was gorgeous, pure 1930s glamour. We stayed in the Beach House. Nestled into the rocky cliffs and facing out to sea, it had a private sun deck and outdoor hot tub and had once been a writer's retreat for Agatha Christie.

Marcus was attentive and loving, the perfect husband. He wrote me poems, tucking them under my pillow so they'd be the first thing I saw when I woke up. He sat at the end of the bed and watched as I put on my make-up, offering opinions on shades of lipstick and helping me choose a dress for dinner. He told me, over and over, that his life began when we met. And if, occasionally, all that laser-focused attention felt a little claustrophobic, well, that was my failing, not his.

It was on our last night that Marcus dropped a bombshell I hadn't seen coming. I could tell something was on his mind. He'd felt distant and on edge all day, snapping at a waitress when she spilled orange juice on the table at breakfast and calling up reception to complain housekeeping hadn't left us enough towels.

He was monosyllabic over dinner, barely answering when I tried to engage him in conversation, even when it was about his favourite subject: himself. Because I'd quickly learnt that stroking his ego was the easiest way to tease him out of a black mood, and when that didn't work, sex usually did the trick. But that night every attempt to lighten his mood hit a brick wall.

He climbed into bed in silence, immediately turning his back to me. I'd been planning to read, but knew I wouldn't concentrate until I worked out what was bothering him. I switched off my bedside light and ran a hand lightly across his shoulder.

'What's wrong, sweetheart? Have I done something to upset you?'

He didn't answer and I tensed, replaying the day in my mind, looking for something I might have done wrong. A curt word or a thoughtless comment, anything that might have annoyed him. But hard as I tried, I couldn't think of anything.

'Please, Marcus, talk to me. I hate to see you miserable,' I pleaded.

Just when I was about to give up hope of him answering, he turned onto his back and stared up at the ceiling.

'It's your course,' he said finally.

I frowned into the darkness. I counted myself extremely lucky that, after missing so much of my final term, my tutor said I could retake the year. I'd been worried how Marcus would react, but he'd been nothing but supportive. We'd talked everything through before the wedding. He was going to spend more time at his London flat during term-time and I'd be back in Cornwall for the holidays. We'd promised each other we'd make it work. My happiness, he said, was his priority. If finishing my master's made me happy, he would move heaven and earth to help me.

And I'd believed him.

'What about my course?' I said, feeling a flicker of disquiet.

'I don't want you to do it.'

'But we talked about this. You're going to spend more time in London, and I'll be home every holiday. And it's only a year. Less than that. Nine months, really. It'll fly by.'

'I can't function without you, Alana.'

'Don't be melodramatic. You've functioned perfectly adequately without me for the last thirty-five years.'

It was the wrong thing to say. He reared up out of the bed, muscles bulging in his chest, and I shrank back.

'All right, Miss Pedantic. I don't *want* to function without you. And I shouldn't have to. You're my wife. Your place is with me, not wasting your time at a second-rate college sketching dresses for flat-chested clothes hangers.'

The contempt in his voice was as corrosive as acid. But it was his complete about-turn that really unnerved me. He knew I'd wanted to be a fashion designer all my life and he'd been not just supportive but proud of my chosen career. At least that was the picture he'd painted. Now I wasn't so sure. Had it all been a play to seduce me?

I tried a different tack. A compromise that should keep us both happy. 'What if I looked at Open University courses? I could study at home then.'

He let out a long, loud sigh. 'You don't get it, do you? You don't need to work. I have plenty of money. I'm your priority now, Alana, and you need to remember that. Now, if you don't mind, I need to get some sleep. We have an early start in the morning.'

He turned his back on me again, and I lay as still as I could beside him, my heart crashing in my chest, wondering how the future I'd planned for so long could be stolen from me in the space of one evening.

Even then, as I clutched the duvet under my chin, craving the oblivion of sleep, I still hoped I could talk him round. It just needed time and a strategy. Surely he'd see, in the light of the morning, that by stifling my career he would stifle me? And he loved me, right? That's what he was always telling me. He loved me more than life itself.

I prayed my optimism wasn't misplaced.

Because one thing was very clear. The honeymoon was over.

29

ALANA

By morning, my mind was made up. I was only twenty-two and I still had my degree. I didn't need a master's to start designing my own collections. I could work when Marcus was working. In fact, he didn't even need to know. All I needed was a sketch pad, a pencil and my imagination. I turned to him to deliver the good news that I was happy to be a stay-at-home wife, only to discover his side of the bed was empty.

'Marcus?' I called. No answer.

Frustrated, I jumped out of bed, wrapped one of the hotel's dressing robes round me, and went in search of him, eventually finding him on the sun deck, his chin in his hands, staring out to sea.

'I've decided,' I said, as if the decision had been mine to make. 'I'm not going back to college. You were right. My place is in Cornwall with you.'

His face split into a huge grin. 'I knew you'd see sense.' He stood, his arms outstretched. 'Come here, Mrs Adams.'

I let myself melt against him, hugging the thought to myself that I wasn't caving in completely. I would still work, even if it wasn't how or where I'd planned.

Marcus nuzzled my neck. 'Come to bed,' he murmured, taking my hand and leading me back across the deck. I followed, glad equanimity had been restored, for now at least.

* * *

Back at Merryn's Reach, our life settled into a routine. Marcus was working round the clock ahead of a new exhibition at Jasper's gallery in St Ives, spending his days travelling across Cornwall with his camera and his evenings in the darkroom.

I came to terms with my new role as mistress of the house. There wasn't much to do: Marcus's cleaner, Mairead, came three times a week, and her son, Rory, looked after the garden. But I took charge of planning and cooking our meals and the weekly online shop.

Marcus was meticulous about food, throwing anything even near its use-by date in the waste disposal unit. Having grown up watching every penny, I found the waste criminal. When he chucked out two perfectly good sirloin steaks two days before their use-by date, I'd challenged him.

'Why didn't you stick them in the freezer if you didn't think we'd eat them in time?'

'I am not risking getting food poisoning because of two steaks,' he said, his voice tight. 'Anyway, they smelt off. Perhaps if you planned our meals better, I wouldn't have to dispose of them.'

I stifled a sigh. Marcus had this knack of making everything that went wrong my fault and it was easier all round to agree. He was the one paying the bills. If he wanted me to throw away perfectly good food, that was his prerogative.

'You're right,' I said. 'I'll make sure it doesn't happen again.'

A month or so after we were back from our honeymoon, I discovered the reason for his fastidiousness over food. He was in north Cornwall, photographing the pretty harbour at Padstow, when Mairead called to say both she and Rory had been laid low with norovirus and wouldn't be coming in to work.

By early afternoon, I began to feel queasy. I tried to ignore it, putting it down to the runny poached egg I had for breakfast, and nibbled on a ginger biscuit. But by six o'clock, the contents of my stomach were churning like cement in a concrete mixer and beads of cold sweat were breaking out across my forehead.

I took myself up to bed, plumped up the pillows behind me and sipped a glass of water, hoping the nausea would pass. But it came in dizzying waves, as relentless as an incoming tide. When the vomiting started, I barely made it to the bathroom in time. I crouched by the toilet, my hands curled around the seat, as my body purged itself of everything I'd eaten in the last twenty-four hours.

I stayed like that for almost an hour, not daring to move, when I heard the click of the front door.

'Alana, where are you?' Marcus's imperious voice carried through the house.

'Upstairs,' I tried to call back, but my reply was little more than a croak, my throat was so tender.

He was muttering to himself as he stomped into the bedroom. Something about the wheelbarrow Rory had left on the lawn. I wiped my sweaty brow and sat back on my haunches.

'I'm in here,' I rasped.

I sensed rather than saw him by the bathroom door and the relief was immense. Here was someone to bring me a glass of water and rub my back. Someone to look after me.

'I don't feel too good.' I groaned and clutched my stomach as another wave of nausea rolled through me.

Marcus didn't rush to my side with a damp flannel. He didn't press a cool hand to my forehead and tell me I was going to be OK. Instead, he hovered in the doorway, and when he finally spoke, his voice was thick with distaste.

'Jesus, Alana, have you *vomited*?'

'Mairead phoned in sick. She and Rory have norovirus. I think I must have caught it too.'

'Christ.' His voice was taut with anger. And something else. Something fraught. Panic? 'Did you touch anything? The fridge? The sink?'

I blinked at him, dazed. 'What?'

'The door handles, Alana. Did you touch the door handles? His eyes slid to the bedroom, then widened. 'You've been in the bed? I'll have to change the sheets. And the handles. I need to wipe all the handles.' He was already backing away, his expression a mixture of horror and revulsion.

I stared at him in shock. I was hurling my guts up and he was worried about the goddamn *bed sheets*?

'Marcus, I—' But I couldn't finish. I lunged over the toilet again, gagging as another ripple of biliousness cramped my stomach. When I finally slumped back onto my heels, wiping my mouth with the back of my hand, he was standing in our bedroom, his arms folded across his chest.

'There are disinfectant wipes and a bottle of bleach in the cupboard under the sink. Please make sure you clean up after yourself.' He pressed his lips together, his face as pale as mine. 'I'll sleep in the spare room tonight.'

Before I could say anything, he was gone.

30

ALANA

I woke up the next morning, hollow, exhausted and alone. The Aston Martin was gone, and so was Marcus. I told myself he was probably feeling guilty for being so unsympathetic the previous day and had driven to the supermarket to pick up a packet of rehydration drinks or a carton of chicken soup, which is what Mom always used to give me when I was sick.

I showered and washed my hair, and although I felt as though I'd been flattened by a steamroller, at least the nausea had passed and I was able to keep a glass of water down and even nibble on a piece of toast.

I called Marcus, leaving a message when his phone went straight to voicemail.

'Hey, honey, it's me. If you get this in time, could you pick up some herbal tea? Peppermint or fennel, if they have it.'

When, by lunchtime, Marcus still wasn't home, I began to worry. The nearest supermarket was only a twenty-minute drive away. He should have been back ages ago. What if he'd had an accident or the car had broken down?

Common sense told me he'd probably stopped off some-where to take some photos and had lost track of time, but when it reached six o'clock and he still wasn't home, my worry turned into a low-level panic. I searched my memory, trying to recall if he'd mentioned an exhibition or a work commitment I'd forgotten about, but my mind was a blank. I combed the house in case he'd left me a note saying he was popping over to St Ives to have lunch with Jasper or he'd been called up to London unexpectedly. There was no note. I shuffled up the stairs to our bedroom to check his wardrobe to see if I could work out what he was wearing in case it offered any clues. A suit would signal a meeting, but if he was in his thick fisherman's sweater and cargo pants he'd be out there somewhere with his camera.

His overnight bag, half a dozen shirts, a couple of merino wool sweaters and some black jeans were missing.

Before my brain had a chance to process this, I was calling him again.

'Where are you, Marcus?' I asked, my voice shrill. 'Phone me, please. I'm worried about you.'

I sank onto the bed, the phone clutched in my hand. We'd been married for less than six weeks, and my husband thought it was acceptable to waltz out without telling me where he was going, with no thought for me and the fact that I would be scared as hell.

I wanted someone to reassure me that there would be a perfectly reasonable explanation. But who could I phone? I couldn't worry Mom, who'd feel powerless to help, stuck on the other side of the Atlantic. It wouldn't be fair to call Dad, George or Hannah: they were all still reeling over Carol's death. I was too embarrassed to phone my friends at college and admit that my fairy-tale marriage had already lost some of its sparkle. And there was no one else. No one.

In desperation, I googled the phone number of The Seaforth Gallery. Jasper was the only person I could think of who might know where Marcus was. I dialled the number, thumping the duvet in frustration when a recorded voice informed me the gallery's opening hours were ten till four, Monday to Sunday. I didn't have Jasper's mobile number, but Marcus kept a contacts book in the darkroom. It was bound to be in there.

I made my way slowly downstairs, hesitating outside the hidden door to the darkroom. Marcus was funny about me going down there on my own. He viewed it as other men might view their man cave at the bottom of the garden, as his own private domain. I hadn't been in it since the day he showed me round Merryn's Reach.

Even though I remembered the code for the door, I took no chances, dragging one of the heavy bar stools over from the kitchen island to prop it open. Marcus could have changed the code for all I knew. I hit the light switch and at once the cavernous space was illuminated by that eerie red glow.

The contacts book was on top of a metal filing cabinet at the far end of the room. I flipped it open and flicked through the pages, not daring to use the torch on my cell phone in case I damaged any of Marcus's prints. It was a struggle to find Jasper's number but eventually I did and, squinting, I punched the number into my contacts.

There was no WiFi in the darkroom – part of Marcus's desire to keep the intrusions of modern life at bay when he was working – so I closed the book, replaced it on top of the filing cabinet, and was about to set off for the stairs when my eye was caught by a string of photos hanging to dry above the steel workbench.

Marcus had asked me to model for him on the cliffs above Merryn's Cove a couple of weeks previously, and he hadn't yet shown me the results. Curious, I stepped over to take a look.

Quick as a flash, my anticipation turned to horror as I realised what I was looking at. A seagull trapped in a fishing net, its neck at an unnatural angle and its beady eye dulled by death. It would be a statement, I told myself. Marcus telling the world through his pictures that humankind needed to take better care of the environment or we'd live to regret it. Bold, but brave. Thought-provoking. I peered at the next photo. This was a zoomed-in shot of the seagull's dead eye and was so high-res I could see my husband's reflection in the glassy orb. I looked closer. His face was half hidden by his camera, but the Canon SLR didn't quite cover his rictus grin.

The hairs on the back of my neck stiffened, and I almost turned on my heels and left then, but my gaze slid to the third picture before I had the chance. It was a line of tiny bird skeletons, laid out so perfectly along the tideline that they could have only arrived there by human hand. I shivered. Had Marcus stumbled across them, or had he put them there himself?

A wave of the nausea I thought had passed rose in me again, and I stumbled up the stairs and into the house gasping for air as though I'd been holding my head underwater. There was so much I didn't know about the man I'd married. Not least his whereabouts.

Where the hell was he?

31

ALANA

My breathing was shallow as I waited for Jasper to answer my call. Just as I was giving up hope, there was a click and his plummy voice filled my ears, as welcome as a mug of hot chocolate on a snowy day.

'Jasper Trelawney speaking.'

'Jasper? It's Alana. Marcus's wife,' I added, suddenly worried he might have forgotten who I was.

'Alana, darling! How's married life treating you? Marcus behaving himself, is he?'

It was an odd thing to say, and only served to ramp up my anxiety.

'That's the thing, Jasper. He's disappeared, and I have no idea where he's gone.'

'Disappeared?'

'He wasn't here when I woke up this morning.' I didn't mention the missing overnight bag. I was too ashamed. 'I assumed he'd come to see you, but it's' – I glanced at my watch – 'almost seven now and he's still not back. I'm getting worried.'

'He's not come to see me, old love. We have a lunch in the diary next Monday, but that's it. Have you tried his mobile?'

'I've left a dozen messages asking him to call me. I'm worried he's had some kind of accident. It's so out of character for him to disappear like this.' Even as I said it, I checked myself. I was beginning to realise I had no idea what was or wasn't out of character for Marcus.

'You two haven't had a lovers' tiff?'

'No. I've been laid low with norovirus.' I couldn't miss Jasper's sharp intake of breath. 'What is it?'

'He hasn't told you?'

'Told me what?'

'I'm not sure it's my place to—'

'Jasper, *please*. What hasn't Marcus told me?'

A beat of silence, then a sigh. 'He suffers from emetophobia.'

I frowned. It sounded like a disease you'd catch from leeches in the Amazon rainforest.

'Emeto-what?'

'It's a fear of vomiting. In Marcus's case, it extends to seeing or hearing someone else being sick.'

'That's a thing?' I couldn't hide my disbelief.

'Oh, yes, a very real thing. Marcus has had it since he was a little boy. It stems from a time he had food poisoning and his father locked him in his bedroom with a bucket and left him to get on with it. He was shut in there for twenty-four hours. Look, I'm not sure I should be telling you all this. You know what an intensely private man Marcus is.'

'No, I need to know.' Compassion for my husband chased away the fear I'd been struggling to contain all day. Now I stopped to think about it, Jasper's revelation made perfect sense. One of my elementary school friends had a phobia of spiders. I used to poke fun at her until I saw her have a full-on panic attack when a tiny money spider crawled across her desk one day. I genuinely thought she was having a heart attack. I never teased her again.

'Have you never wondered why Marcus never has more than a couple of glasses of wine?' Jasper said. 'And why he's so fussy in restaurants? Eating out is a big trust thing for him. He has to be sure he's not going to end up with food poisoning.'

'He never eats shellfish,' I said slowly. 'And he's really finicky about sell-by dates at home. No wonder he was so upset when I was ill yesterday.'

'Try not to worry, Alana, darling. I'm sure he'll be home before you know it. Enough about Marcus. How are *you* feeling? Is there anything I can do?'

Tears unexpectedly welled in my eyes at Jasper's concern.

'Thank you, but I'm fine. I'm already feeling so much better.' And it was true. Understanding the reason for Marcus's behaviour had eased the panic that had gripped me when I realised he'd gone.

'You take care of yourself, d'you hear me? And Alana? Best not make a big thing about this when Marcus does come home. He's a bit sensitive about it, as you can imagine.'

'Of course.' I thanked him, ended the call and stared at my cell for a moment. Finally, I tapped out a text.

*Hey, baby, just wanted to tell you I'm feeling so much
better. Let me know when you'll be home and I'll make
us something delicious for dinner. A xx*

Just over an hour later, the Aston pulled into the drive. I'd given the door handles a cursory wipe, squirted some bleach down the toilet and changed the sheets on our bed, figuring that it would be enough to keep Marcus happy.

Play it cool, I told myself as I opened the front door. Jasper was right. My husband was a proud man, and if he thought I knew about his phobia, he might feel exposed – even emasculated.

'Hi, honey. How was your day?' I beamed at Marcus, feeling a little like a Stepford wife.

He grunted, dropping his overnight bag on the floor.

'Are you hungry? There are some fishcakes in the oven and I've made a salad.'

'Did you wash the lettuce properly?'

'I did. And I've chosen us a nice Sancerre to go with it. Do you want to freshen up while I lay the table? I've cleaned the en suite.'

He grunted again and disappeared upstairs. I poured myself a large glass of wine and was halfway down it when he reappeared, dressed in white lounge pants and a tight black T-shirt, his dark hair still wet from the shower. Conversation was hard work, but I steered it towards his upcoming exhibition and, eventually, his mood lifted.

'The problem is, these kids fresh out of art school have no idea about composition and what makes a truly great photograph,' he pontificated.

'You're so right,' I said automatically, but my mind was back in his darkroom, staring at the photos I'd seen earlier. The dead seagull with its glassy eyes and the tiny, brittle birds' carcasses in a line on the beach. They weren't great photographs, they were twisted. Macabre. I wanted to ask him about them but stopped myself. Nothing would be gained by antagonising him, especially tonight.

'Coffee?' I asked, standing to clear our plates. Suddenly, the room span and I had to grip the table to steady myself. Too much wine on an empty stomach.

'I think that's a very good idea,' Marcus said, and I bristled. I loved the man but sometimes he could be so damn patronising.

Maybe it was resentment at how he'd left me to cope on my own when I was ill. Maybe it was the condescending way he spoke to me. Maybe it was the half-bottle of Sancerre sloshing around in my stomach. It was probably a mixture of all three, but I found myself addressing the elephant in the room.

'You could get help for your emetophobia, you know,' I said. 'There are all sorts of ways of treating it. Cognitive behavioural therapy, exposure therapy, talking therapies, even anti-anxiety medication. And I'd be there every step of the way.'

I prattled on, my voice growing more strained as I clocked his darkening expression. A muscle twitched in his jaw and his eyes had narrowed to slits.

'Anyway,' I finished lamely. 'We can beat this together.'

'Who've you been talking to? Mairead? No, let me guess, Jasper.' The words were fired like ball bearings from a slingshot, hard and fast.

'No! No. I figured it out myself. I had a friend at elementary school like you.'

'"Like me?"' His lip curled. 'You make it sound like a disability.'

My eyes widened. 'I didn't mean to. I just feel sorry for you, honey. I mean, I want to help. Let me help?'

This time his whole face twisted with rage.

'I don't want your pity, do you hear me?'

'I hear you,' I said in a small voice.

'I'm going to bed. Make sure you disinfect the kitchen properly. One more thing.' He leaned towards me, so close I could feel his hot breath on my cheek. It took all my self-control not to gag. 'You shall never, *ever* speak of this again.'

32

ALANA

That was the moment I realised that the man I married had been an illusion. Charismatic, affable Marcus Adams didn't exist, not really. The man behind the mask was cold and emotionless. Manipulative and self-absorbed.

The man I married wasn't my Prince Charming. He was the evil villain.

From that point on, everything I did seemed to annoy him, from the meals I cooked to the clothes I wore. He would mock my accent and denigrate my country. If I dared to voice an opinion on anything, from the state of the world to the weather, he had a counter-argument. He found fault with the cup of coffee I brought him every morning and the way I arranged the cushions on our bed. He thrived on conflict and, rather than rise to the bait, I retreated into my shell.

A month or so after I was sick with norovirus, Mom called, asking if we wanted to fly home for Christmas. It was a beautiful time of year to be in New England. The snow transformed our pretty town into a perfect winter wonderland. But that wasn't the real reason I was desperate to go home. I missed Mom badly despite our weekly FaceTime chats. I hadn't told her how our short marriage had hit the skids because, in an open-plan house like Merryn's Reach, it was impossible to find somewhere private to talk and, invariably, Marcus would find an excuse to hover in the background, listening in. But if I could see her, I was sure I would be able to ask her advice on what I should do, because the current situation was intolerable.

I knew Marcus well enough by then to realise that if I showed him how badly I wanted to go back to the States, he would find a reason why we couldn't make the trip. So I dropped Mom's invitation into the conversation one night over dinner almost as an afterthought.

Marcus carefully placed his knife and fork in the centre of his plate and watched me closely.

'Do you want to go?'

I shrugged. 'I don't know. It's such a long way. And Mom only gets a week off work. Perhaps we should leave it this year.'

'No,' he said. 'I think we should go. I'll have a look at flights.'

It was almost impossible to hide my delight, but somehow I managed it. I told Mom the good news the next time I called. As I suspected, she was thrown for a loop.

'I can't wait to show Marcus a Maine Christmas,' she said, her smile almost as wide as the laptop screen. 'We can go to the Christmas by the Sea Festival and take him tobogganing at the Camden Snow Bowl.'

'He wants to visit a Christmas tree farm, don't you, honey?' I said, throwing a glance over my shoulder to where Marcus was pretending to read the paper. To the outside world, we were still blissed-out newlyweds. It was only inside the four walls of the house that the cracks were apparent. To Marcus, for whom image was everything, the pretence was non-negotiable.

'I do, Kathryn.' He was the only person to call my mom Kathryn and she loved it. 'I want the whole works, please. Carol-singing, clam chowder, Christmas movies, the lot.'

As December approached, my excitement grew. Marcus took

care of everything, from booking the flights to renewing my passport, which had expired that summer. He even chose my outfits for the week-long trip. Being in control was not just important to him, it was fundamental. I suspected this was a direct result of a childhood in which his father would fly off the handle for the most minor of transgressions. Marcus was just paying it forward. I understood, even if I didn't agree with his behaviour, and so I let him take charge.

The morning we set off for the airport I couldn't believe the trip was actually going ahead. Marcus loaded our bags into the trunk of the Aston and I locked up the house.

'Tickets, passport, money,' I chanted. Then a thought struck me. 'You did pick up the right passport for me, didn't you?'

'Of course I did,' he said impatiently. 'What kind of idiot do you take me for?'

'Sorry,' I said, quick to keep the peace. Marcus had been uncharacteristically jovial in the days leading up to our trip. The last thing I wanted was to rock the boat and spend the five-hour journey to Heathrow in stony silence. I settled in the car and watched the countryside whizz by as the Aston covered the miles.

'Will you stop fucking humming? You're doing my head in,' Marcus snapped, as he pulled onto the A30 at Camborne.

'Sorry.' It was all I seemed to say. I looked sidelong at his profile. His jaw was set, as it so often was these days, but there was a tiny speck of blood on his cheek where he'd nicked himself shaving, a reminder that he was human.

'Marcus?' I began.

'What?'

God, this was difficult. 'D'you think we need help?'

'Help? What kind of help?'

'I don't know. Counselling or something. Everything used to be so perfect. If we do the work, I'm sure we can get back to how things were when we first met.'

'"If we do the work,"' he mocked, mimicking my accent. 'You're such a cliché, Alana. That's not how we do things over here.'

'No, you Brits just repress everything, which is *so* much better,' I hit back, before I could stop myself.

'Actually,' he said smoothly, 'I'm glad you brought the subject up, because you are right. Things haven't been as I'd envisaged before we were married. However, I do have some thoughts on the way forward.'

I sat straighter in the seat, all ears.

'I think we need to establish some ground rules,' he said.

It made sense. You read about them all the time in women's magazines. Respect each other. Set boundaries you're both happy with. Communication is king. Never go to sleep on an argument. That kind of thing.

'OK,' I said.

'Good. I'm glad you agree. These, Alana, are the rules. I am to approve every outfit you wear outside the house. You will answer every call I make to you immediately. Missed calls will not be tolerated.'

'*What?*' I jerked my head towards him, sure he must be joking, but his mouth was set in a hard line, and he gripped the steering wheel so tightly his knuckles were completely bloodless.

'Dinner must be served on the dot of seven unless I'm in London, in which case you will FaceTime me at six o'clock precisely,' he continued, as if I hadn't spoken. 'I expect you to keep the house spotlessly clean at all times, though that's hardly a rule when you have Mairead doing the hard yards,' he sneered. 'You will not see anyone other than Mairead and Rory without my prior consent and you will hand me your mobile phone. Finally, I would like a daily affirmation.'

'A daily what?'

'I want you to tell me how much you love and appreciate me every day.'

I frowned, then my face cleared as everything became clear. Marcus was winding me up. This was all his idea of a joke. It had to be, because the alternative was too crazy to contemplate.

I laughed. 'Nice try, buster.'

He turned to me, his eyes sharp as flints. 'I'm not joking, Alana. I'm deadly serious. You will do as I say.'

'And if I don't?'

He exhaled loudly, as if he was addressing a contrary child. 'If you don't, there will be consequences.'

33

ALANA

I sat in stunned silence, trying to process what Marcus had just said. He wanted me to follow a set of rules. Rules that dictated what I could wear, who I could see and how often I was expected to call him. To top it off, I had to tell him every day how much I loved and appreciated him.

The more I turned it over in my head, the madder it seemed. Normal marriages were built on foundations of love and respect, not rules and sanctions. Marcus, the man who swept me off my feet, who penned love poems and showered me with flowers, now wanted not just to clip my wings and keep me in a gilded cage but to follow his orders like I was a servant and he was my master.

The contents of my stomach curdled and for one horrible moment I thought I might be sick. The man I married wasn't just intractable, he was certifiable. Where the hell had this come from?

I concentrated on my breathing until the nausea faded, my mind spinning. Deep down, I knew these demands stemmed from his need to control, a legacy of his turbulent childhood, but that didn't mean I was OK with it. There was no way in hell I was going to agree to his power trip. But it was fine. The moment I was back in the US, I'd tell him our marriage was over. Mom would fight my corner if the need arose. One thing was clear: I was done with Marcus, and I was done with the UK. In fact, I'd be happy if I never set eyes on either my husband or Cornwall ever again.

But I couldn't let him get even a whiff of my intentions. I had to play the game. So I swallowed hard and said, 'What consequences?'

Finally, his face broke into a smile. 'Ah, I'm glad you asked. For minor indiscretions, such as leaving a mess in the kitchen or being late serving dinner, you'll forfeit your morning swim. Severe transgressions will result in' – he glanced sidelong at me, the corner of his mouth twitching – 'well, let's just say the consequences will be commensurate with the crime.'

Crime? Since when was it a crime to leave crumbs on the countertop or wear the wrong goddamn dress? I sneaked a look at this stranger I called my husband, wondering if he was having some sort of psychotic episode. He must have felt the prickle of my gaze, because he turned to me and smiled, and it was the wide, easy smile he'd employed to seduce me. He wasn't having a mental breakdown. He was *enjoying* himself. And the realisation chilled me to the core.

'What's the matter? Cat caught your tongue?' he asked, amused.

I shook my head. 'Say I went along with this. What's in it for me? Do I get to set some ground rules, too?' Because I could think of a few. No gaslighting. No belittling me. And no manipulating me.

'There are women who would sell their souls to take your place, Alana. To live at Merryn's Reach. To be Mrs Marcus Adams. So, in answer to your question, you do not. But I can see this has come as something of a surprise. We'll park the idea for now and return to it when the time is right.'

'But I—'

'I said, we'll talk about it another time. For now, I've had enough of your tone.' He leaned across me and turned on the radio.

I angled my body away from him and closed my eyes, feigning sleep. Instead, I did the math in my head. Three more hours to Heathrow. Another three or so at the airport. Almost eight hours in the air and the three-and-a-half-hour drive to Camden. Add a couple of extra hours for collecting our bags and picking up a hire car, and I was looking at twenty hours to endure before I could tell Marcus we were over. Twenty hours before I could escape our charade of a marriage. Twenty hours until I could be free.

* * *

After the relative isolation of Merryn's Reach, Terminal 5 at Heathrow Airport was an assault on my senses. The bright lights and noise, the sheer number of people, made me want to shrink into myself. But I plastered a smile on my face and followed Marcus through the concourse to departures, every step I took a step closer to home.

Marcus lifted our bags onto the conveyor belt at the check-in desk, handing our passports and tickets to a pert blonde, whose eyes widened a fraction when she clocked him.

'Is it business or pleasure?' she asked.

'Always pleasure,' Marcus said, smooth as a polished stone, and the woman dimpled as his gaze lingered over her. I had to hand it to him, when he switched it on, his charm was irresistible.

Just as she was about to check our passports, I became aware of a commotion to our right. A brawny guy with meaty hands and a shaven head was berating the woman a couple of desks down.

'What d'ya mean, you won't let me on the flight?'

'I'm sorry, sir, but the boarding gate has closed.'

'It's not my fault the M25's a fucking car park. You need to let me on that fucking plane, or so help me God, I'll—'

We never found out what he would have done, as just then two security guards arrived and escorted him out of the terminal.

The blonde woman turned back to us, one eyebrow hitched, and handed Marcus our passports.

'Takes all sorts,' she said.

'It certainly does,' Marcus agreed as our bags disappeared from view.

She flashed him a seductive smile. 'Have a good trip.'

Before long we were through security and sipping champagne in the club lounge. As the alcohol fizzed on my tongue and worked its way into my bloodstream, I let myself relax for the first time in weeks. I would soon be home, and I could put this chapter of my life firmly behind me. I could study for my master's in New York, maybe even get an internship at one of the big fashion houses. I would start divorce proceedings the minute I was able to. I'd look back on my time in the UK as an unfortunate blip. A lesson learnt. And I would never be taken in by a man like Marcus again.

'Excited?' he asked, and I nodded, finally having the confidence to show it.

'I can't wait to see Mom. It's been such a long time.'

'Cheers,' he said, tipping his flute towards me, and I smiled right back at him as we clinked glasses.

* * *

It took a moment to register the expression on the gate agent's face as she flicked through my passport to the back page. Her brow furrowed and she tugged at her earlobe. I think I knew what she was going to say before she even opened her mouth.

'I'm sorry, madam, but your passport expired four months ago.'

I forced myself to smile. 'I'm sure that can't be right. We applied for a new one, didn't we, Marcus?'

Marcus frowned. 'You said you'd taken care of it, yes. Are you telling me you picked up the wrong one?'

'No. You were looking after the passports and tickets, remember?' I said through gritted teeth. When I'd realised my old passport was out of date Marcus had picked up a form from the post office, insisting he would fill it in for me. He'd taken my new passport picture and had asked Jasper to countersign the back. He'd even sent the completed application off by recorded delivery. Knowing his need for control, I'd left him to it. Anything for a quiet life.

I was paying for that decision now.

I fought the panic rising inside me. 'Is there anything we can do?'

The gate agent looked at me pityingly. 'I'm afraid not, madam. We can't let you travel without a valid passport.' She glanced over my shoulder at the people queued behind us. 'I'm going to have to ask you to step aside.'

'Please,' I begged. 'I need to be on this flight.'

'I'm sorry,' she said, beginning to lose patience. 'You need to step aside,' she repeated. 'People are waiting.'

I gazed out of the plate-glass window at the Boeing 777 standing on the runway. Baggage handlers ran about loading luggage into the hold like worker ants gathering food for their colony. Our cases were probably on the plane already. Beside me, Marcus's face was a picture of concern, but I knew that beneath the mask he was congratulating himself on his ingenuity.

He'd let me build up my hopes, only to knock them to the ground. *Bastard.* But two could play at that game.

I touched his arm. 'You can still go, honey.'

For a moment, the mask slipped, and a flash of annoyance crossed his face so fleetingly you'd have missed it if you didn't know him as well as I did.

'What?' he snapped.

'It's only my passport that's not valid. Yours is fine. You go. You know how much you were looking forward to meeting my mom. It seems crazy for us both to miss out. Honestly, I'll be fine at home on my own.'

The gate agent's gaze tracked from me to Marcus and back again.

'Your wife is right, sir,' she said. 'You're fine to fly.'

I held my breath. If Marcus got on that plane, it would give me a week to figure out a way to leave him. I still had Dad, George and Hannah, even though Marcus had done his best to isolate me from them since I moved to Cornwall. I could go to them, explain everything. Marcus might have charmed them at our wedding, but I was confident they would take my word over his.

'Sir?' the gate agent asked.

Marcus stepped back, shaking his head, and the tiny flame of hope inside me flickered and died.

'Don't be silly,' he said, snaking an arm around me and squeezing my shoulder so tightly I had to suppress a gasp. 'How could I leave you on your own at Christmas? I'm sorry to have wasted your time,' he told the gate agent with a sorrowful smile. 'We'll make sure everything's in order next time, won't we, darling?'

I smiled and agreed, even though in my heart I knew there would never be a next time.

34

ALANA

Marcus whistled tunelessly as he drove out of the airport car park, a sure sign he was pleased with himself.

I waited until we were on the motorway before I tackled him.

'I know what you did,' I said. 'And it was cruel, Marcus. Getting my hopes up like that. Mom'll be devastated.'

'You're telling me like I give a damn. This is why we need ground rules, Alana. Basic principles by which you live your life in order to make our marriage tolerable.'

The anger that had been simmering inside me since the woman at the boarding gate told me I couldn't fly finally boiled over.

'Tolerable? Don't make me laugh. You pursued me!'

'You have a short memory, Alana. I think you'll find you were the one doing all the running.'

I blinked. 'What about the roses and the tickets to London Fashion Week? Whisking me down to Cornwall on our second date? I imagined all that, did I?'

'This is exactly the problem I'm talking about. Being

married to you is like walking a tightrope. There's no reasoning with you. One minute you're inventing stories, the next you're hysterical. It can't go on.'

Marcus accelerated past a caravan, then pulled back into the inside lane. In the distance, the brake lights of an articulated truck flashed on and off, the red lights reminding me of Marcus's darkroom and those disturbing photos of dead birds I'd found when I was looking for Jasper's phone number. I could not stay married to this man. I had to get out. I played my trump card.

'Then divorce me.'

'No.'

'Why not? If I'm as unhinged as you claim, free yourself of me. I'll sign anything and I won't ask for a penny, you have my word.'

'Divorce is not an option, I'm afraid.'

I slumped in the seat. Of course it wasn't. Marcus enjoyed belittling and controlling me. It fed the monster inside him. The monster spawned from the scared little boy who was terrified of his father's rages. But even though I thought I understood what made Marcus tick, I wasn't prepared to stick around. There would be other opportunities to leave. I just had to bide my time.

'All I'm asking is that you cooperate,' he continued.

'Comply, more like,' I muttered under my breath.

'There you go again, questioning everything I say. It is wearing, Alana. You are wearing. Just follow my ground rules and life can return to how it was when we first met. That's what you want, isn't it?'

'What if I refuse?'

'If you refuse, we have no future. Please believe me when I say I will never entertain the idea of separation or divorce.' He paused, his eyes fixed on the truck ahead. It had a Spanish number plate and a picture of some tomatoes on the back. 'I will not have people thinking I have failed at something, do you understand?'

He stamped on the accelerator and the Aston surged towards the truck.

I shot him a look of concern. 'What are you doing?'

'If you're not prepared to meet me halfway, I don't see the point of us. We may as well be dead.'

Dread solidified in the pit of my belly. What was he talking about?

'I can end it now, Alana, if that's what you want. I can drive into the back of this lorry, and it'll all be over in an instant.' He accelerated harder and the car leapt forwards with a guttural growl.

'You're mad!' I yelled, spittle flying from my mouth as I leaned across him to grab the steering wheel. He pushed me away with such force that my head ricocheted off the window, my vision blurring.

'I can assure you I'm perfectly sane.'

I couldn't believe how freakishly calm he sounded. He was about to kill us both, yet it was as if he was discussing the weather.

'Just say you'll do it. Say you'll follow my rules and I'll hit the brakes and we can go home and start over.'

We were bearing down on the lorry fast. A roaring noise filled my ears as images of twisted and bloodied metal danced before me.

'Say it, Alana.'

I grabbed the door handle, clinging onto it like a lifeline. I had three options. Hurl myself out of the car onto the hard shoulder and suffer catastrophic injuries. Stay in the car and hope Marcus was bluffing. But I knew my husband well enough to recognise he was deadly serious. Or capitulate. Follow his ridiculous rules until I could work out a way to leave him.

Put like that, I didn't have a choice. But forcing the words out was the hardest thing I'd ever done.

'All right,' I said. 'I'll do it. I'll follow your rules.'

Marcus eased off the accelerator, a self-satisfied smile on his face.

'There you go,' he chirped. 'It wasn't so hard, was it?'

35

ALANA

'Marcus, I love you and appreciate everything you do for me. I count my blessings that we found each other every single day.'

As always, I was trying to avoid sounding robotic, but it was hard. So damn hard. The words meant nothing to me, but to Marcus they were evidence that he had me exactly where he wanted me. He leaned back in his seat, crossed his arms and smiled.

'You're very welcome.' He pushed his empty plate towards me. 'I'd like a coffee now. Though you can make it stronger than the dishwater you gave me last night.'

I nodded mutely, carried our plates over to the kitchen and flicked on the De'Longhi. I stacked the plates in the dishwasher and disinfected the worktops, then pulled a coffee cup from the cupboard. As the coffee machine did its thing, I turned my back to Marcus and concentrated on pooling every drop of saliva in my mouth until I had enough to spit into his cup. I filled it with coffee, poured in a splash of milk and gave it a good stir so he'd never know.

'Here you go, honey. I put two shots in this time, but please let me know if it doesn't measure up and I'll make you another.'

Marcus nodded and I headed back to the kitchen, a secret smile on my face.

It was these little acts of rebellion that had kept me going in the months since our aborted trip to the States. My life was no longer my own. I couldn't go anywhere, speak to anyone or do anything without Marcus's prior approval. Merryn's Reach was no longer my home, it was my prison.

Not long after our return, Marcus took the SIM card from my cell phone, handed me the kitchen scissors and ordered me to cut the card into tiny pieces and throw them in the trash. Next, he rang Dad to tell him I'd been so upset he hadn't been down to Cornwall to visit after the wedding that I wanted to cut all ties with him and my step-siblings. It was all lies, of course, but Marcus was so credible that Dad believed him. When Mom FaceTimed, Marcus stood just out of sight, listening in, and I didn't dare to even hint at the darkness that lurked beneath the surface of our marriage. As far as she knew, I was still happy with the life I'd chosen.

If I transgressed, if Marcus found crumbs under the toaster or supper was five minutes late, punishments were swift and sharp. A hand twisting my arm behind my back until I cried out in pain. My dinner tipped in the bin before I'd eaten a mouthful. A favourite dress slashed to tatters with a kitchen knife.

Isolated from the people I loved and stuck in that soulless mausoleum of a house with only a psychopath for company, my life was a living nightmare, and in my darkest moments I wished Marcus had driven into the back of that damn truck and killed us both.

His punishments were always worse when I dared question his authority. His need for control underpinned his very existence, and he couldn't cope when it was threatened. But if I followed the rules, he didn't lash out.

I learnt to follow the rules.

Sometimes, weeks would pass without incident, weeks

when I saw flashes of the man I'd fallen in love with, the charming, handsome, courteous guy who'd swept me off my feet. And I would question my own sanity, because it was impossible to believe that he was the same man who'd held my head in the toilet and pulled the chain because he'd found a hair in the sink.

In company, Marcus played the part of the perfect husband better than any Oscar-winning actor, though sometimes I caught Jasper looking at me with his head cocked to one side and concern in his heavy-lidded eyes.

Once, during a meal at a fish restaurant in St Ives to celebrate Marcus's latest sell-out exhibition, I found myself alone with Jasper. Marcus had been collared by the restaurant owner, who was, it transpired, a big fan of his work.

'You seem quiet tonight, darling girl. Is everything all right?' Jasper's voice was uncharacteristically gentle, and I'd had to bite the inside of my cheek to stop myself from breaking into noisy sobs.

I glanced over at Marcus, who was holding court on the other side of the restaurant, the restaurateur hanging on his every word. 'What if I told you it wasn't?' I asked, in a low voice.

Jasper had broken a bread roll in two and rolled a piece between his thumb and forefinger. 'That would put me in a very difficult position, Alana, old love. Marcus is the one who keeps the champagne flowing.' He tipped his head towards the bottle of Laurent-Perrier chilling in an ice bucket on the table. 'But if things were to become too much, you know where I am.' And he'd reached across and touched my hand, only pulling away when Marcus strode back to the table.

Even though I knew I'd never ask him for help, the fact that he'd offered was a comfort of sorts.

As the months turned into years, I became an expert at playing the game, so much so that Marcus would grow bored and change the rules just to catch me out. He'd tell me to cook pork tenderloin one day and refuse to eat it the next. He'd smear toothpaste over the bathroom floor, then make me scrub it clean with my toothbrush. He'd take a sudden dislike to my favourite perfume and tip the whole bottle down the sink.

Meanwhile, his reputation as one of the UK's most talented photographers grew, even though he only left Porthmerryn when he absolutely had to. Ironically, this self-enforced exile from the London art scene worked in his favour. The more reclusive he was, the greater regard his contemporaries seemed to hold him in. His mystique was his USP. Lucky son of a bitch.

As time went on, I knew Marcus believed he'd broken my spirit, and sometimes, when the constant bullying and belittling got too much, I was inclined to agree. But then a sliver of the old Alana buried deep inside me gave me a nudge and reminded me I wasn't beaten just yet.

I found unexpected allies in both Mairead and Rory. They were both too dependent on Marcus for their livelihoods to overtly challenge him, but they made sure to be' around when he was spoiling for a fight.

I took pleasure in the small freedoms I was granted, like my morning swim at Merryn's Cove. I went in all weathers, from New Year's Day to New Year's Eve, unless Marcus was feeling particularly vindictive and had hidden my wetsuit and float.

And I had a secret.

Whenever he was out, I drew. I'd spent months collecting loose change from his pockets, scraping together enough to ask Rory to buy me a sketch pad and pencils.

'You can't tell Mr Adams, Rory,' I'd said. 'He... he likes to be the breadwinner and says I don't need to work.'

Rory nodded slowly. He knew his boss well enough to read the subtext. 'What are you going to draw?'

'Clothes. I wanted to be a fashion designer before I met Mr Adams, you see.'

'You can keep your drawings in the shed, if you like. 'E never steps foot in there.'

'Thank you,' I said, pathetically grateful. 'Mr Adams will be in St Ives tomorrow afternoon. Perhaps you can bring them then?'

The next day, when he knocked on the door empty-handed, I could have wept with disappointment.

'It's OK, Mrs Adams,' he said quickly. 'Didn't want to risk bringing them to the house in case' – his gaze darted to the tiny camera above the front door – 'anyone saw. They're in the shed. Smuggled 'em in under a bag of compost.' He grinned at his own ingenuity and I grinned back, anticipation ballooning in my chest. How ridiculous, to be excited over a sketch pad and a few pencils.

I drew every minute I could, pouring everything into the pages of that secret sketchbook while Marcus was out taking photos. The emotions I'd buried, the betrayal, the hurt, the vulnerability, bled into the lines and seams of my designs. The collection grew. Floaty, ephemeral pieces, delicate but not fragile. Never fragile. Dresses that caught in the wind. Billowing skirts with double-breasted military-style jackets. Ruffled shirts in muted, earthy shades. It was the best work I'd ever done. And that wasn't arrogance. It was the truth. I knew it.

I also knew the collection was my ticket out of this place.

36

ALANA

I smelt the smoke before I saw the flames. I was on my way home after my morning swim, my swimsuit and float in a canvas bag on my shoulder. It was the middle of August, and the air was already sticky, a trickle of sweat sliding between my shoulder blades as I climbed slowly up the narrow cliff path. It hadn't rained for weeks, and the grass was as dry as a tinderbox. Which is why I froze when the acrid smell hit me.

Firefighters had been called out to half a dozen small grass fires already that summer, so I quickened my pace, anxious to get back to the house so I could phone them if I needed to. I paused at the top of the cliffs, shading my eyes from the sun as I scoured both directions looking for a telltale black plume, but there was nothing. It was only when I turned towards home that I saw it: a cloud of smoke spiralling into the air. And it was coming from our garden.

I broke into a run, dread spurring me on. Merryn's Reach had burned down once before. Surely it couldn't happen again? When the architect designed the house, Marcus had insisted on a sprinkler system being fitted, and every room had a fire alarm. It was better protected than most public buildings. But the knowledge was no comfort when the black smoke continued to billow from the garden, settling in a pall over the house.

I hit the entry code on the pin pad with trembling fingers and hopped from foot to foot as I waited for the gates to open. The house looked fine. The smoke was coming from behind it. I tore round the side and stopped in my tracks.

Marcus was standing by the cast-iron fire pit feeding screwed-up balls of paper into the fire. I could feel the heat from the flames from where I was standing. He must have heard the crunch of gravel because he turned to me and smiled.

'Good swim?'

I nodded. 'What are you doing?'

'Having a bit of a spring clean. I found a pile of old papers in the shed. I probably should've put them in the recycling but I thought burning them would be more... *symbolic*.'

The dread I'd felt morphed into a dazed horror as I glimpsed a black and white sketch of a pair of palazzo pants being devoured by flames. I swivelled back to Marcus. My sketchbook was tucked under his arm. As I watched, he tore another couple of pages out, crumpled them in his fist and tossed them onto the fire.

'What is it, Alana? You're gaping like a goldfish,' he taunted. The sneer on his face spurred me to action.

'Those are mine!' I yelled, lunging forwards and trying to grab the sketchbook from his grasp. But he was too quick for me, hurling it onto the flames before I could stop him.

I darted forwards, then hesitated for a second. Those sketches were my way out of this nightmare of a marriage. I had no copies, no back-up. They were it. I didn't have a choice. I plunged my hand into the flames.

At first, I felt nothing as my fingers curled around the sketchbook. Then a searing, white-hot pain exploded across the back of my hand like nothing I'd ever felt before and I screamed in agony. Marcus yanked me back from the fire pit by my shoul-

ders and my scream turned into a howl of despair as my drawings dropped back into the flames.

'You bastard!' I yelled, turning on him. It was as if I was
possessed: every slight, every snide comment, every decree and
every punishment solidifying into one deadly surge of anger.
The pain in my hand was forgotten as I pummelled him with
my fists. 'You complete and utter shit! They were mine. *Mine!*'

Marcus gripped my wrists and twisted them till I gasped
out in shock.

'That's enough!' he yelled, his face so close to mine I could
see the flecks of hazel in his eyes. He let go, pushing me away,
and I turned back to the fire, but the pages and pages of designs
I'd spent years perfecting were nothing but ash.

He motioned to a bucket of water on the ground beside him.
'Put your hand in that.'

I sank to my haunches and did as I was told, the fight in me
gone. The water brought momentary relief and I opened and
closed my fingers experimentally. The skin on the back of my
hand was red and blistered, the smell of burnt flesh clawing the
back of my throat.

'Keep it in there,' Marcus instructed, before turning and
striding back to the house. He reappeared a few minutes later
with a glass of water, a packet of ibuprofen and a roll of
clingfilm.

'You need to keep it in the water for twenty minutes,' he
said, popping two painkillers from the blister pack and handing
them to me, then holding the glass to my lips. I swallowed them
both, a dribble of water running down my chin. He thumbed it
away before I had a chance to.

'How's your hand?'

'Throbbing,' I admitted. We both stared at the puckered
skin.

'The clingfilm's to keep it clean and protect the exposed

nerves. I'll put a dressing on it later. It should be fine, but you're going to have a scar.'

I shrugged. What did a scar matter when my entire collection had been destroyed?

'Did you really think I wouldn't find out?' Marcus said, reading my thoughts. 'Perhaps if you'd come to me and asked my permission I might have let you do some of your pointless doodling. But you kept it from me, Alana. Which is tantamount to lying. And you know how I feel about liars.'

'It's all right for you,' I said heavily. 'You have your photography, your career. But I have nothing, Marcus. Nothing.'

He frowned. 'You have me.'

I let out a sharp bark of laughter. So what if he was pissed at me. I was past caring. At this point I had nothing left to lose. 'Let's not pretend. This marriage is a sham, and we both know it.'

Hurt clouded his eyes. 'I don't know what you're talking about. I love you, Alana. I have loved you from the moment I saw you.'

'You don't love me,' I spat. 'I'm just one of your possessions, like the house or your fricking camera. You don't know the meaning of love. If you loved me you wouldn't destroy my work.' I lifted my hand out of the bucket to wave at the fire pit, instantly regretting it when a scorching pain shot along my arm. I plunged it back in the water with a grimace.

His mouth twisted. He seemed genuinely pained by my outburst and I wondered yet again how badly wired his brain must be for him not to realise he was batshit crazy. But, I supposed, mad people thought they were the normal ones.

'I don't want to punish you, but what else am I supposed to do when you continually go against my wishes?' He lifted my hand out of the water and inspected it. 'How's it feeling?' he asked solicitously.

'It's fine.' I stared at the ground, trying not to wince as he laid a length of clingfilm over the burn.

'There you go. Good as new.'

'Thank you.'

He held out a hand and I let him pull me to my feet. He held me close. 'My poor baby,' he crooned. I was so starved of affection that, despite everything, I melted into his embrace, hating myself for being so weak.

'Please, let me leave,' I whispered.

'Oh, I can't do that,' he murmured, his breath hot in my ear. 'You're mine, don't you see?' He laced his hand in mine, pinching the burnt skin until I yelped in pain. 'I will never let you go, Alana. Never. And the sooner you understand that, the better.'

Something inside me cracked. That tiny flicker of defiance that had helped me survive years of a loveless, controlling marriage was extinguished. He had finally broken me.

Tears rolled down my cheeks and dripped off my chin, but I didn't wipe them away. It didn't matter. Nothing mattered.

A feeling of nothingness settled over me, like my brain was looking the other way. My body felt numb, my burnt hand nothing more than a dull throb at the end of a limb that barely felt like mine. Suddenly I was watching from above. Marcus gripping me, his hands digging into my collarbone. Me, slack. Compliant. I watched dispassionately until Marcus kissed the top of my head and broke away. His lips were moving and it took a moment to work out what he was saying, but eventually I did.

I'm glad you saw sense.

He had won.

37

ALANA

It was the perfect morning for a swim. Cold enough to ensure I had the beach to myself, but so still the sea was as flat as a mirror. I walked down the path with a spring in my step. Marcus had left for the station after an early breakfast, headed for a series of meetings about an upcoming exhibition. It was the first time I'd had the house to myself for weeks and I was relishing the prospect of kicking back without him breathing down my neck.

I pulled off my dry robe, heeled off my sneakers, attached the float to my waist belt and crossed the sand to the shore. I used to be a fair-weather swimmer until I moved to Cornwall. The first time I waded into the rolling Atlantic, inch by inch, my skin prickling like gooseflesh, I almost gave up and retreated to the beach. But an innate bloody-mindedness kept me in the water till I was brave enough to plunge in up to my neck, gasping and shrieking, even though there was no one there to hear me. It wasn't long before I had my breathing under control and managed a few strokes, and when I got out, the endorphins hit and I was addicted.

I once watched a documentary that explained the physiology behind my body's reaction. When we swim in cold water we go into fight or flight mode, our bodies flooded with adrenaline, cortisol, dopamine and serotonin. When I was in the water, I felt weightless, like I was floating on a cloud. Sea swimming helped me sleep better. It made me feel alive. As if anything was possible.

Like Marcus, the sea was an unpredictable beast. Sometimes calm and crystal clear, sometimes so rough I was glad of my float. A couple of times it was so wild I feared I might be sucked underwater by the force of the currents. But it never stopped me from going in.

That morning, I swam the length of the cove, turned and swam back. That's when I saw the woman standing motionless halfway down the path, shading her eyes from the sun's glare as she watched me.

When I reached the beach she was there waiting for me.

My doppelgänger.

All I could do was stand and stare. She told me her name was Laura and she'd seen a photo of me in The Ship. She thought it would be fun to say hello.

Fun.

As she wittered on about living in Kent and how she once came to Porthmerryn on holiday, I couldn't drag my eyes away. It was uncanny. I'd seen her from my bedroom window when she came to the house, of course, and even from a distance I'd been shocked by our similarities. But seeing her up close blindsided me. We had the same brown eyes, so dark it's hard to tell where the iris ends and the pupil begins. The same chin, the same nose, the same hair.

'I should get out of this,' I said eventually, waving a hand at the wetsuit. It gave me a chance to collect my thoughts. Laura continued to prattle on about how she was hoping we could hang out together. It sounded so simple. That's what normal women did, right? They went out for a drink or a meal to shoot the breeze. It wasn't her fault she assumed it would be as straightforward as that. How was she to know what my life was like?

But I wasn't like other women, and I was about to make my excuses and retreat to my prison of a home when I saw her shoulders slump and the hard kernel inside me softened.

'I'll be here again tomorrow,' I told her. 'Bring a flask and a blanket.'

* * *

Did our friendship blossom so quickly because we looked alike? Was there some kind of elemental pull, some deep-rooted instinct that made us gravitate towards each other? A subconscious preference for the familiar? Or maybe it was something simpler. Maybe we recognised the same emptiness in each other.

I could tell Laura was reeling from her break-up with Vinnie, even if she tried to put on a brave face. And there was something else, too. Sometimes I would catch a look of desolation in her eyes that mirrored my own. Once, I asked her if everything was OK, but she brushed it off and changed the subject. I let it go, knowing I'd get to the bottom of it eventually.

I had secrets to hide, too, but by then I was an expert in concealing my true feelings. Since the terrible day Marcus burned my sketchbook, I'd played the part of a doting wife meekly and without complaint. It didn't stop the punishments, but I had learnt to dissociate, watching my husband do his worst from a safe distance.

I was numb, and I was alone.

Perhaps that's why we clicked. Two lost souls. Two sides of the same coin. Was it any surprise I'd started to wonder what life would be like if she were me, and I was her?

38

ALANA

Laura and I sit with our backs against a rock and she hands me her cell phone so I can scroll through the selfies she insisted on taking. Even though I should be used to it by now, I can't help but gawp at the photos of the pair of us. It's freaky how alike we are.

'Look at us, two peas in a pod.' I squint at the screen. 'If I narrow my eyes I can't tell us apart.' I pause for a beat. 'Funny to think we could swap lives just like that.'

Beside me, Laura purses her lips but says nothing. I give her back her cell, fearful I've somehow upset her.

'I should get back,' I say, scrambling to my feet. 'Marcus will be phoning home soon and he'll be worried if I'm not there.'

Laura jumps up and grabs my arm. 'Worried?' she asks, her eyes searching mine. 'Or angry?'

I pull my features into a frown. 'What are you talking about?' I bluster.

'C'mon, Alana. Be honest. Why does it matter if you're there to answer his call? Sounds to me like he's checking up on you. That's not worry. That's control.'

I let out a forced laugh. 'You've got it all wrong.'

'Have I?' Her eyes are blazing. She grabs my hand and turns it over, exposing the puckered skin of my scar. 'How did you get this?'

'I knocked over a pan of boiling water. I'm such a klutz.'

'I don't believe you. And what about the way he love-bombed you when you met? The flowers and the tickets to the fashion show? It's textbook, Alana. What man tells you on your first date he wants to spend the rest of his life with you? It's not normal behaviour.'

'You moved in with Vinnie after a month,' I protest.

'That's different. Vinnie might be a lot of things, but he's not a love-bomber, and he's not a control freak. He never made me feel like I had to ask permission to breathe.'

I jerk my hand back, rubbing the scar as if I can smooth it away. 'Marcus isn't like that. I came to yours the other night, didn't I?'

I don't tell her that the only reason I was able to leave the house was because I'd tripped the electricity meter, rendering Marcus's array of security cameras useless. It's a trick Rory unwittingly taught me after a thunderstorm last winter. Lightning had cut the power supply when it struck a nearby pylon, and when the lights went out, he showed me how to reset the trip switch in the fuse box under the stairs.

'It's good to know in case you ever need to turn off the electric,' he said. 'Like if a plug starts sparking or something shorts out.'

'You mean, if I turn that switch off, the power for the whole house goes out and Mr Adams would just think it was a faulty plug?'

He nodded solemnly and I filed the information away, knowing it might come in handy one day.

Now, Laura folds her arms across her chest. 'So if you told

him you were going out for a drink with me tonight, he'd be fine with that, would he?'

'I... I don't know. Probably not.' I force a smile. 'But that doesn't make him a monster. He just likes to know where I am, that's all.'

Laura drags her hands down her face. 'I know we haven't known each other for long, but I have to tell you what I see. I'd never forgive myself otherwise. You hear about men like Marcus all the time. There are even podcasts about them, for God's sake. The type of bullying bastards who track their partners' every move, who isolate and manipulate and control because they're too insecure and paranoid to have a healthy, balanced relationship.'

'OK, so he can be a bit prescriptive at times, but that's only because he expects everyone to have the same high standards as he does.'

'Course he does,' Laura mutters. 'Look, I saw the way he was with you at the restaurant the other day, OK?'

'Harbour Lights?' I don't bother to hide my shock. 'You were spying on us?'

'No! I was walking past when I saw Marcus's car parked outside. You looked... I don't know. Sad. Yes, you looked sad, Alana, when you should have looked happy.'

I stare at Laura in surprise. I have underestimated her. She's more perceptive than I thought. It takes a moment for me to realise she's still speaking.

'...and I would never forgive myself if something happened to you.'

'Nothing's going to happen to me.'

She throws her hands up in frustration. 'Have it your way. But don't say I didn't try.' Shaking her head, she sets off down the path towards Porthmerryn.

'Wait!' I call after her. 'Laura! Please?'

She stops and spins round. 'What is it?'

I catch her up. Take a deep breath. Try not to think about what I'm going to do, and the consequences it could have for us both.

'You're right,' I say finally. My voice sounds high. Reedy. 'About everything. Only it's worse than you could ever imagine. So much worse.'

PART THREE

39

LAURA

Blood whooshes in my ears as I follow Alana down the rocky path to Merryn's Cove. My instincts had been right. I'd known something was amiss the moment I saw Alana and Marcus together in Harbour Lights. The dynamics between them were all wrong. Never mind the deferential way she spoke about him and that burn on her hand. To me, it added up to a pattern of behaviour I couldn't ignore.

It was Alana's suggestion to talk on the beach, away from the house. I can only guess it's because she doesn't feel safe in her own home. Maybe Marcus is spying on her. I wouldn't put it past him, the cretinous bastard.

Alana sinks gracefully onto the sand and I follow suit, sitting with my legs crossed and my elbows on my knees. Alana hugs her legs to her chest and stares out to sea. We watch the waves roll in for a minute or two, the soft swishing noise they make as soporific as any sleep app.

Now we are here I don't know where to start, but I needn't worry. Alana sighs, then glances at me, a sad smile on her face. I'm pretty sure I have a matching one.

'There's a saying, isn't there? That if things look too good to be true, they probably are.'

I nod.

'It was a fairy tale in the beginning, Laura. You have to believe me. Marcus was my Prince Charming, the kind of boyfriend every girl dreams of. Kind, considerate, generous. Spontaneous. Exciting. Maybe even a little dangerous. He fell head over heels in love with me, he—'

'That's not love, Alana. That's love-bombing.'

'No, it wasn't like that. He was just... passionate. Yes, he liked me to look a certain way and could get a bit possessive when I wanted to see my friends, but it was only because he loved me so much.'

'Jealousy and love aren't the same thing.'

'I know that now.'

'When did things change?'

'On our honeymoon.' She gives a hollow laugh. 'He waited until he had a ring on my finger, then told me he didn't want me to go back to college.'

'And you agreed?'

'I didn't see that I had a choice.'

'Everyone has a choice.' The wind blows a strand of hair across my face, and I tuck it behind my ear. 'Does he... hurt you?'

'Sometimes,' she admits. 'But it's not his fault. He didn't have a happy childhood. His father had a nasty temper.'

'That's no excuse!' I explode.

'I know.' Her chin drops to her chest and, instinctively, I drape an arm across her shoulders and pull her close.

'What really happened to your hand?'

'I'd been designing a catwalk collection behind his back. I knew he'd be angry, because my job was at home looking after him, so I hid my designs in the shed.' She sniffs. 'Anyway, he found them and threw them on the fire. I burned my hand trying to save them. I wasn't lying when I said it was my fault.'

Frustration rises inside me, hot and fierce. Why is she continually trying to defend him? The man's a monster, any idiot can see that.

'Have you reported him to the police?' I ask, already knowing the answer.

'There's no point. Marcus went to school with the chief constable and knows half his senior management team socially. Plus, he has this way of making people believe him. I did, didn't I, all those years ago? They'd never take my word over his.'

'Then leave him.'

She pulls away from me. 'It's not that straightforward.'

'It seems straightforward enough to me. He's abusive, Alana. No one should have to put up with that.'

'He's not always like it. Weeks can go by when nothing happens, and I start wondering if I imagined it.' A flush creeps up her neck and across her cheeks. 'Perhaps a tiny part of me thought I could fix him.'

I harrumph.

'Anyway,' she continues, 'I have to stay. I have no money, no home. Where would I go?'

'To London, to your dad?'

She shakes her head. 'I told you. He has dementia and lives in a nursing home. Even if he didn't, Marcus turned him against me years ago.'

'Your brother or sister?'

'I haven't heard a word from either of them in over ten years. I can't suddenly rock up on their doorstep after all this time, even if I did know where they lived, which I don't.'

'What about your mum?'

'She doesn't know about any of this.'

'You haven't told her?'

'Don't look at me like that. You haven't told your mom you and Vinnie broke up.'

'Fair enough,' I concede. 'But she'd help you, right? If she knew what was going on?'

'Of course she would.'

'So why haven't you told her?'

'You make it sound so easy. But Marcus is always there whenever I FaceTime her and I don't have my own phone.'

'You could call her from the landline.'

'I could. But even if she knew what was happening, she's too far away to help. Marcus could have killed me before she's even halfway across the Atlantic.' Alana picks up a handful of sand and lets it run through her fingers. 'The first year we were married we were supposed to fly home for Christmas. I was going to tell Mom how bad things had gotten the moment I was home, but when we reached the boarding gate at Heathrow the gate agent spotted my passport had run out. Marcus had promised me he'd renewed it, but of course he hadn't.'

'Wow, what a bastard.' I picture Alana at the airport, thinking she was almost free, only to be thwarted at the final hurdle. It must have been devastating. Is that what her whole marriage has been like: years of power games and gaslighting?

'Imagine what he'd do if he found out I'd told her.' Her shoulders sag. 'And there's always this worry in the back of my mind. What if she *doesn't* believe me? Marcus is so goddamn convincing. He knows exactly how to twist things and make me sound unhinged. Can I really take that chance?'

Sympathy for her wells in me and my mind races.

'Couldn't you apply for a passport yourself? I'll help you. I'll even lend you the money. I'll lend you enough for your flight home too, if you like.'

Alana smiles. 'That's so kind of you, Laura, but I don't think you understand. Marcus monitors everything I do. There are... oh goodness, this is hard to admit,' she says, rubbing her face. 'There are cameras all over the house. He likes to watch me when he's not there.'

'He literally spies on you?'

She nods.

'Bloody hell.' I swallow. 'But that means he'll have seen me at the house.'

'We had no power today, remember.' For the first time a grin creeps across her face. 'Something must have tripped the switch. It keeps happening,' she adds. 'I really should call an electrician.'

She lets out a peal of laughter and, in that moment, I see the girl she must have been before Marcus broke her spirit: fearless, trusting, ready to take on the world. A girl who crossed the Atlantic to pursue her dreams. A girl who took a chance on love after a whirlwind romance. A girl who put her faith in the wrong man.

'What would Marcus do if you did try to leave?' I ask.

The laughter stops abruptly and a shadow falls across her face. 'Isn't that the six-million-dollar question. Truth is, Laura, I don't know.'

I pound my thigh with my fist. 'Bloody men. It's the twenty-first century and they still think they can walk all over us. First, my dad, then Vinnie, now Marcus. I even had to stop some creep letching over the girl from the shop yesterday. All she wanted was to go for a run without being hassled, for fuck's sake. Honestly, it drives me mad.'

As I stare out towards the horizon, my mind races. Alana doesn't deserve to be imprisoned in a toxic marriage with a controlling, abusive man, just as I didn't deserve to be cheated on. There's nothing I can do about Vinnie's infidelity, but there has to be a way I can help Alana, because it's clear she can't stay with Marcus. Every day she spends with him is another day he will grind her down until one day there will be nothing left.

But how do you leave someone who tracks your every move?

How do you disappear from a house with hidden cameras in every room? And then it hits me. An idea so wild, so insane, it might just work. I don't think about the consequences. I don't consider the risks. I simply turn to her, pulse pounding, resolute. It's time we stopped taking everything lying down.

'We'll swap.'

'What?'

'You and me. We'll swap places.'

She laughs again, but I'm not joking. I've never been more serious in my life.

40

ALANA

I stare at Laura in bemusement.

'What d'you mean, we'll swap places?'

'Don't you see?' she cries. 'It's the only way you'll ever escape. I'll become you, and you'll become me, just long enough for you to get away.'

'I still don't understand—'

'I've got my passport with me, here in Porthmerryn. It's in my handbag back at the cottage. You can use it to get back to the US.'

'But that's illegal.'

'And so is what Marcus is doing to you. If there was any justice in the world he'd be behind bars doing time for controlling and coercive behaviour, but he's not. So don't worry about it. I'll book a flight in my name, and I'll drive you to the airport. You don't need to do a thing. Just be ready for when I come to pick you up.'

She makes it sound so simple, even though I've spent the best part of the last hour describing our sham of a marriage and how Marcus wields power over every single aspect of my life. I suppose it's impossible to understand unless you've been in that situation yourself.

'Even if I did use your passport to get home, I'd never be able to leave the house. Marcus would know I'd gone. Flicking the trip switch might do the trick for a couple of hours, but that's all. I appreciate you trying, Laura, I really do, but it just won't work.'

'He's in London till Saturday, isn't he?'

'Yes, but—'

'There you go. I'll book a flight for tomorrow.'

'*Tomorrow?*' Colour leaches from my face. 'I can't go tomorrow. I'm supposed to be cleaning the house. We have people coming for Sunday lunch.'

'Sod the cleaning. Do you want to go back to America or not?'

'Of course I do, but this is all so sudden. I just... I just don't know if I can do it.'

Laura's forehead creases in sympathy. 'It's OK, I get it. You've spent so long doing what he tells you that you've lost all sense of autonomy. But you're not on your own any more. You have me now.'

'Why would you want to help me? You don't owe me anything. You didn't even know I existed a week ago.'

'I know. But I do now.' Laura's concern deepens into a frown. 'Thing is, I've had enough of men taking the piss. Why should they get away with treating us like shit all the bloody time? It's not fair.' She lifts her chin. 'All I'm doing is helping redress the balance.'

I hug my knees closer to my chest. Laura makes it sound so simple. *I'll become you, and you'll become me.* How can I tell her that it won't work? Marcus isn't stupid. The minute he realises I've gone he'll move heaven and earth to track me down. We need to think smarter than that. We need to be not one, not even two, but three steps ahead of him.

'Tomorrow's too soon,' I say. My voice comes out breathless. Panicked.

Laura exhales loudly. 'What is it you're worried about?'

I grind my heels into the sand. How can I find the words to describe the violent rages Marcus flies into at even the slightest of perceived misdemeanours? Alongside the original set of ground rules, like the daily affirmation and having dinner on the table at seven on the dot, Marcus is always announcing new ones, which are arbitrary and ever-changing. I'll be punished for not answering his call before the third ring or leaving the wheelie bin in the wrong place in the garden. I'm not stupid. I know he does this to keep me in a constant state of anxiety, my cortisol levels spiking, as I try so goddamn hard to negotiate a safe path through our marriage that doesn't involve stepping on a land mine.

'Alana?' Laura asks gently.

Our eyes meet. Can I really trust her?

I make a choice. One I hope I won't live to regret.

41

ALANA

Laura watches wordlessly as I pull my T-shirt up and show her an area of lighter skin just below my ribcage.

'This is what happened the first time I tried to leave.'

Her eyes are like saucers.

'It was when I was still allowed to drive the Aston. I drove Marcus to the station to catch the train up to London one day, waited until the train left, then began to drive. I had no idea where I was going, I just knew I had to get away. I made it to Somerset before the car ran out of petrol. Of course, I couldn't fill it up because I didn't have any money. I sat in the car for hours, wondering what to do. I must have dozed off at some point, because I woke up to find him sitting in the passenger seat, watching me.'

'Oh my God, that's so creepy.' Laura inhales sharply. 'How did he know where you were?'

'He'd put a tracker on the car. When I hadn't gone straight home, he jumped off the train and into a taxi. He stopped to buy a can of petrol on the way.' I paused, remembering the look of unbridled fury on Marcus's face when I'd woken up, bleary-eyed and disorientated. 'I thought he was going to kill me there and then. But that isn't Marcus's style. He made me wait a week before he tricked me into his darkroom, tied me to a chair and poured acetic acid over me.'

'Jesus.' Laura drops down to her haunches and traces a finger over the scar. 'That's... sick. I suppose he did it here so no one would see.'

I nod. 'That would involve too much explaining. He never leaves marks where they'd show.'

Laura stares at me, her mouth agape. I'd probably be the same in her shoes. Stories like this belong in psychological thrillers, not real life.

In her shoes.

'Wait,' she says, her forehead creasing. 'You said that's what he did the first time you left. How many other times have you tried to go?'

'Just once more. I got as far as Wales that time.'

'Wales?'

'I thought I'd be safe in the middle of nowhere.'

'Makes sense, I guess.'

'I thought so. That time, I didn't leave anything to chance. There was no way I was going to make the same mistake again.'

I'd hit upon the idea of holing up in a remote bed and breakfast while I worked out how I could renew my passport and fly home to the States. I'd chosen Snowdonia after watching a programme about the place and being mesmerised by its craggy mountains and steep valleys. It was as wild as Cornwall yet different too. It was also three hundred miles – and at least a seven-hour drive – from Porthmerryn.

Planning my escape consumed me for weeks. Not only did I have to find somewhere to stay, but I had to work out how I was going to get there and how I was going to pay for it.

This was a major problem. I hadn't had a penny to my name since our wedding. Marcus had taken my bank cards 'for safe-keeping' the day we returned from our honeymoon and I had no idea what he'd done with them. He did a weekly online shop for our groceries and handled all the other bills. I could have asked Mairead or Rory for a loan but I'd be putting them in an impossible situation. Marcus was their boss, after all. I could sell a piece of jewellery, but where? And collecting the change in Marcus's jacket pockets would take too long.

Even if I did somehow get my hands on a supply of cash, I knew booking train tickets and accommodation would be virtually impossible. Marcus changed the WiFi password whenever he left the house, and without a cell phone I had no access to the internet. The landline was no help either. Marcus checked the itemised bill every month and, anyway, I had a sneaking suspicion he'd bugged the phone. The obstacles seemed too huge to overcome.

In the end, Jasper unwittingly provided the solution when he invited us to his townhouse in St Ives for supper one night. After we'd eaten, he and Marcus decided to take their port and cigars out into the garden.

'Coming, old love?' Jasper asked. 'Or would you be happier checking out my new first edition of *Jamaica Inn* while we talk work?'

I grinned. 'What do you think?'

'Thought as much. It's on my desk.'

I headed to the library, an opulent room that doubled up as Jasper's office. Collecting antiquarian books was one of his passions, and the floor-to-ceiling bookshelves housed an enviable collection of first and special editions. The mulberry crushed-velvet curtains were already drawn so I flicked on a couple of side lamps on my way over to the huge, leather-topped desk.

I spied the book in its faded cream dust jacket immediately, but what really caught my attention was Jasper's laptop open beside it. I cast a furtive glance over my shoulder to check I was alone. Marcus had a nasty habit of following me round the house, my silent shadow, so I was never completely off guard. Just to be sure, I sidled over to the curtains and peeked through, relaxing a fraction when I spied the two men deep in conversation under the pergola at the end of the garden, illuminated by strings of fairy lights.

Reckoning I had twenty minutes before they returned to the house, I slid into Jasper's chair and hit the enter key, my eyes widening as the home screen lit up.

Jasper had once admitted to me, after a few glasses of Marcus's vintage burgundy, that he was a hacker's dream. Not only did he store his bank card on his laptop but he kept the same password for everything. Seaforth1959. The name of his gallery and the year of his birth. With trembling fingers, I typed in his password and there it was, bright in the dimly lit room. The Google search page.

It took ten minutes to find a B&B on the outskirts of Betws-y-Coed, and another five to book train tickets from Penzance to Betws-y-Coed via Reading, Chester and Bangor leaving in a week's time, when I knew Marcus had a meeting with his accountant. Panic began to set in. What if Jasper checked his laptop and saw the booking? Spying his printer, I quickly printed the e-tickets and the B&B booking confirmation, folded both into my bra and deleted the browsing history.

Laura's eyes are round as I recount the story.

'You managed to escape?' she asks, slightly breathlessly.

I nod. 'Everything went to plan. I left the moment Marcus set off for his meeting. It took almost eleven hours, but I made it to the B&B in Betws-y-Coed just after eight o'clock that night. I was so bushed I went straight to bed—'

Laura appears to be holding her breath, waiting for the 'but' she knows is coming.

'—and when I came down for breakfast the next morning, the owner bustles over with a smile on her face and says, "You should've told us your husband was joining you. We'd have given you the master suite." And I look over and there is Marcus at the table in the bay window, sipping a coffee and reading the *Telegraph*. And he looks up and smiles and says, "Darling! There you are. I was beginning to think you'd never surface.""

Laura's shock is tangible.

'But how did he—?'

'Know where I was? If you want the honest answer, I'm still not sure. I don't think Jasper told him. I think he followed me from the start. He often says he's going someplace then doesn't, just to keep me on my toes.'

'What happened then?'

'What choice did I have? I went home with him. Two weeks later he stubbed out a cigar on the inside of my thigh. So, yeah, I'm worried what he might do to me,' I finish. 'That's why, though I really appreciate your offer of help, I can't leave. I can't risk it. He always finds me in the end.'

Laura winds a strand of her hair around her index finger, then chews the end. She looks up at me.

'What if... what if I took your place, just until we knew you were on the flight?'

'I don't understand what you mean.'

'When I said swap places, I meant you impersonate me. But what if we did actually switch? I could stay at your house and pretend to be you. You can drive Beatrice to the airport and catch your flight pretending to be me. Marcus wouldn't think to look for you because as far as he was concerned, you'd still be at home. Only it wouldn't be you, it'd be me. And if he comes home early, I'll just play my part... as you.'

'That's crazy. He'd never fall for it. I know we look alike, but he's my husband. We've been married for ten years. He'll tell in seconds you're not me.'

'Not if we're clever about it,' Laura says, but I shake my head, because she's delusional if she thinks it'll work.

'Hear me out. I'll be busy in the garden or something.

Around, but not in his face. I'll be wearing your clothes. Maybe a hat and sunglasses. We only need to keep up the pretence till you're in the air, then you're safe and I can go.'

'But what if he realises, Laura? I've told you what he's capable of. God only knows how he'd react. I can't put you in that kind of danger.'

Laura tsks. 'You needn't worry about me. Marcus is your classic bully. I can handle him.' She says it with a smile, but I notice her swallow hard, just once. She must see my worried expression because she adds, 'Seriously, Alana, I deal with pet owners every day of the week. You have no idea how terrifying they can be. If I can handle them, I can handle your husband. Besides, egomaniacs like him have a fatal flaw.' She taps the side of her nose. 'They think they're the smartest person in the room, so they never see it coming when they're outplayed. Trust me. I'll be fine.'

Unconvinced, I'm about to disagree, when I stop myself. Who am I to argue if Laura so desperately wants to help? And besides, there is a way we might actually get away with it. Because Marcus has an Achilles heel which, if we're clever, could be the key to making Laura's crazy plan work. She's studying my face and cocks her head.

'What is it? What are you thinking?'

I smile, a nub of excitement forming in my chest. 'There might be a way. A way we can fool him.'

42

LAURA

I pace up and down the beach, waiting for Alana to elaborate.

Finally, she says, 'Have you heard of emetophobia?'

'Nope.'

'It's a phobia of vomiting. Either of being sick yourself, or of someone else being sick. Marcus has suffered from it since he was a child. I had norovirus when we were first married. He couldn't cope with it at all. At the time, I was shocked, but now I'm thinking it could work in our favour.'

My brain is joining the dots. 'Are you saying that if I pretended I was ill, he'd keep his distance?'

'He couldn't even be in the same house when I was sick. You'd need to be convincing, but it's our best chance of fooling him.' Her face falls. 'Except he'd know as soon as you spoke that you weren't me.'

'Ah,' I said, holding up a hand. 'That's where you're wrong. I was a pretty good mimic at school. My impression of Rachel from *Friends* was legendary. You, for example, have a soft New England accent, honey. Must be all those years living this side of the pond,' I say, mimicking her accent perfectly.

Her eyes widen.

'Of course, I'm gonna need shorter hair and a fringe like yours, and I'll have to borrow some of your clothes, and—'

'Wait,' she says. 'There's something else you need to know.' She drags a hand down her face. 'Marcus has these... guidelines I have to follow.'

'Guidelines?' I stare at her, thrown. 'What guidelines?'

She can't meet my eye. 'Who am I kidding?' she mutters. 'They're not guidelines. They're rules. For example, I have to keep the house spotlessly clean and have Marcus's dinner ready for seven on the dot. I have to answer his calls immediately, and I'm not allowed to see anyone other than Mairead or Rory without his consent.'

'Bloody hell.' I shake my head as I digest this latest revelation.

'And there's the daily affirmation. I have to tell him once a day how much I love and appreciate him.'

'What happens if you don't? No, don't tell me. I can guess. Jeez, Alana. How have you put up with him for so long? I'd have been out of there the minute he started bossing me about.'

'Believe me, if you'd told me in the beginning my marriage would be like this, I would have laughed you out of the room. But it's insidious. He's so good at twisting things to make me think I'm in the wrong.'

I'm quick to reassure her. 'You shouldn't blame yourself. And I'm sorry. I don't mean to sound critical. None of this is your fault, OK?'

'OK.' She gives me a watery smile, and I hold out a hand to pull her to her feet.

'C'mon,' I say. 'We should make a start. The sooner we get you away from that bastard, the better.'

If, for a moment, a shadow of doubt flits across my mind, I am quick to push it aside. This isn't about me, it's about Alana, and doing the right thing.

* * *

We head back up the path to Merryn's Reach, but when we reach the gates, I stop.

'What's up?' Alana asks.

'Are you sure he won't see me on the security cameras?'

'I told you. I've flipped the trip switch. It'll be fine.'

She leads me through the gates and into the house, and I follow her upstairs to her bedroom. My eyes are on stalks as I take in the ivory, deep-pile carpet, the super-king bed and the huge windows that look out to sea.

'Wait there,' she says, disappearing back downstairs.

I walk round the room, fingering the gauzy, voile curtains and running a hand along the crisp Egyptian cotton bedlinen. Two doors lead off the bedroom, and I peek my head around them both. One is a huge walk-in wardrobe with floor-to-ceiling mirrors covering the end wall. The other is a sumptuous bathroom, complete with a rainfall shower, clawfoot bath and his and hers basins. It's so far removed from any house I've ever lived in that I find myself wondering how Alana can bear to leave it behind. But then I remind myself that it's all an illusion and behind the perfect facade, evil lurks.

I hear footsteps and turn to see Alana waving a pair of kitchen scissors at me.

'Sorry,' she says. 'They're the only ones we have. Come into the en suite. We'll flush your hair down the toilet so Marcus doesn't find it.'

I perch on a chair in front of the sink and Alana stands behind me, combing through my hair with her fingers.

'Are you sure about this?' she asks, waving the scissors at me.

'In for a penny.' I pull a face. 'Just do it before I change my mind.'

She hesitates for a second, then takes a length of my hair

and snips off a couple of inches. I watch as she works, neatly and efficiently, her face a picture of concentration. I can imagine her with pins in her mouth, altering the hem of a dress on a catwalk model, and my resolve hardens. Alana has wasted so much of her life on Marcus. She deserves a second chance. She already looks as if a weight has lifted from her shoulders. The tightness around her eyes has gone, and she's humming softly to herself as she snips away.

'Do you always hum?'

'I do.' She glances at me in the mirror and grins. 'Drives Marcus nuts.'

'Noted. You hug yourself when you're nervous, too. And you have a habit of inspecting your fingernails before you answer an awkward question.'

She raises an eyebrow. 'Do I?'

'Yup. What do you call Marcus?'

'Um, honey or sweetheart.'

I nod. Alana steps beside me, checks her own fringe in the mirror, then starts cutting mine. Long locks of hair fall to the ground.

'I haven't had a fringe since primary school.'

'Bangs,' she corrects me.

'You're right. Bangs.'

She tidies up the edges and then stands back and gives a small bow. I stare at my reflection in shock, my hand creeping up to touch my hair, an involuntary reflex.

'I look... I look...'

'Like me,' Alana finishes. 'You look just like me.'

She sweeps up my hair and flushes it down the toilet, then we move to the bedroom and she sits me down in front of her dressing table and pulls open the top drawer.

'I never bother much with make-up,' I admit, staring in wonder at the array of foundations and blushers, eye shadows, mascaras and lipsticks.

'Marcus likes the type of make-up that looks effortless but takes an hour to perfect. You know the kind. Dewy skin, neutral eye shadow and nude lips. Just enough mascara to make my lashes look long. Look, I'll show you.'

Alana gets to work, applying a primer and sheer foundation, concealer, blusher and highlighter, before she moves on to my eyes. Finally, she applies lipstick, then stands back to admire her handiwork.

'Pretty good, even though I say so myself. Come with me.' She leads me into the walk-in wardrobe and slides open the door on the right, pulling out a knitted wrap dress in burnt sienna. 'Try it on,' she says. 'It's one of Marcus's favourites.'

I step out of my jeans, pull off my sweater and slip the dress over my head. It fits like a second skin, and I give a twirl, then we turn to face the mirror together and my breath catches in my throat.

We are two halves of the same coin. Two peas in a pod. I am her, and she is me. We might not share the same blood, but it doesn't matter. Our similarities bind us together.

Alana reaches out and squeezes my hand. Her palm is as damp and clammy as my own.

'D'you think this will work?' she asks quietly.

That nagging doubt is back. *What the hell have I let myself in for?* I force myself to smile at her reflection. 'It has to, doesn't it?'

In the bedroom a phone rings, making us both jump. Alana's face drains of colour.

'Oh, God. It'll be Marcus.'

I act before my brain has a chance to engage, racing out of the room. There's a clunky old-fashioned handset on the bedside table nearest the door and I grab it. Alana has followed me, her eyes wide with fear. I answer the phone and press it to my ear. My pulse races.

'Hey, honey,' I drawl. 'Everything OK?'

43

ALANA

Laura leans towards me, so close the scent of her shampoo fills my nostrils. She angles the handset so I can hear Marcus's voice. Assured, familiar and sharp with irritation.

'No, everything is not OK. The damn power's tripped again,' he snaps.

I hold my breath. My heart is fluttering so hard in my chest it's in danger of bursting free. If he suspects anything's wrong, our plan is over.

'Oh,' Laura says in a perfect Maine accent. 'Sorry, honey, I've been in the garden most of the day. I'll go check it right away. And I'll make sure to call the electrician.'

'Ask him about his meeting,' I mouth.

She gives a quick nod. 'How was the meeting, sweetheart?'

'Fine,' he says shortly. 'I'll be on the four o'clock train from Paddington on Saturday, OK? I won't have eaten.'

'No problem. I'll fix you something for when you're home. Talk tomorrow, yes?'

The line goes quiet apart from the muffled roar of traffic, then Marcus says, 'Have you forgotten something?'

Laura looks at me, panicked. I mouth, 'Affirmation', but she is staring at me like I'm talking in a foreign language. I grab the phone.

'Sorry, honey. You were breaking up. I love you, and I'm so grateful for everything you do for me. I'd be lost without you.'

He exhales sharply. 'There, that wasn't so hard, was it? I'll see you Saturday. And sort out the fucking trip switch.'

The line goes dead.

'Oh my God, Laura. You were amazing. He had absolutely no idea he wasn't talking to me. I can't believe it. I think this crazy plan of yours might just work.' I raise my hand to high-five her, but she doesn't move. She's staring at the phone as if it might bite. I pause, telling myself to tone it down. I'm so used to Marcus's bullying ways that I'm almost immune to them. I need to remember that while Laura might understand what he's like on an intellectual level, the reality is somewhat harder to stomach. What if she's wondering what she's let herself in for? What if she changes her mind about swapping places?

'Are you all right?' I ask gently, slipping the phone back into its cradle.

She visibly shakes herself. 'Of course.' Her mouth finally curves into a smile. 'Told you I was a good mimic, didn't I?'

We head back downstairs and I pour us both a large glass of wine. Laura's fingers are trembling as she takes hers and drinks deeply. I watch her out of the corner of my eye as I lay out the cheese and crackers we didn't finish at lunch. I didn't ask her if she would stay for something to eat. It was implicit she would.

Dusk has fallen while we were upstairs, and I find half a dozen tealights and light them, liking the way they make even this warehouse-like space cosy.

Laura picks up her cell and starts scrolling. Her face falls. 'The first available direct flight from Heathrow to Boston isn't till Saturday evening. I'll try Gatwick.'

'No.'

'What? Why not? The sooner you fly the better.'

I grip the stem of my wine glass. How can I explain to her that I've been institutionalised for so long I'm scared to make the break, even though I've been dreaming about leaving Marcus for years? I need twenty-four hours to mentally prepare myself. Twenty-four hours to summon the courage to walk away.

'I'll go Saturday. We need time to run through the plan, and you need to show me how Beatrice works. I can't remember the last time I drove a car, let alone one with gears.'

Laura chews her lip. 'I suppose you're right.' She waves her phone at me. 'So shall I book you a seat for Saturday?'

The hairs lift on the nape of my neck. I can't tell if it's through excitement or terror. 'Um, I guess.'

She taps away, then pulls her purse out of her bag and has me read out the number of her credit card. 'There,' she says, finally looking up at me. 'You're on the flight. I'll check in online for you, but you need to be at the airport by four thirty. Which'll mean leaving here by half eleven. Will you get your mum to meet you at the airport?'

'I'll call her once I land.' I shave off a piece of cheddar and pop it in my mouth. 'The fewer people who know what we're planning, the better.'

'Agreed. I'll drive Beatrice over in the morning so you can have a practice go in her. And I was thinking, you need to take my phone so you can access your boarding card and stuff. I'll pick up a cheap pay-as-you-go in Penzance in the morning.'

She slides her phone across the table to me. 'You might as well have it now. But if you post something embarrassing on my Instagram there'll be trouble, all right?' she jokes.

I'm about to ask for her passcode when a thought strikes me. 'I wonder if facial recognition will work?'

'I don't know.' She frowns. 'It somehow seems easier to fool people than AI.'

'There's one way to find out.'

Laura's screensaver is a cute photo of her and Vinnie on a pebbly beach, wide grins on their faces. Holding my breath, I swipe to open. There's a pause – just half a second, but enough to send a ripple of anxiety through me. Then, I'm staring at her home screen. I look up at her triumphantly.

'Oh my goodness. I'm in!'

We toast our success with a second glass of wine. Laura doesn't have to say a thing, but I know her thoughts mirror mine. If the latest artificial intelligence can't tell us apart, no one can. It's like we've been given permission to carry out our plan.

Which just leaves one thing. I push the cheeseboard towards Laura, but she shakes her head. I cross and uncross my ankles. Open my mouth to speak, then close it again. Should I even be saying this? But the sight of her still-trembling fingers is the prompt I need.

'You need an exit strategy for once I'm safely in the air,' I say, gripping the countertop and glancing up at the ceiling. 'There's a box of Tampax in the bottom drawer of my bedside cabinet—'

Laura snorts. 'I don't think they're going to be much help.'

'Listen, this is important. There's a bunch of keys in the box.'

'Keys?'

'To my lock-up.'

Laura's head snaps up. 'You have a lock-up?'

'In the village. You know Back Street? The road behind the fish and chip shop? It's the grey garage door.' My gaze slides to the wall clock. 'Number twelve.'

'Why d'you have a lock-up, Alana?'

'Because last summer I bought myself a car. A Toyota Aygo.'

She cocks her head and regards me steadily. 'I thought you said you didn't have any money.'

'I don't. I sold my grandmother's Cartier brooch to pay for it.'

'So why haven't you already used it to leave Marcus?'

I can't blame her for being suspicious. I would be too in her shoes. I rub the puckered skin on my right hand. 'I kept telling myself I would, but when it came to the crunch, I always bottled it. I'm a coward, Laura. That's the long and short of it. A spineless, gutless coward.'

Laura's expression softens and she reaches across and touches my arm. 'It's OK. I understand. It's hardly surprising, living with a sociopath like Marcus. He's made it his life's work to erode every shred of your self-confidence. So,' she says, checking. 'Box of Tampax in bedside cabinet. Keys for car and lock-up at number twelve Back Street.'

'I'll text you when I'm at Heathrow to let you know where I've left Beatrice. Just leave the Aygo in the airport car park when you come to fetch her. I won't be needing it again.'

At seven o'clock, Laura makes noises about heading back to the holiday cottage. I offer to see her home, but she assures me she'll be fine. I'm rummaging around in a kitchen drawer looking for the spare torch when a movement outside catches my eye. I jump out of my skin, stifling a gasp.

'What's wrong?' Laura cries, staring at me in concern.

'I... I saw someone out there, looking in.'

'Holy shit.' Her face drains of colour. 'Are you sure?'

I nod, and turn back to the window, sick with fear. It wouldn't be the first time Marcus has claimed to be somewhere else when he was really at home, spying on me. But there was traffic in the background when he phoned. It *can't* be him.

Laura is already pulling on her coat.

'What are you doing?'

She takes a knife from the block on the kitchen counter. My mouth hangs open.

'Laura!' I screech.

Her jaw is set. 'I'm going to see who the hell is out there.'

44

LAURA

The knife feels reassuringly heavy in my hand. I don't even remember why I grabbed it, to be honest. But Marcus's voice – so cold, so dismissive – reminded me this isn't a game. I wasn't joking when I called him a sociopath. He has tortured and tormented Alana for the last ten years. God only knows what else he's capable of.

Not for the first time, I worry I'm walking into a danger I don't fully understand. But then I think of Alana and every other woman whose life has been ruined by a bastard like Marcus, and my anger crystallises into something solid and utterly uncompromising.

Alana watches in stupefied silence as I stride across the kitchen to the back door and wrench it open. As I hover over the threshold, she cries, 'Wait!' and crosses the kitchen at a trot, pressing a torch into my free hand. 'Be careful,' she urges. I nod, tuck the knife into my belt and step into the darkness.

I wave the torch in front of me as I picture the layout of the garden. The window Alana saw the prowler through faces the back, so I turn right and head in that direction, my head cocked, listening for footsteps or the sound of someone breathing. I sweep the torch from left to right, every shrub, every terracotta pot, looking for a potential intruder.

'I know you're there,' I call, tightening my grip on the torch. 'We've called the police, so you might as well come out now.' I'm bluffing, but who cares if it flushes him out. I creep past the window and glance in. Alana is gripping the worktop and staring out into the garden, her face creased with worry. Something inside me tightens. That urge to protect her from the man who has made her life a misery, whatever the cost.

She startles when she sees me, then the tension leaves her body and she gives me a little wave. I'm about to wave back when a hand grabs my shoulder and spins me round.

I act without thinking, dropping the torch, grabbing the knife from my belt and twisting round using the intruder's momentum to slam him onto the ground. My knee digs into the small of his back as I pin him there, the tip of the knife on the base of his neck. With my left hand, I snatch up the torch, shine it into his face and freeze. It's Rory.

'What the fuck?' I yell, my face up against his.

He shrinks back, his pupils dilating when he sees the knife.

'The lights were off,' he stutters, his head jerking towards the house. 'I was checking she was all right.'

'Why should I believe you?' I growl. 'You could be a dirty little peeping Tom for all I know. Is that what you were doing? Spying on her?'

'I would never do that!' he cries. 'I was... I was looking out for her, I promise.' The words catch in his throat and I loosen my hold.

'Get up,' I tell him, and he scrambles to his feet, his eyes fixed on the knife. Even though he towers over me, I don't feel threatened by this strange boy-man. 'It's all right, I won't hurt you. Come with me.'

I lead him to the back door where Alana is waiting.

'Rory! What are you doing here?'

'I came to check you was all right. Then your double jumped me.' He rubs his back and scowls at me.

'So I saw,' Alana says, ushering him into the kitchen. She raises an eyebrow. 'It was pretty impressive.'

'Did I forget to mention I was a brown belt in judo when I was a teenager?' I stalk across the kitchen and slot the knife back in its block. My breathing is still heavy, adrenaline flowing through me, making my movements jerky.

Alana gestures at Rory to take a stool at the island and asks if he wants a beer.

'Just a glass of orange squash please, Mrs Adams.' His gaze falls on the nearest tealight. 'Have you called the electric people?'

She shakes her head.

'I can phone them for you, if you like.'

'There's no need, Rory. I... I flipped the trip switch.'

He blinks. 'Why would you do that?' When Alana doesn't immediately answer, comprehension dawns on his face. 'Because of her,' he says, dipping his head towards me. 'And Mr Adams's cameras.'

'That's right.' Alana hands him a glass of squash. 'He can't know about Laura.'

'Why not?'

I make a cutting motion across my throat but she ignores me.

'Because we're planning to—'

'Alana!' I say sharply. 'I thought the less people who knew about this the better?'

'It's OK. We can trust Rory, can't we, honey?'

He nods slowly. 'You can. I won't say a word to no one.'

'Loving the double negative.' My voice drips sarcasm.

'I mean it. You can trust me.'

'Laura and I are going to swap places so I can fly home to my mom,' Alana tells him.

'When?'

'Saturday evening. My flight's at half seven. Laura's lending me her car to drive to the airport.'

'I would'a taken you on the bike. You know that. You only had ter ask.'

She reaches across the table to touch his hand, and his ruddy cheeks turn a deeper shade of red. 'I know, but I don't want to get you into trouble with Mr Adams, do I?'

'I wouldn'a minded. Is there anything else I can do to help?'

'Nothing, thanks. We have everything covered,' I say, before Alana has a chance to answer.

Rory ignores me. 'You can park 'er car outside ours, if you like. You needn't worry. Mam's in hospital to sort out her breathing. No one need know.'

'Thank you, Rory. That would be a help.'

He downs his drink in one and carefully places the glass on the worktop. 'How long are you staying with your mam?'

He assumes she's coming back, I think. Will he still help us if he realises he's never going to see her again? He might tell Marcus what we're planning if he thinks it'll stop her from leaving.

Alana must read my mind, because she pats him on the hand again, briskly this time.

'Just a couple of weeks,' she says. 'Then I'll be home.' She pushes her stool back and he takes the hint.

'I oughta get going. I promised Mam I'd call her. I'll see myself out.' His gaze flickers from me to Alana. 'Have a nice holiday,' he says finally.

Alana smiles. 'I will.'

Once he's gone, Alana clears the food away and I sit slumped at the island, resting my chin in my hands.

'I know what you're thinking,' she says, her back to me. 'You're wondering why I haven't asked Rory to help me leave before.' She turns to face me, plucking at the scarred skin on the back of her hand.

I shake my head. 'I told you. You don't need to justify anything to me. I'll never judge you, Alana. How can I, when I have no idea of the hell you've been through?' I push my stool back and carry my glass and plate over to the sink. 'I should go. You need to get the power back on, or Marcus'll be suspicious. I'll see you in the morning.'

'With Beatrice?'

'With Beatrice,' I agree.

I'm halfway home when I realise I'm still wearing Alana's clothes, and that, while our phones couldn't tell the difference, Rory had no problem telling us apart.

My stomach flips and I stumble as I realise what this means.

Perhaps we aren't quite as identical as we think.

Because if Rory, Alana's *gardener*, can tell us apart, Marcus surely will too.

45

LAURA

My legs are heavy as I walk through the cobbled streets to the car park at the top of the village the next morning. I slept badly, my dreams like a slasher film on repeat, only I was the one wielding the knife. Freud would have something to say about that, I think, as I unlock Beatrice and slide into the driver's seat. It's been a few days since I've driven her, which is never good, and I hold my breath as I turn the key. But my doubts are misplaced and the engine fires first time.

I drive to the big Tesco on the outskirts of Penzance and buy the cheapest pay-as-you go phone I can find. It'll have to do until Alana can send mine back to me once she's home.

Beatrice's tank is less than a quarter full, so I top her up at the petrol station, then turn her towards Porthmerryn. It's not long before we've passed the glamping place and are approaching Mairead's chalet bungalow. I brake sharply. Two police patrol cars and an ambulance are parked outside, blocking the lane. My heart pumping and my palms sweaty, I swing onto the verge and kill the engine.

I pull the keys out of the ignition and twist them in my lap, wondering what the hell is going on. Perhaps Mairead's had a fall or has taken a turn for the worse. What was it Alana said she had? I search my memory. Lung cancer, that was it. Rory said she was in hospital while they sorted out her breathing but it's possible she was discharged last night.

An officer notices the car. I wind down the window and wait nervously as he marches over.

'Can I help you, madam?'

Instinct kicks in. If he thinks I'm just some random walker he's not going to let me through. But if he thinks I'm Alana...

'I live here,' I say, turning on my American accent. 'Why, what's happened? Is Mairead all right?'

He answers my questions with another of his own.

'You live *here*?' He jerks a thumb at the bungalow.

'Merryn's Reach,' I clarify. 'The house at the end of the lane.'

'Marcus Adams's place?'

I nod, feeling a sudden tug of anxiety. Alana said Marcus knew half the local police force. What if word gets back to him that she's not at home where she should be? I might end up paying for my lie. But my fears prove groundless, because he's already losing interest.

'We're dealing with an incident, Mrs Adams. You're going to have to leave your car here and walk.'

'Of course.' I grab my bag from the passenger seat and jump out. He watches inscrutably as I lock the door and ball the keys in my fist. I'm desperate to ask what kind of incident they're dealing with, but I have a feeling I'd have better luck getting blood out of a stone.

Another police officer is standing by Mairead's front door, talking into his radio. I strain to catch a snippet of the conversation as I set off up the lane towards the sea.

'...The postman called it in... We've left the scene as we

found it, sir... No, it was a leather belt... The duty DI and SOCO are on their way... No problem, I'll call the coroner's office now... Next of kin's aware... The mother's in hospital... PC Bellamy is with her now... Understood... I'll see what I can do.'

I quicken my pace, turning his words over in my mind as I hurry towards Merryn's Reach. Why was he talking about a belt? And why do they need the coroner's office? My first theory, that Mairead has been taken ill, doesn't fit the narrative. There is only one scenario that does, but that can't be right. It can't be.

'Wait!' a voice commands, and I freeze, swallowing down a yelp of fright. I turn slowly to see the police officer who was on his radio behind me, a pocket notebook in his hand. 'Sorry if I startled you,' he says, though he doesn't look very sorry. He's a big guy, with a neat beard and muscular forearms.

'Not a problem.'

'You're American.' He seems surprised.

'Uh-huh.' I extend a hand. 'Alana Adams. I was on my way home when I saw the ambulance. Is Mairead OK?'

'Mrs O'Cleary?'

I have no idea what Mairead's last name is, but O'Cleary sounds suitably Irish, so I nod. 'Is the ambulance for her?'

The officer glances at his colleague, who has stopped a guy with a red setter and is directing him back down the lane towards the village.

'Mrs O'Cleary's currently in hospital.'

I don't have to feign my shock. 'It's for *Rory*?'

He shifts his weight from one foot to the other. 'I'm afraid I can't divulge—'

'It's fine,' I say quickly. 'It's none of my business. I shouldn't have asked.'

'Not a problem, Mrs Adams. You go easy, OK?'

I thank him and tramp towards Merryn's Reach, my mind whirring. I didn't need the cop to say who the ambulance was for. He was as easy to read as a book. So why is it not roaring off to hospital, lights flashing and sirens blaring?

My heart skips a beat, because there's only one explanation. Rory is dead.

46

ALANA

I'm in the laundry room at the back of the house when Laura's cell pings with a text message from a number I don't recognise. To my relief it's Laura on her new phone, telling me she's arrived.

Give me five, I type back. *I'll trip the switch and come down and open the gates manually.*

I find her loitering just out of sight of Marcus's cameras. She's pale, her hands thrust deep into her pockets, and there's no sign of her car.

'Where's Beatrice?'

She glances behind her, then shakes her head. Her mouth is a grim line. 'I'll explain inside. Are the cameras off?'

'They are.'

I trot after her, trying to damp down the groundswell of fear that is compressing my chest, making every breath an effort. I shepherd her into the kitchen and she slumps on a stool and drops her head in her hands.

'What is it, Laura? You're scaring me.'

She looks up. Purple shadows ring her eyes and her jaw is

tight. 'Did you see the police cars outside Mairead's? The ambulance?'

'What police?' The vice-like grip around my chest tightens another notch. 'What ambulance?'

'Mairead's in hospital, so it can't be her. It must be Rory.' She looks at me. 'I think something's happened to Rory.'

The colour drains from my face. 'What?'

'One of the police officers said the bungalow was a scene and was talking about the duty DI and SOCO being on their way. SOCO stands for scene of crime officers, doesn't it? And I heard him mention a leather belt. Plus, the ambulance was going nowhere, which can only mean one thing.'

Laura is talking so quickly it takes a moment for her words to sink in, but when they do, I stare at her with growing horror.

'What are you saying?'

'I think Rory's killed himself. It's the only thing that makes sense. That's why the house is a crime scene and the forensics people are on their way.'

'No!' I gasp, the pressure around my chest almost unbearable. 'He wouldn't do that.'

Laura runs her hands through her hair. 'I know it's a shock, but there's no other explanation.'

'But we saw him last night and he was fine. He was offering to help me, for Chrissakes.'

'He could have had mental health problems for all we know. He was a bit...' She trails off.

'A bit what?'

Her eyes widen at my sharp tone. She pulls an apologetic face. 'Unworldly...'

Anger ignites inside me and I ball my fists at my sides.

'Does it matter? Rory is one of the most kind-hearted, gentle people I have ever met.' I can't talk about him in the past tense because we don't know what's happened for sure. Laura could be putting two and two together and coming up with twenty-six.

'Call her,' she says. 'Call Mairead and ask.'

'I can't do that. She's in hospital.'

'Say you've seen the patrol cars outside the house and you're checking everything's OK.'

When I make no move to pick up the landline, Laura exhales loudly. 'It's the neighbourly thing to do, and you need to be acting normally right now. The last thing we need is for people to start getting suspicious.'

Reluctantly, I do as she says. Mairead's number rings and rings, and I'm about to hang up when she finally answers with a wobbly, 'Hello?'

'Mairead, it's me. Alana. I hate to bother you while you're in hospital but there are a couple of squad cars and an ambulance outside yours. Is everything all right?'

There is silence, though I can hear her breathing.

'Mairead, are you there?'

'Oh, it's awful, Alana. The police are saying Rory's dead. Hung himself from the banister with the belt you gave him for Christmas.'

The shock I feel is visceral. It blasts through my body like a lightning strike, first searingly hot, then as cold as splinters of ice. *He can't have.* Rory, that gentle giant of a man who was willing to risk his job to smuggle me in a sketch pad and some pencils. Who offered to take me to the airport on his bike. Who would have done anything for me if I'd asked him to.

'Are you sure?' My voice is strangulated. Hardly surprising considering the hard ball of grief that has settled at the back of my throat.

Mairead hiccups. 'Suicide. That's what they're saying. But they're wrong. He wouldn't do that.'

It's the same thing I told Laura just minutes ago. Mairead

and I are in our own echo chamber of two. But we are the people who knew Rory best.

'Did he... did he leave a note?'

'That's the thing, Alana. He didn't. And the last time I spoke to him, he was his usual self.'

'When was that?'

'He called me last night, just before nine. When did you last see him?'

'Um.' I pause. Should I tell her he was here just before that? Laura and I must have been the last people to see him alive. Even if the police are right and Rory killed himself, would they want to talk to us as part of their investigation? I can't risk saying anything that might disrupt our plans. I feel the heat of Laura's gaze on me as I say, 'I haven't seen him since first thing yesterday morning, Mairead. I'm sorry.'

'You've no need to apologise, love. I'm struggling to take it all in. I just can't believe my boy would do that to himself.'

'Is there anything I can do?'

'No, you're all right. The police are going to secure the house after they've taken away the... they've taken Rory away.' Her voice breaks up into a series of strangulated sobs. I close my eyes, wishing there was something I could do to ease her pain. In the ten years I've lived here, Mairead and Rory are the only people who've had even an inkling of what really goes on behind these four walls. Apart from Mom, they're the closest I have to family. Mairead's loss is my loss, and I ache for her.

Eventually, she collects herself, and I tell her to call if she needs anything, before saying goodbye.

'Well?' Laura asks.

'He hanged himself with a belt I gave him for Christmas.'

Laura whistles. 'Did you know he suffered from depression?'

'That's the thing. I don't think he did. Mairead doesn't, either.'

'People are good at hiding it.' She is quiet for a moment, then looks up. 'He must have been worried about his mum. Perhaps he couldn't imagine life without her.'

I shake my head. 'He was worried about her, but he wouldn't have left her, not when she's so poorly.'

'Perhaps it was a sex game gone wrong. It does happen.'

I recoil. 'No. Not Rory.'

'If it wasn't suicide and it wasn't an accident, what are you saying? That someone did this to him?'

It sounds ridiculous, and I tell her that no, that's not what I'm saying. But a tiny voice whispers inside my head. *Are you sure?*

47

LAURA

Alana hugs her chest, the coffee in front of her going cold. She's been in this almost catatonic state for the last ten minutes. Her face is deathly pale, and every now and then she gives an involuntary shiver, like she's trapped in a memory and can't escape.

'Hey,' I say softly. 'You OK?'

Her gaze darts to me, but her eyes are opaque, unfocused.

'Alana—'

She starts, jerking her head back as if I've raised a fist to her. I try a tentative smile and gradually her shoulders drop and her hands fall to her lap.

'The police have got it all wrong,' she says, finally. 'It wasn't suicide.'

'Then what do you think happened?'

'Me?' Her hand flutters to her throat. 'Why would I know?'

'Because you seem so certain Rory didn't kill himself.' She flinches at the sound of his name. *And because you seem rattled.* Something feels off-kilter. But what? Before I can dwell on it further, she jumps to her feet and announces that she's going for a swim. Alone.

'You don't want me to come?'

'Not today.' Her tone is flat and I'm about to tell her I don't think it's a good idea for her to go on her own, especially not this morning, with Rory's death so raw, when she disappears upstairs, returning a few minutes later in her dry robe, her float under her arm. She hands me my phone.

'I'll be forty minutes max. You can amuse yourself, can't you?' She sounds distracted, like she's already reached the end of the narrow path down to the cove and is about to step into the rolling swell of the Atlantic.

I bite my lip. 'It looked rough this morning. Be careful.'

Finally, she smiles. 'I'm always careful.'

When I hear the front door slam, I wash up our mugs and give the worktops a wipe. I run through our plan in my head. It's almost eleven. This time tomorrow Alana will be setting off for Heathrow, leaving me in the house awaiting Marcus's return from London. I'll be making sure the already spotless house is gleaming, before setting the stage for my bout of gastric flu. I practise a couple of affirmations. My voice sounds feeble in the atrium-like space.

'Marcus, you are my north, my south, my east, my west. Every day I wake up grateful that I get to have you all to myself.' I snigger and try another, my voice growing stronger, the American accent sharper. 'Marcus, you are the light of my life. The icing on my cake. My one and only. Jeez, how does Alana keep a straight face when she's trumpeting this bullshit?'

Bored with stupid affirmations, I head upstairs to Alana and Marcus's bedroom. The thick carpet sinks luxuriously under my feet as I walk over to the dressing table. I pull out the stool and spend the next ten minutes following Alana's make-up routine. Next, I cross the room to the dressing room and pick something to wear for tomorrow. It takes ages because there's so much to choose from, but eventually I settle on a pair of Calvin Klein tailored wide-leg trousers in a charcoal grey, a fitted white shirt and a soft-green cashmere sweater. I pull off my jeans and hoodie and try them on, catching my reflection in the mirror. I no longer look like Laura, the rather scruffy, disorganised vet nurse from Kent. I look elegant. Poised. I look like Alana.

I'm striking a pose when my phone rings, and I grab it and answer without checking the screen.

When will I learn?

'Laura, it's Vinnie. Don't hang up.'

'What do you want?'

'I know you're mad at me, and I get it. But Sam's been in touch—'

I don't bother to hide my disbelief. 'Sam's been in touch with *you?*'

'—and she really wants to talk to you, babe. I've got her number. I'll text it to you. Will you give her a ring?'

'No!' I explode. 'I will not give her a bloody ring. When will she realise I don't want anything to do with her? Or you, for that matter. So why don't you both piss off and leave me alone!'

I end the call and fling the phone onto the floor, shaking with anger. How dare Sam call Vinnie behind my back, using him to get to me? And how dare Vinnie let her? He always was a sucker for a sob story. He'd take in half the waifs and strays at work if our landlord allowed pets. *His* landlord, I remind myself bitterly. I don't have a home any more.

Once again, the stark reality of my situation hits me. I have no partner, nowhere to live and a stalker of a sister. Coming down to Cornwall, meeting Alana and forging a plan to help her leave Marcus has been a convenient – and welcome – distraction from my car crash of a life.

I glare at my reflection in the mirror. Swapping places with Alana is proving easier than I ever imagined. Surrounded by rails of her designer clothes, in the sumptuous elegance of her beautiful home, it's easy to be seduced into thinking I could stay here forever. But if I think my life is bad, hers is a million times worse. Vinnie and Sam are mere irritants compared to Marcus. The man is a monster.

I can't think about my feckless fiancé and my maddening half-sister right now. I need to focus on Alana and our plan. I know I'll have to face up to my own problems once this is over.

But setting Alana free comes first. It has to. Because if I can help her escape, maybe I'm not a total failure. I'll have done something meaningful. Something that makes a difference.

And, just maybe, I'll find the courage to start over, too.

48

ALANA

Laura was right. There is a strong swell today. I can feel the currents tugging at my feet as I wade in. When the water is chest-deep I start to swim, half a dozen easy strokes of breast-stroke while I regulate my breathing. Sea swimming is all about discipline and control. Assessing risks and seeing things through to the end, even though it might be well out of your comfort zone.

Outsmarting Marcus has required the same focus, the same determination. To do whatever it takes.

Whatever it takes.

I'm in a strange mood. Rory's death has thrown me for a loop. He has been a permanent fixture in my life since I married Marcus and I assumed he always would be. Always in the back-ground, but there, as solid and dependable as a faithful dog.

The fact he's gone has me questioning my truth.

I switch to freestyle, my arms powerful as they slice through the water. I suck in a cold lungful of air every third stroke. *Stroke, stroke, breathe.* My body knows this rhythm, it is as familiar to me as walking. It's predictable. Unlike everything else.

This time tomorrow I will have left Marcus and Merryn's Reach behind. I should be excited. At the very least relieved. But all I feel is a weird kind of numb, as though I'm watching myself from the top of the bluff. I stop, treading water, and stare at the horizon. I'm dissociating. I recognise the signs. I concentrate on the feel of the saltwater on my skin, the way the swell lifts and drops me. The sound of my breathing.

What even is my truth?

A wave rolls over me, bigger than the others, and for a moment it pulls me under before I kick back to the surface. I gulp air, my lungs burning. Maybe I should keep swimming, let the water take me. At least then it would all be over. The scheming, the games, the subterfuge. No one else would get hurt. It would be so easy. So, so easy.

But I can't, because there is a chink of light in the darkness. There is hope that one day I might be able to live a normal life, free of fear, thanks to Laura. I picture her up at the house, concern carving deep lines on her forehead as she waits for my return. Laura, who is willing to risk everything for me.

I have no choice. I set off back to the shore, tears mingling with the spray of seawater on my cheeks.

* * *

Later that afternoon, once Laura has left, I walk through the house, reliving the last ten years. Our en suite, where Marcus once held my head under the bathwater until I almost lost consciousness because I went swimming without his permission. The spare bedroom, where he locked me for forty-eight hours with a two-litre bottle of water and a packet of crackers because he was going to London and didn't want me to leave the house. The landing, where he shoved me in the back, laughing spitefully when I stumbled and almost fell down the stairs. The kitchen, the scene of so many verbal and physical assaults. A finger 'accidentally' trapped in a drawer. A carefully prepared meal upended on the tiles. A hissed barb. A globule of spit in my face.

I don't go down into his darkroom. I have no wish to relive those memories.

At six o'clock, Marcus calls. I take a deep breath and answer, hoping it's the last time I ever have to speak to the sadistic bastard.

'Hi, honey. I'm missing you.'

'Are you?' There is a ring of suspicion to his voice that catches me off guard.

'Of course I am. It's been... it's been a horrible day. Rory's dead.'

Silence. My grip on the phone tightens.

'Did you hear what I said, Marcus?' My voice rises. 'Rory is *dead*.'

'I heard you the first time. What happened?'

'The police say it was suicide.' I'm about to add that I think they're wrong because Rory would never kill himself while Mairead needed him, when I stop myself. Best that Marcus thinks I accept the police's version of events.

'It's bloody inconvenient,' he huffs. 'It's going to be a nightmare trying to find someone else to do the garden.'

His callousness takes my breath away. But why would I be surprised? Marcus only ever thinks about himself. He certainly wouldn't spare a thought for poor Mairead. He only helps her get to her hospital appointments because it reflects well on him.

'If you give me the WiFi password I'll check out some local firms,' I offer.

'No, I'll do it when I'm back.'

'You're still planning to catch the twelve o'clock train tomorrow?'

He grunts an affirmative.

I dig my nails into the palm of my free hand so hard I wince, then take a deep breath. 'I can't wait to see you, sweetheart. The house has felt so empty without you. I love you so much and—'

'Yes, yes,' he interjects irritably. 'I'll text when I'm on the train. And, Alana,' his voice turns smooth, honeyed, 'I have a surprise for you.'

Coming from any other husband, it would be something to look forward to. A box of chocolates, maybe even a piece of jewellery. But from Marcus, who feeds off my fear, it simply sounds like a threat...

49

LAURA

Back at Gull Cottage, I fix myself scrambled eggs on toast, only to find I'm too wired to eat. I tip it into the food waste and pour myself a large glass of wine with trembling fingers, hoping the alcohol will settle my nerves.

I don't bother with the television. I'm not in the mood for inane Friday-night TV, and the Netflix true crime documentaries I usually love feel a bit too close to the bone. Is what we're doing a crime? I've never been in trouble with the police in my life. I've always followed the rules, been a model citizen. Not just a model citizen but a protector of the weak. A crusader for justice. I was never afraid to stick up for the poor kids who were picked on at school. Never frightened to stand up to the bullies.

But standing up to Marcus is something else entirely. I slop wine onto my leg as the sheer magnitude of what we're about to do hits me. Have we lost our *minds*? What if he takes one look at me and realises I'm not his wife? I already know he has a vicious temper. He's left Alana – the woman he promised to love and cherish – with both mental and physical scars. What the hell will he do to *me*?

My eyes flick to my phone, lying on the coffee table. Alana insisted I take it in case Mum rang.

'You might be able to do an American accent, but my English accent is as bad as Dick Van Dyke's in *Mary Poppins*. Just bring it back in the morning. I'll keep the prepaid phone so you can call me if you need to.'

She was in a funny mood when she came back from her swim, her cheeks wind-bitten and her hair dripping wet. Maybe she's having second thoughts too. After all, if Marcus ever discovered what we were planning, the consequences would be brutal.

Despite my misgivings, I know we can't back out now. We're doing the right thing. I can't begin to imagine what the last ten years have been like for Alana. Vinnie wasn't perfect, but he was kind and funny and he treated me with respect – until he was dazzled by a bubbly sales rep, at any rate.

Out of nowhere, the urge to speak to him rises in me and I reach for my phone before I can talk myself out of it.

'Hey,' he says, answering on the second ring.

'I'm sorry I yelled at you.'

''S'OK. 'Spect I deserved it. Everything all right?' He sounds so concerned my eyes prickle with tears. 'How's Cornwall?'

'Fine.'

'I miss you, Laura. I wish I hadn't—'

'Let's not talk about that now.'

'I just want you to know how sorry I am. I've been such a fucking idiot. I wish I could turn back the clock.' He makes a strange choking noise and with horror I realise he's crying. I've only ever seen him cry once before, when a litter of puppies was dumped outside the surgery so emaciated they were scraps of skin and bone. Only two of the six survived. We all shed a tear that day.

'Vinnie—'

'Sorry.' He sniffs. Clears his throat. 'Ignore me. Tell me what you've been up to.'

What would he say if I told him the truth, that I'd met my double and we were planning to trade places so she could escape her abusive husband? It sounds so far-fetched I doubt he'd believe me, and if he did, he'd certainly try to talk me out of it, telling me I was crazy to risk my life for someone I hardly knew.

'Laura?'

I give a start. Collect myself. 'Oh, you know, the usual. A few walks. Fish and chips. A boxset or three.'

'Good. I'm glad you're having a rest.' He pauses. 'D'you want to talk about Sam?'

I shake my head, forgetting he can't see me. 'Not really. Listen, I need to go. There's something I want to watch on TV.'

'Oh, OK. I'll leave you in peace.'

'I called you, you idiot.'

'So you did.' He lets out a low laugh and a smile creeps across my face, catching me by surprise.

'Thank you,' he says.

'What for?'

'Talking to me. You're not due to leave till next Saturday, right? Maybe we can talk again next week?'

'Maybe.'

I'm still smiling when I end the call. Just because we're not together any more doesn't mean we can't be friends. Better that than not having him in my life at all.

I log onto the airline's website and check in, picking Alana a window seat over the wing, because I once read it was less bumpy than the back of the plane. I'm rinsing out my wine glass when the phone rings. Recognising the number of my new pay-as-you-go, I dry my hands on my jeans and snatch it up.

'I can't do it,' Alana says breathlessly. 'I can't leave.'

'*What?*'

'You don't know what Marcus is capable of. If he finds out what we're doing he'll kill me.'

'He won't find out.'

'But how can you be sure?'

'Because we've been so careful. Our plan is foolproof, and the only person who knew about it is dead. You'll be halfway across the Atlantic by the time he realises what we've done. You'll be safe.'

'But what about you?' she cries.

'I can look after myself. I was a brown belt in judo, remember. You saw how I took Rory down. And I have my escape route planned, don't I, thanks to you and your little Toyota Aygo. I'll be fine.' I sound so breezily confident I'm almost fooling myself. 'Has he rung you tonight?'

'A couple of hours ago.'

'And did he sound suspicious?'

'I guess not, but—'

'Then don't worry. I've checked in for you. Have you packed?'

'Just a few things, yes.'

'Good. We should both get an early night. Big day tomorrow.'

'Laura, I—'

'Alana, it will be all right. I promise. I'm a great believer in karma. Don't worry, Marcus will get what he deserves. We all will.'

* * *

I sleep surprisingly well, waking just after seven. After a shower and a couple of slices of toast, I pass the time until I'm due to leave practising my American accent in the empty cottage. At half eight, I set off through the village to the car park. It's raining, a light drizzle that makes the cobbles gleam and gums my eyelids together. I pull my hood up and quicken my pace. I'm breathing hard by the time I reach Beatrice.

It's just after nine when I pull up outside Mairead's bungalow. The police have long gone and the place is deserted. Mairead must still be in hospital. What must it be like, having to deal with the death of your son *and* cancer? Poor woman.

I ping Alana a text to let her know to flip the trip switch, then lock Beatrice and wander up the track to Merryn's Reach. The Boston flight leaves Heathrow at seven thirty tonight and check-in's three hours before that. According to Google Maps, the journey's currently taking just over five hours. Leaving at ten gives her an extra hour and a half as a contingency.

The gates are open and I walk straight up to the house. My heart is fluttering in my chest. Once again, this hare-brained plan of ours, so simple in theory, seems ludicrous. Who in their right mind would possibly think that Marcus could mistake me for his wife of ten years? It's ridiculous. Not just ridiculous but fraught with danger. Was I not listening when Alana recounted example after example of Marcus's abuse? The man isn't just a violent bully, he bears all the traits of a psychopath, and I'm walking straight into his lair.

I hesitate, my hand halfway to the door ready to knock, fear pumping adrenaline through my veins. I can't go through with it. I can't—

The door swings open and I bite down on my lip to stifle a yelp of surprise. Alana's brow creases and she beckons me in. I follow her to the kitchen, shrugging off my coat, averting my gaze from the photo of the old woman whose face is gripped by a silent scream.

Alana's hands are trembling as she takes my coat and runs me a glass of water. She's as nervous as me. Inexplicably, this knowledge makes me braver. I am the strong one. I can do this. I paste a smile on my face and ask how she's feeling.

'I'm kind of freaking out,' she admits. 'Trying not to, but... you know—'

'I do. It's OK to be nervous. I am too, if you must know.'

An emotion I can't read passes across her pale face. Worried she's about to dissociate again, I reach out and touch her hand, my fingers grazing the scarred skin of her burn.

'Shit,' I say, pulling my own hand back. 'Marcus will see I don't have a scar.'

'It'll be fine. He won't come near you while you're sick.'

'Are you sure?'

She nods. 'A hundred per cent. I told you, it's a full-blown phobia. He's paranoid about getting ill himself.'

I have to take her word for it. It's too late to change our minds now. We swap phones and Alana hands me her rock-like engagement ring and diamond-studded wedding band. I slide them both onto my ring finger. We run through the plan a final time and at five to ten I push my stool back.

'Time to hit the road.'

She nods and picks up her handbag and a small carry-on. 'I've left the bucket and disinfectant in the utility.'

'Thanks.'

'And you'll remember to reset the trip switch when I've gone?'

'I will.' I make a mental note while trying to stem my rising panic. There is so much to remember. 'I'll keep an eye on the flight tracker app, but you'll text me when you arrive at the airport, yeah?'

'Of course.' She straightens her shoulders, takes one last look around the cavernous kitchen, then marches towards the front door. I grab my car keys and follow.

* * *

Alana sits in the driver's seat and stares at the VW Beetle's dashboard doubtfully.

I lean on the open door and give her a crash course in Beatrice's quirks. The stiff gearstick, the temperamental heater, the way her front wheels lose grip in the wet. 'I know she's no Aston Martin, but she's pretty simple to drive. Windscreen wipers are this side, lights are there. That's the choke.' I tap the small black knob below the dash.

'What the heck is a choke?'

'It makes starting easier when the engine's cold. The Aston probably does it automatically but Beatrice is old school and you have to do it by hand. Just don't overdo it or you'll flood the engine.'

Alana's eyes widen and she clutches my arm in panic.

'I don't think I can do this.'

'Nonsense. Beatrice will look after you, won't you, Bea?' I close the driver's door and pat the roof. 'Start her up and have a quick drive up and down the lane to get a feel for her. Then you'd better go. It's already a quarter past ten.'

I shove my hands into my pockets and step back onto the verge. Alana closes her eyes briefly, then flicks the ignition. The engine turns over once, then dies.

'Try again,' I call. Beatrice makes a high-pitched whirring sound, like her heart isn't quite in it. I'm about to walk over and tell Alana she's flooded the engine when the hairs on the back of my neck stiffen as I sense someone's gaze on my back. I spin on my heels and scan the scrub, then shake my head. Nerves are getting the better of me.

There's no one there.

50

ALANA

Blood whooshes in my ears. I try the ignition again, but the car just makes that goddamn whirring sound that grates on my already shredded nerves.

I drag my hands down my face and turn towards Laura. She is completely still, one hand shielding her eyes from the drizzle as she stares into the bushes. It's enough to send another ripple of fear through me. I wind down the window.

'What's wrong?'

She turns, sees my worried expression and shakes her head. 'Nothing.' She marches over and lifts the trunk. Petrol fumes waft in through the open window. 'I thought I said go easy on the choke,' she mutters as she peers at the engine.

I'm about to let rip. If she owned a proper car instead of this heap of crap, none of this would've happened. But I bite my tongue. For some inexplicable reason she seems inordinately fond of it and the last thing I want to do is hurt her feelings. Instead, I ask if there's anything I can do.

'Give her a minute. Then, next time you try, press the accelerator to the floor and hold it there when you turn the ignition.'

'You mean the gas pedal?'

'Exactly.'

I do as instructed, and this time the car wheezes into life. Leaving the engine running, I clamber out of the driver's seat and hug Laura.

'Thank you,' I whisper in her ear. Her hair brushes against my cheek as she nods. We both pull back and once again I get that flip of recognition, like I'm staring into a mirror.

Laura. My doppelgänger. My fetch. My saviour.

'Drive carefully,' she says.

'I will.' A lump forms in the back of my throat and I quickly swallow it down. I can't let my emotions get the better of me, not now, not when I'm so damn close to escaping.

She breaks away from me. 'Go. It's already half ten.'

I nod, climb back into the car and coax it into first gear, watching Laura grow smaller and smaller in the rear-view mirror as the car bumps down the track towards freedom.

* * *

I make steady progress until tail-lights ahead of me flash red five miles before the M4 junction. I grab Laura's cell from the passenger seat and check Google Maps. There's a thirty-minute delay, pushing my ETA back to four fifteen. I'm going to be cutting it fine.

The flickering tail-lights remind me of the journey back from Heathrow the last time I tried to fly home. The day Marcus introduced me to his rules. To think I'd thought he was joking. I was such an innocent back then. A fatherless daughter who craved security and stability. Ripe for the picking for a man like Marcus, my manipulative, charming, handsome monster of a husband.

I picture Laura alone at Merryn's Reach, counting down the minutes till he comes home and she has to give the performance of her life. Beneath all her bravado she seemed nervous this morning. It's understandable. I'm not sure I would have been so quick to offer help in her shoes. But Laura's a vet nurse, the kind of person who picks up strays, patches them up and sends them on their way. The kind of person who not only hates injustice but is brave enough to do something about it. The kind of person I wish I'd been.

Maybe I was, in another life.

The traffic starts to move again. I take my foot off the clutch too quickly and the Beetle bunny-hops forwards. Christ, I hate this car. I force myself to concentrate on the road ahead, watching out for signs for the M4. I've just turned off the slip road when my cell – *Laura's cell* – rings. I glance down, my heart missing a beat when I see the number of Laura's prepaid phone on the screen.

Keeping half an eye on the road, I accept the call and turn on the speakerphone.

'Everything OK?'

'No.' Laura's voice is shrill. 'Everything is not fucking OK. Marcus just called to say he's at the station.'

'Paddington?'

'No, not Paddington. Marcus is at Penzance. He's going to be back in fifteen minutes!'

51

LAURA

I end the call and run my hands through my hair. I'd wanted reassurance but Alana sounded as shocked as I was that Marcus was already in Cornwall. I can guess why. It's only a quarter past two. If he realises what we've done he'd just about have time to drive to Heathrow and stop her leaving.

Shit. *Shit.* I was in the garden when I heard the landline ringing. For a moment I considered ignoring it, but then I remembered the rules: Alana has to answer the phone immediately or she'll be punished.

Maybe the smart thing would have been to let it ring out and flee. Grab my bag and race down the coastal path to the safety of Gull Cottage. But I couldn't let Alana down.

Instead, I told myself it was good he was calling as I sprinted into the house. It gave me a chance to plant the seed that I was sick.

I answered with a flat, 'Hey, honey.'

'Why didn't you answer immediately?'

'I was in the garden, getting some fresh air. I'm feeling a bit off-colour.' I paused, my mind suddenly blank. What would Alana say now? I stared skywards for inspiration. Marcus was a man who needed his ego massaged. I cleared my throat. 'I can't wait to see you, sweetheart. The house feels so empty without you.' When he didn't reply, I worried I'd laid it on too thick, but I ploughed on anyway. 'You'll be back just after five, right?'

'Actually, the breakfast meeting was cancelled. I caught the nine o'clock. I'm at Penzance now.'

My stomach clenched. Penzance? It was ten miles from Porthmerryn, which meant... which meant he could be home in twenty minutes.

Fuck.

'Oh, that's... great.' I was scratching around for a way to end the call when he spoke again.

'I've missed you, Alana. I hope you've missed me, too,' he said silkily. The meaning was clear, and a wave of revulsion ripped through me. I hoped to God Alana hadn't exaggerated his fear of vomit. Otherwise I was in trouble. Big fucking trouble.

'Of course I have, honey.' I forced the words out, trying to sound like I meant them. 'I'd better go freshen up. You drive safe and I'll see you soon.'

I put the handset down with trembling fingers, hoping I hadn't made the biggest mistake of my life.

* * *

Telling Marcus I was feeling off-colour was a self-fulfilling prophecy as my stomach is pitching like a ship at sea as I kneel on the cold floor tiles in the en suite, the bucket in front of me. Though I've had a few stomach bugs over the years, I've never made myself sick before. I take a deep breath and shove two fingers down my throat. My eyes water and I gag, my stomach clenching. It doesn't work, so I do it again. It takes three attempts before I vomit.

'Make sure you're sick in the bucket, not the toilet,' Alana had instructed. 'Marcus needs to be able to smell it. And leave the bathroom door ajar.'

'What if he comes in?' I'd said, last-minute nerves getting the better of me.

'Trust me, he won't. The minute he realises you're sick he'll be outta there.'

My stomach curdles some more and this time I'm sick without trying. I rock back on my heels and check my watch. It's been fifteen minutes since Marcus rang. He could be here any moment. I stagger to my feet, grimacing as I rinse my mouth out with water from the tap. I wipe my face with my sleeve and stare at my reflection. My mascara has run and my cheeks are ghostly white. I look terrible.

Which, I guess, is the aim.

The sound of a car has me scuttling over to the small bathroom window. It overlooks the side of the house but if I stand on my tiptoes and crane my neck, I can just see the tip of the Aston Martin's silver bonnet. He is here.

I hotfoot it back to my position in front of the bucket. The huge diamond on my ring finger catches the light almost mockingly. The engagement ring Vinnie bought me was tiny in comparison, but I prefer it over this ostentatious rock any day of the week.

The front door slams. Moments later, footsteps cross the landing.

'Alana?' Marcus's voice is imperious. 'Where are you?'

'In here,' I call feebly. 'You'd better not come in. I don't feel too good.' The bathroom reeks of vomit. I only hope the stench is wafting into the bedroom.

'Poor baby. Can I get you anything? A drink? A flannel? Some fresh clothes?'

I freeze. This is not what's supposed to happen. He's supposed to be so phobic he can't even stand to be in the same house as me. He shouldn't be offering to *help*.

All of a sudden, I am filled with panic. What if Alana got it wrong? It's been clear to me for a while that she dissociates as a way of coping with her abusive marriage. Her expression goes curiously blank when she talks about Marcus, and I can't say I blame her. But, what if... what if the last ten years have taken such a toll on her mental health that she's made his emeto-phobia up? What if she's so out of touch with reality that she's mistaken, confusing bossiness for abuse? She said herself the scar on her hand wasn't his fault and she put her own hand into the fire. And the acid burn on her stomach. Could she have done that to herself?

But as soon as the doubts crowd into my mind, I force them out. What am I thinking? Of course she wouldn't pour acid over herself. And if she did put her hand in the fire, it was only to try to save the drawings Marcus had done his best to burn.

This Mr Charm act won't fool me. I've seen them together, read their body language. Marcus, like all serial abusers, is a master manipulator, an expert in deflection. He uses his charm to coerce and control. I know Alana is telling the truth and this knowledge strengthens my resolve. I decide to call his bluff.

'Could you bring me... oh God, I'm going to be sick again.' I wave the bucket under my nose and it's enough to trigger another retching session. When I've finished, I groan and say, 'Some Pepto-Bismol, please, honey? It's the pink and yellow bottle in the medicine cabinet in the kitchen.'

When his footsteps disappear, I pull myself up, rinse my mouth out again and check the time. It's three o'clock. Alana should be arriving at Heathrow soon. Even if Marcus jumped in his car now and broke every speed limit between here and the airport, he'd never get there in time to stop her escaping. But I can't leave Merryn's Reach until I'm sure she's actually on the plane. I made her a promise.

A promise I will keep, no matter what it costs me.

52

ALANA

The Beetle shudders as I ease it into a space in the short-stay car park at Heathrow's Terminal 5. I kill the engine and sit for a moment, massaging the small of my back. After two hundred and sixty bone-shaking miles, I'm as stiff as a board. I won't miss this pile of junk, that's for sure. God only knows why Laura hangs onto it.

I grab my carry-on from the passenger seat, lock the car and leave the keys on top of the driver's side tyre, just like we agreed. A stab of guilt needles me as I walk straight past the machine without buying a parking ticket, but the car's going to end up getting towed anyway, so what's the point?

My heart hammers harder the closer I get to departures, and every few paces I steal a glance over my shoulder, half expecting Marcus to step out from behind a parked car and grab my arm. Rationally, I know he can't because he's in Cornwall with Laura. But I quicken my pace anyway, heading for the self-service check-in desks. Even though we checked in online I still need to print out the boarding pass.

I join the queue and fish Laura's passport from my bag, flipping through it to the page with her photo. Even though the real test is still to come, a thread of fear prickles along my spine as I hold the passport over the scanner. Five long seconds pass before the machine spits out my boarding pass and I can breathe again.

Head down, I follow the straggle of people heading towards security, the passport digging into my sweaty palm. As the queue inches forwards, I sneak another look at Laura's photo. Her expression is serious, almost grim. Surreptitiously, I adjust my features to mimic her poker face. I can't risk anything going wrong, not when I'm this close.

I'm so lost in my thoughts that I jump a foot in the air when someone taps my shoulder. I spin round to see a guy in his sixties in a Hawaiian shirt and cargo shorts frowning and pointing.

'Wake up, love. They're waiting for you,' he says.

I follow his gaze to where the security guard on the furthest desk is beckoning. My cheeks redden as I mumble an apology and scurry over.

I smile a hello and slide Laura's passport and boarding pass across the desk to him. He's young, mid-twenties at a guess, with gelled hair and deep-set eyes. He picks up the passport, glances at the photo, then back at me. I force myself to hold his gaze, willing my face to stay neutral even as my heart threatens to burst out of my chest. Seconds feel like a lifetime. And then he hands the passport back with a smile.

'Have a good trip.'

'Thanks, I will.' My attempt at an English accent is sketchy as hell. Fortunately for me, he's already turned his attention to Hawaiian Shirt Guy.

Exhaling, I slip the passport into my bag and place it and my carry-on into a tray along with my watch and belt and step through the scanner.

The arch wails. My nerves are so shredded I flinch, I can't help it.

'Step aside please, madam,' a butch-looking female security guard instructs. She sweeps her handheld scanner slowly up and down. 'Are you wearing a bracelet?'

I glance down at the silver bangle circling my wrist. The one Marcus gave me not long after we met, when I still thought he was the man of my dreams.

'Oh, crap. I'm so sorry.' I slip it off and hold it in my outstretched palm like an offering for the gods.

'In the tray, please, madam,' the blank-faced guard says. I skitter back through the arch and dump the bangle in the tray. This time it stays mercifully silent as I walk through, and I scoop up my belongings with relief.

Finally, I'm airside.

53

LAURA

Once I'm sure Marcus is downstairs, I whip out the pay-as-you-go phone and check the flight app. The flight to Boston is on time. In a little over two hours Alana will be in the air, and I can leave. Two more hours at Merryn's Reach. Two more hours of pretending to be Marcus's wife. It sounds so simple.

The bedroom floor creaks and I shove the phone into the waistband of my trousers and bend back over the bucket, letting my hair fall forwards to hide my face from Marcus. I slip my right hand under my thigh, masking the fact that there's no scar. My anxiety cranks up a notch as he knocks gently on the door to the en suite.

'Here you go,' he says, pushing it open. 'Want me to pour you out a dose?'

'No!' It comes out sharper than I intend, and I bite my lip. 'Sorry, honey. Just leave it there. I'll be fine. Go fix yourself something to eat.'

'Let me at least pour you a glass of water.' He's in the bathroom now, and it's all I can do not to shrink into the corner and bury my head in my knees. He takes a glass tumbler from the shelf above the sink and fills it from the tap, then bends down and offers it to me. I take it wordlessly, and he tucks my hair behind my ear and gives me a crooked smile.

'My poor darling. You always were a terrible patient. Do you remember when you had the flu the same week as my exhibition at the National Portrait Gallery? You tried to talk me into going but there was no way I was leaving you, the state you were in.'

I nod, even though I don't remember, of course. I wasn't there.

'Take a sip,' he orders. I do as he says, watching his face for the smallest tell. A muscle pulsing in his jaw, a tightness around his eyes, anything that might suggest he knows I'm not his wife. But there is nothing. He believes I am Alana. The relief is heady and for a moment I sway, then Marcus's arms are tight around me, and he pulls me gently to my feet.

'Let's get you into bed,' he whispers, his breath hot against my ear. And even though I know I've fooled him, that our plan is working, my blood runs cold as two separate thoughts collide. I can't believe they haven't occurred to me already.

Either he is lying about his vomit phobia, or Alana was.

* * *

Once Marcus has settled me into bed, a fresh glass of water on the bedside table and a clean bucket on the carpet beside me, he announces that he has to pop out.

'Now?' I say, hope blooming in my chest.

'I have some prints for Jasper. He needs them for the morning.' He perches on the end of the bed and squeezes my thigh over the duvet. It's all I can do not to physically cringe. 'Though I hate leaving you like this.'

'Don't worry about me. I'll be fine. Really. I'm already feeling so much better.'

He studies my face and I shift against the pillows. His scrutiny is unbearable. I feel so exposed I might as well be parading around the room butt-naked.

'If you're sure,' he says finally. 'I'll only be an hour or so. Call me if you need anything.'

The front door slams moments later. I slip out of bed and cross to the bedroom window. There's a better view of the drive from here. Marcus appears, blips his key fob and the Aston's lights flash once. Before he climbs into the car he pauses, one hand on the roof, and looks up at the house. I stare in fascinated horror as he lifts a hand and waves at me cheerily. How the hell did he know I was watching? Just as I'm wondering if the man is telepathic, he turns, slides into the driver's seat and revs the engine once, twice, before shooting out of the drive, gravel flying.

I fumble for my phone, my fingers trembling as I tap out a text to Alana.

Have you boarded yet?

Minutes pass as I stare at the screen but although two ticks show the message has been delivered, they don't turn blue. I pace the room, doing swift calculations in my head. Alana must have passed through security by now, may have even been called to the boarding gate. Airside, she is safe, whereas I am... well, I'm not so sure. I have played my part perfectly. I have done what I promised I would do. Marcus has given every impression of falling for our plan hook, line and sinker. So why do I feel like the protagonist in a horror movie, waiting for the next jump scare?

There's still no answer from Alana. I phone Vinnie, telling myself it's insurance, not just because I'm suddenly desperate to hear his voice. Someone needs to know where I am if it all goes pear-shaped.

'Who is this?' he says when the call connects.

'It's me, Vin. I—'

'Laura?' He cuts across me, his voice loaded with concern. 'Are you all right, babe? What's happened? Why aren't you on your own phone?'

I can picture the worry lines creasing his forehead.

'It's a long story and I don't have time to tell you now. I just... I just wanted to say that if anything happens to me, tell the police I was at Merryn's Reach, OK? Merryn's Reach,' I repeat. 'It's just outside Porthmerryn.'

'Babe, you're scaring me. What's going on?'

'I wanted to do the right thing, but I think I've bitten off more than I can chew.'

'You're not making sense. Is that where you are now?'

'Yes.' It comes out as a half-sob. I'm surprised to realise I'm crying. 'I just wanted to help, that's all. Look, I've got to go. Maybe I can see you when I get home?'

'Of course you can, babe. But there's something I need to—'

'Bye, Vinnie,' I say, brushing the tears away impatiently. I can't afford to lose it now. There's too much at stake. My gaze falls on Alana's bedside table. If I'm quick, I can get out of here before Marcus is back from the gallery. Once I'm home, Vinnie and I can talk properly, work out exactly where things stand between us and what happens next. I can't do it now. Not here. 'I'll phone you, OK?'

'OK, but Laura—'

I hit end call and stumble across the room, replaying Alana's voice in my head. *There's a box of Tampax in the bottom drawer of my bedside cabinet. There's a bunch of keys in the box.* I pull open the bottom drawer. There at the back is a small box of Tampax. I breathe a sigh of relief as I take it out, thumb open the end and shake the contents onto Marcus and Alana's thick cream carpet.

Half a dozen paper-wrapped tampons fall out like a weird game of pick-up sticks and I burrow among them looking for the keys to Alana's lock-up and the Toyota Aygo she bought with the proceeds of her grandmother's Cartier brooch.

There are no keys.

I give the box another shake and a folded piece of paper flutters into my palm. I open it with trembling fingers.

One word is scrawled on the paper in jerky letters.

When comprehension dawns, it is swift and savage.

The bitch has set me up.

54

LAURA

As soon as the thought enters my head, I dismiss it. Of course Alana hasn't set me up. She's the victim here. Marcus has spent years belittling, controlling and gaslighting her. He has stripped her of all her self-confidence and taken away her independence. He poured chemicals over her in his darkroom, for God's sake. I can't begin to imagine what other emotional and physical abuse he's subjected her to over the last ten years. To doubt her would be to do her a grievous injustice. It would make me as reprehensible as Marcus. Besides, how can I blame Alana when it was *my* idea to swap places?

I check the note again, just to be sure. There it is in black and white. One word.

Sorry.

Sorry for what, exactly? The question eats away at me as I pull the entire contents of the bedside cabinet onto the carpet. A box of tissues, a hairdryer, a tub of earplugs, a cosmetic bag full of hair clips and an old fitness tracker tumble out. Next, I upend the drawer. Lipsticks, blister packs of antihistamines and painkillers, half-finished tubes of hand cream, pens, a couple of charging cables and a manicure set join the pile on the carpet. Even as I search through the flotsam of Alana's life I know I'm not going to find any keys.

Perhaps, in her spiralling anxiety, she forgot to leave them where she said she would. I think back to the conversation we had over a glass of wine in her kitchen only two days ago, though it feels like a hundred.

'You need an exit strategy for once I'm safely in the air,' she'd said, then she'd told me about the lock-up. Number twelve, Back Street. Grey door. And she'd clearly said the keys for both the Toyota and the lock-up were in the Tampax box in her bedside cabinet.

Except they aren't.

Another thought occurs to me. Alana also promised to text me when she arrived at the airport.

Except she hasn't.

I scroll through the settings on the pay-as-you-go phone, just in case I've accidentally set it to airplane mode. I check WhatsApp and Messenger, too. But there's nothing from her. What if she's crashed the car? She told me herself she hasn't driven in years. She could be lying on a trolley in an A&E department right now, her one chance of freedom lost. More likely she's broken down and is parked up on a hard shoulder somewhere on the M5 wondering what the hell to do.

Not knowing what's happening is intolerable. But then I have a brainwave. I phone Vinnie again. This time he picks up immediately.

'Vinnie, I need you to see where I am on the Find My app,' I blurt, before he has a chance to speak.

'You told me you're somewhere called Merryn's Reach.' He sounds confused and I can't say I blame him.

'I am. I need to know where my phone is.'

'Oh. Right. Hold up.' There's a muffled noise, then an intake of breath. 'It's at Heathrow!'

'Where exactly?'

'In departures at Terminal 5. Why? What's going on, Laura?'

'I don't have time to explain right now. I'll phone you. I promise,' I add, then end the call and rock back on my heels, my head spinning.

Alana said she'd text me when she arrived at Heathrow. She also said she'd leave me the keys to her lock-up and car. She's done neither. No text. No keys. Nothing.

Why? *Why?*

There's only one explanation. My first instincts were right. Alana has used my car and my passport to escape her abusive marriage. And in doing so, she's sacrificed me to save herself.

*   *   *

I stumble to my feet, dark spots peppering my vision. How could she? How *could* she? I thought we were friends. I swallow a sob. More than friends. We had a connection deeper than that. She was me and I was her. This time it's not a sob but a hollow laugh bubbling up inside me. Because she *is* me now. And I am her.

Marcus, her psycho husband, thinks so anyway.

I force myself to focus. Keys or not, I need to make a run for it. Fifteen minutes have passed since Marcus left for St Ives. Assuming he drops the prints at the gallery then drives straight home, I have just forty-five minutes to get the hell out of here. It's a twenty-minute walk into Porthmerryn. I can pack my stuff in another ten. The station at Penzance is a fifteen-minute taxi ride away. I could be on the platform waiting for the next train to London before he's back.

I dart into the dressing room and rootle through a couple of drawers until I find a pair of Nikes. I pull them on, then scan the bedroom, snatching the nail scissors from the manicure set and stuffing them into my back pocket before hurrying onto the landing and taking the stairs so quickly my feet are a blur.

Outside, I pause. The gates are closed but that's OK, because Alana gave me the code. I just need to remember it. It was Marcus's birthday, I know that, and it was definitely sometime in September. The twentieth? No. I close my eyes, trying to focus. The twenty-fourth, that was it. Two-four-zero-nine.

I've tapped in the first two digits when, out of nowhere, a hand clasps my mouth and jerks my head back in one fluid movement. My knees buckle.

'Not so fast,' hisses a voice in my ear.

A scream rips through me, but with the hand clamped over my mouth, it has nowhere to go.

55

LAURA

Marcus.

Muscle memory kicks in and I twist my body and drop my weight but what worked with Rory doesn't with Marcus. He is bigger, stronger, more ruthless. Somehow, I manage to grip his wrist and start the throw, but he shifts his weight and grabs a handful of my hair with his free hand, yanking me off balance. I cry out as my legs are swept from under me.

We both crash to the ground, Marcus on top of me. For a second I am winded, the air smacked out of my lungs by the force of the fall. I thrash about in the gravel trying to wriggle free, but Marcus is already hauling me to my feet and frog-marching me towards the house.

At the front door, I try again, a sixth sense telling me that if I end up inside that mausoleum of a place, I'll never come out. I take a deep breath and slam an elbow into his ribs as hard as I can, but he just tightens his grip and laughs.

'Feisty,' he pants as he drags me into the house. 'Alana never fought back.'

Dread seeps into my bones. He knows I'm not her.

'Let me go!' I yell, dropping the American accent, because what's the point? We are past that now. No more games.

'What, and spoil my fun? I don't think so.' His nails bite into my arms, as sharp as tacks, but I refuse to cry out. I will not give him the satisfaction.

In the kitchen, he pulls a roll of duct tape from a drawer and binds my wrists behind my back, then marches me into the living room and shoves me onto the sofa.

'Where is she?' he demands.

I stare back at him defiantly.

He takes a step forwards until he is towering over me. 'I *said*, where's my wife?' He lunges towards me and grips my chin, forcing me to look at him. 'I know who you are. Laura Jarvis, a nobody from Kent. You really thought you could swap places with my wife and I wouldn't notice?'

He lets go and I fall back onto the cushions, my eyes darting this way and that, looking for a way out. He is speaking again, and I drag my gaze back to his face.

'I've been keeping tabs on you since the day you turned up here pretending you had a parcel to deliver.'

What? I push myself up. 'How?'

'I saw you on the gate camera.'

I blink. Alana told me she'd wiped the footage that first time I went to the house. Not quickly enough, apparently. Marcus seems to find my discomfiture highly amusing. His eyes gleam.

'Alana thought she was so clever, tripping the power every time you came over, but the security cameras are solar-powered. I've been watching you both all week.'

I slump back again, the fight draining out of me. Marcus has the upper hand, and he knows it.

'Tell me, did you come to Cornwall looking for her?'

'No! I had no idea she even existed until I saw your photos of her in the gift shop and pub. We looked alike and I was curious. I asked around and found the house. That's it.'

'And now you're besties,' he mocks, his head tilting to one side. 'At least, that's what she wants you to think.'

I lift my chin, staring him out. I know exactly what he's doing. He's trying to gaslight me. But I refuse to fall for it. 'We saw each other a couple of times when you were in London. It's not a crime, is it?'

He smirks. 'I never went to London. I stayed here to watch you two idiots hatch your little plan.'

For the first time, I start to doubt myself. 'What?'

'Let me guess. Alana told you what a bastard I was and how desperately she wanted to leave me. At what point did she ask you to swap places with her?'

'She didn't. It was my idea.'

'You might think it was, but she planted the seed. I guarantee it. She'd have spotted an opportunity the moment she met you.'

I am silent as his words settle. Could it be true? Had Alana decided the first time we met that I was her ticket out of her abusive marriage? No. I refuse to believe it.

But she's stitched me up, hasn't she? She's left me in this godawful house with her psycho husband, while her promised escape plan – the lock-up, the car – was just smoke and mirrors.

'Where is she, Laura?' Marcus says in a sing-song voice that sends a chill down my spine. 'Where is Alana? Plymouth? London? Come on, you owe the bitch nothing. Tell me where she is.'

I gaze over his shoulder at the huge art deco wall clock above the fireplace. It's almost seven o'clock. Alana will be on the plane by now. Safe. Whatever she's done, I still feel the need to protect her, or this has all been for nothing.

'She's flying back to the States on my passport,' I say finally. 'You're too late to stop her.'

His expression is unreadable, but his voice drips sarcasm.

'There, that wasn't so difficult, was it? Surprise, surprise, Alana has gone running home to Mommy.'

'Can you blame her?' I watch him carefully. 'I know what you did, Marcus. She told me everything.'

'Why are you defending her when she's hung you out to dry? Genuinely, I'm curious.'

'Because she needed my help,' I say, but though it's true, it's not the whole truth. The rest is harder to admit. I envied her. My life had hit the skids, but hers seemed perfect. She lived in an amazing house with a famous husband. She looked like me, yet she was everything I wasn't. Sophisticated, stylish, affluent. And then, when she showed me the cracks in that apparently perfect life, I'd wanted to fix it. Fix her.

'You thought I wouldn't notice the difference?' Marcus sneers. 'Give me some credit. You're ten pounds heavier with the grace of a fucking hippo, for starters.' He laughs. 'I wouldn't go near you if you were the last person on earth.'

'Then let me go.'

He sits beside me on the sofa and runs a finger down my cheek. 'I told Alana once that divorce was never an option because I don't fail at anything.' He smiles, though his eyes remain cold. 'You wanted to swap places, yes? Then you can play my fucking wife. I'll wheel you out for the occasional opening night and you can keep house, smile for the cameras and play your part. I might even grant you conjugal rights if you play your cards right.' He pinches my thigh. 'Though you can lose a bit of weight first.'

'You're mad!' I yell, squirming away from his touch. 'Out of your fucking mind!'

The mask slips and he lunges forwards, curling a hand around my throat and squeezing. I try to wrench my head away, kicking and twisting, but he's too strong. The edges of my vision blur as I fight for air, but his grip just tightens. I can't... breathe.

The last thing I see before everything goes dark is Marcus's gloating face leering at me, centimetres from my own.

And then, nothing.

56

LAURA

When I regain consciousness, I'm lying prone on the floor, my cheek squashed against rough concrete, my head pounding so badly it's impossible to marshal my thoughts. I prise my eyes open, but it's so dark I struggle to focus and what little I can see is blurry. I blink twice, then go to rub my eyes, but I can't. With a surge of shock, I remember why. My hands are pinned behind my back.

Swearing under my breath, I wiggle to a sitting position, yelping at the pins and needles in my arms. Trying to ignore the stabbing pain, I take in what little I can see of my surroundings. I seem to be in some sort of basement, the only light coming from a red strip light on the low ceiling.

I shuffle onto my knees to get a better look. The narrow room is lined on one side by steel worktops on which plastic trays are set in rows. Above them, sheets of paper hang from a line of wire. Not just paper. Photographs. With a jolt of clarity, I realise where I am, but the knowledge brings no comfort. I'm in Marcus's darkroom. The place he brought Alana to torture her.

Piece by piece, I stitch together the splintered fragments of my memory. Alana leaving for the airport, me heading back to Merryn's Reach to await Marcus's return. The call to say he was already at Penzance. Rushing up to the en suite to make myself sick. Thinking I'd fooled him. Realising I hadn't.

Darker still, memories I wish I could forget. Looking for the keys to Alana's lock-up and finding an apology instead. The crazed look in Marcus's eyes as he taunted me. The creeping fear that he was right and Alana had engineered the whole thing so she could escape. That I was nothing more than a sacrificial lamb.

The flashbacks keep coming. Phoning Vinnie, my port in a storm, my comfort blanket, despite everything. I still love him. The realisation is a slap in the face. Whatever this thing was with Tammy, I want to believe there's a way through it. Lunch and a few flirty texts don't make him a serial adulterer. Vinnie is not my dad, and I was wrong to punish him for the mistakes Dad made. I shiver, craving the feel of his strong arms around me, wishing with all my heart he was here in Cornwall and not on the other side of the country.

A tear trickles down my cheek and I can't even wipe it away because my sodding hands are tied. I stagger to my feet angrily, colliding with one of the steel worktops, which topples to the ground with a satisfying clatter that echoes around the walls of the darkroom.

The anger morphs into pure rage at the injustice of it all. I was trying to help and look where it got me. I've been locked up by a bloody psychopath while Alana gets to waltz home to New England.

Thud. I aim a kick at the next worktop along. It too crashes to the floor, trays, goggles and tongs flying onto the concrete. 'Fuck you, Marcus!' I roar as I work methodically around the room wrecking everything I can. 'Fuck you, Alana! Fuck the fucking pair of you!' It's cathartic, seeing Marcus's carefully ordered darkroom descend into chaos. I just wish I could see his face.

'Take that!' I launch myself at a filing cabinet, which wobbles then crashes onto its side, the drawers tipping open. Dozens of black and white prints spill out and I kick through them like they're autumn leaves. Pictures of cliffs and beaches, of fishermen and farmers, pretty harbours and rockpools. The rage inside me is building. I stamp on the photos like a toddler mid-tantrum, grinding them into the floor with my heels until the paper snags and tears.

I attack the next filing cabinet. More photos spill out. But these aren't Marcus's trademark pictures of landscapes and people. I bend down, shuffling through them with my toe, my breath catching as they swim into focus under the red strip light. Dead birds on a beach. Mangled carrion on a country lane. The bloodied body of a badger half hidden by cow parsley. Images so disturbing, so macabre, it's hard to believe they were ever meant for anyone to see. Which means Marcus must have taken them for his own warped gratification.

'You're one sick bastard, Marcus Adams!' I yell at the empty room. My gaze drops back to the floor and another pile of photos that have spewed out of the bottom drawer. And if the dead birds were vile, they have nothing on these.

They depict parts of a woman's body. An arm. The inside of a thigh. A slender midriff. Each shows an imperfection on otherwise flawless skin. I bend down to get a closer look. Not an imperfection. An injury. Burns, bruises, cuts and scars, photographed in graphic detail. With growing horror I recognise the pale, puckered skin on the back of a slender hand. Alana's hand. My chest tightens. The photos are all of her. The sick bastard has catalogued his abuse and, judging by the dozens and dozens of photos, he's been doing so for years.

Just like that, my rage dissipates, leaving me hollow and unaccountably sad. Even though Alana described the physical and verbal assaults she'd received at the hands of her husband, it's clear she gave me the edited version. Perhaps she thought the truth was too hard for me to handle. Perhaps she was protecting him. Maybe she was protecting herself. I'll probably never know.

I sink back down onto the concrete floor, my back against the filing cabinet, and rest my forehead on my knees. I've seen animals come into the surgery after years of cruelty and neglect. The scars they carry, the ones you can see and the ones you can't. The trust issues and the learned helplessness. The way some lash out even once they're safe, because it's how they've always survived, even if it means biting the hand that feeds them.

I never blame the battered cats and dogs, so would it be so hard to forgive Alana? After all, she did what she felt she had to do to leave Marcus.

Maybe in time I'll be able to.

Right now, I have more pressing problems, because I now know exactly what he's capable of, and it's far worse than I ever imagined.

I need to get the hell out of here before he comes back.

57

ALANA

Mom used to say that no one should ever need a man's approval to feel validated.

'You are your own person, Alana. A clever, funny, beautiful person. You don't need a guy to tell you your worth.'

Easy for her to say. She had parents who adored her, a career she loved and heaps of unshakeable self-confidence. She brought me up single-handed while holding down a high-pressure job. She dated men when she wanted and on her terms, and she saw no stigma in being a single mom. I, on the other hand, had craved male approval for as long as I could remember, never happier than when my grandaddy paid me a compliment, or my Uncle Bob found one of my jokes funny.

Later, when I started dating, I overanalysed every encounter, every conversation, with the opposite sex. A single negative comment or unread text sent me into a downward spiral of self-doubt. In the small hours, I'd lie awake, convinced I wasn't pretty or clever enough to bag myself a man.

I wasn't stupid. I knew it came from a deep-rooted fear of rejection because my dad hadn't been around when I was growing up.

Maybe that's why I fell so hard for Marcus at the end-of-term fashion show all those years ago. Maybe, deep down, I thought he could be the father figure I never had. The irony is, not only did he set out to destroy what little self-esteem I had, he also wrecked the tentative relationship I was finally building with my dad.

My thoughts drift back and forth like the ebb and flow of the tide as I order a glass of champagne in the Club Aspire Lounge while I wait for my flight to board. I feel detached from my memories, like I'm watching a Netflix biopic on someone else's life. My childhood at our pretty, clapboard home in Maine. Flying to London for my master's. Meeting Marcus. Falling in love. The first time I saw Merryn's Reach. Thinking I'd found not just my Prince Charming but my happy ending. And then realising I'd fallen through the cracks into a living nightmare.

And then along came Laura. Not quite a knight in shining armour, but the next best thing. Jasper had called me the minute she left the gallery, bursting with the news that he'd met my doppelgänger.

'You wouldn't credit it, Alana, darling. She's the spit of you.'

'Really? Sounds like a wind-up to me.'

'It's not, I promise. I thought she *was* you at first. I didn't believe her until she showed me the photo in her passport.'

'She showed you her passport?' I quietly filed that information away.

'She did. You could be identical twins. She's desperate to meet you, darling, I could tell. It was rather sweet. She spent the whole time grilling me about Marcus.'

'Does she know we're married?'

'I did mention it. And I have a horrible feeling I let slip your address, so don't be surprised if she pays you a visit.'

'You think she will?'

'I do.' Jasper's voice rang with certainty. 'You don't mind, do you?'

My mind was spinning. A girl who looked just like me, actively looking for me. Did I mind? Was he mad? Of course I didn't mind. I'd be counting down the minutes till she turned up on the doorstep. No, not the doorstep. That was too risky. I couldn't have Marcus knowing I had a lookalike.

'Alana?' Jasper said.

'Of course I don't mind,' I assured him. 'If she comes in again, tell her I'd love to meet up. Only...' I paused, unsure how to frame it.

'Don't tell Marcus?' Jasper guessed.

I let out a long breath. 'I think it's probably best he doesn't know, don't you?'

I spent the next twenty-four hours in a state of nervous excitement, hoping this girl – my double – didn't visit the house. I had to think of another way to meet her that didn't involve Marcus. I was running through scenarios and getting nowhere fast when Rory popped his head round the kitchen door to let me know he'd finished for the day.

'Have you got a minute before you go?'

'Course, Mrs Adams.' He heeled off his boots and clumped into the kitchen, his hands hanging stiffly at his sides. 'Everything all right, is it?'

It was the same question he and Mairead had been asking me in some form or another for the last ten years. Nothing ever was all right, but there wasn't a damn thing any of us could do about it, so I always assured them that everything was fine. But this time, there was something Rory *could* do.

'Jasper says there's a woman who looks like me staying in the village.'

'It's true. Mam thought she was your bloody fetch.' He laughed, a curiously high-pitched honking sound that juddered his whole body.

'Where did Mairead see her?'

'She came to the house looking for you.'

Shit. I'd need to check the CCTV and erase any footage before Marcus saw it.

'Have you seen her, Rory?'

'She came back when you and Mr Adams went down to the village to have your dinner. She got stuck in the garden. I had to let her out.'

'Did she see you?'

'Nope. She came in all cocky like, having a good old nose around. Didn't look quite so cocky when the gates shut on her.' He chuckled again.

I did some swift calculations in my head. I'd need to wipe her second visit from the cameras too. Funny how I was already covering my tracks, even if I didn't really have a plan at that point. Just an innate sense that this girl – my double – mattered and I needed to keep her well away from Marcus.

I reached out and touched Rory's arm. 'Rory, will you do something for me?'

'Course.' He frowned. 'You want me to warn her off?'

'No! No, don't do that. I want to meet her. See if she really does look like me. It would be... fun. Yes, it would be fun to see how alike we are, don't you think?'

'I s'pose,' he said slowly, chewing his bottom lip. 'But I don't know where she's staying.'

'Ask around. You know what this place is like. Someone's bound to know. But don't tell her to come to the house. Tell her... tell her that I swim every morning. Tell her to come to Merryn's Cove.'

He nodded, as I knew he would, and I smiled slowly.

Even though I had no idea what might happen next, I knew it was the start of something.

58

ALANA

Even though I'd been told how alike we were, seeing Laura that first time took my breath away. It wasn't just a resemblance. We were carbon copies.

Laura was clearly as nervous as I was, desperate for me to like her. I was keen to see if my half-formed plan had legs.

And I did. Like her, I mean. It wasn't just because her face was as familiar to me as my own. Laura was everything I wasn't. Impulsive, determined, brave. Kind, too. She spent her days looking after sick animals, for Chrissakes. If that wasn't enough, she was an excellent mimic and, having just left her cheating fiancé, she'd had enough of men.

She was... perfect.

I hoped that when she found out what Marcus had done to me, the cruelty he'd subjected me to over the years, she would want to make everything better, but it was still a relief when she suggested we swap places.

Dear, sweet Laura, thinking it was all her idea.

I felt more than a flicker of guilt as I left the note in the box of Tampax. *Sorry.* It seemed inadequate. But what choice did I have? I couldn't tolerate another second with Marcus. I was already a husk of the girl I once was. If I stayed any longer there'd be nothing left. I could see Laura was getting jittery and I needed her to believe she had an escape plan. If that meant telling a white lie or two, it was worth it. Anyway, she's gutsy and resourceful. Didn't she tell me she was as tenacious as a terrier? She'll find a way to leave.

Even so, I can't help thinking how livid Marcus will be when he finds out I'm halfway across the Atlantic. And what he might do...

To take my mind off that bastard, I scroll through the photos on Laura's cell phone as I sip my champagne. There are half a dozen of Porthmerryn. Boats bobbing in the harbour. Narrow cobbled streets lined with pretty whitewashed cottages. The harbour at night, lights reflecting in the oily-black water. She has a surprisingly good eye. After living with Marcus for so long I'm a bit of an expert. I scroll further back through her camera roll, coming to the pictures of her and Vinnie. He's a nice-looking guy. Broad-shouldered and ever so slightly overweight, he has curly brown hair that tickles his collar and steady green eyes. A bit rough and ready for my liking, but why should we have the same taste in men just because we look alike?

It's hard not to feel sympathy for the poor guy. Ceremoniously dumped for flirting with a pretty sales rep. It seems like a bit of an overreaction when you think of the hell Marcus put me through. Maybe Laura will see sense once she's back home.

If she ever makes it home, whispers the voice in my head.

To quash it, I go to the bar and ask for another glass of champagne, tapping Laura's cell on the card reader. It was a bonus, realising she had Apple Pay. I've already bought a Ralph Lauren silk scarf. Oh, and a bottle of Yves Saint Laurent Libre. I wish I could share the joke with her. Part of me thinks she'd see the funny side. I do the next best thing, raising my glass in a silent toast.

'Cheers,' says a voice behind me, making me jump. I turn to

see a tall, blond man in his forties with an expensive-looking suntan and crinkly aquamarine eyes. He's smiling at me so broadly my heart skips a beat.

I match him smile for smile and we chink glasses. He too is drinking champagne.

'It seems we're both celebrating,' he says. His accent is West Coast. Californian, probably. Though it could be Oregon. 'I've just sold the UK arm of my business for a sum that'd make your eyes water. What about you?'

I lower my eyes demurely. I can't exactly tell him I'm running away from my abusive husband. Nor that I've left my doppelgänger in my place. I settle for, 'Flying home to visit my mom. I haven't seen her in a long time, so...' I dip my head towards my glass.

'An excellent excuse.' His smile widens. 'Justin Sullivan,' he says, holding out a hand. His grip is firm and he holds my hand a little longer than necessary, though I find I don't mind at all.

I hesitate for a beat. Who am I? Alana Adams: housewife, people-pleaser, victim? Or Laura Jarvis: working girl, risk-taker, survivor?

'Laura,' I say finally. 'Laura Jarvis. Nice to meet you.'

'The pleasure's all mine.' He holds my hand to his lips for the briefest of moments, then lets it drop and clicks his fingers at the waiter, who throws a tea towel over his shoulder and scurries over.

'A bottle of Taittinger. The 2012 if you have it,' Justin says, indicating I take the next bar stool. 'So, tell me, Laura Jarvis, what brought you to this grey and rainy little island?'

I run a finger round the rim of my glass with a thrill of anticipation. I'm shedding my old life like a snake sheds its skin and the feeling is intoxicating.

'Well, I came over to study for a master's at the London College of Fashion eleven years ago and never left.'

This piques his interest.

'You work for one of the big fashion houses?'

I glance over his shoulder at a beige, black, red and white check handbag hanging from the back of a chair.

'Burberry.'

'No way! I know the chief financial officer there.'

'Really?' My voice comes out scratchy, my pulse rocketing. I need to be more careful. Lying for the sake of it could land me in a whole heap of trouble if I'm not careful. I change the subject. 'What line of business are you in, Justin?'

'Me? E-commerce. Put it this way – if you've ever bought anything online, there's a good chance we were involved.'

He starts telling me in great detail how he grew his business from a tiny start-up to a Fortune 500 success story. I glance at my watch. The sooner my flight is called the better. Marcus would struggle to find me now, but I wouldn't put it past him to book a last-minute flight just to access departures.

Perhaps I'll feel safe once the plane takes off. Maybe once we finally land in Boston.

There is another very real possibility: that I'll never feel safe again.

59

LAURA

Panicking will get me precisely nowhere, so I force myself to stop and take stock. According to my watch it's ten o'clock, but I have no idea how long I was out cold and as there's no natural light in the darkroom, I have no way of knowing if it's ten at night or ten in the morning.

The room looks like it's been ransacked by burglars, every tray upended, every piece of Marcus's precious photographic equipment on the floor. At the far end of the line of steel counters is a shelf I must have missed. It is full of containers, some small, some large, but they all have labels warning that they contain hazardous liquids. One in particular catches my eye. Acetic acid. It's the chemical Marcus poured over Alana's midriff the first time she tried to leave. Using my shoulders and chin, I right an upended chair, climb onto it and push the bottle off the shelf with my elbow. It rolls across the floor, coming to a stop at the bottom of the stairs.

I shuffle back across the room and start to climb the stairs to the door, which isn't easy with my hands tied behind my back. At the top, I'm hit by a wave of dizziness and for one heart-stopping moment I think I'm going to topple down onto the concrete like one of Marcus's filing cabinets. But the dizziness passes and I squint at the metal door looking for the handle.

There isn't one.

There is a keypad though, and I try the code for the gate. Two-four-zero-nine. I have no option but to use the tip of my nose to type in the numbers and it takes a couple of attempts. It doesn't work.

Swearing under my breath, I try four-three-two-one for no other reason than that it's the code for the keysafe at Gull Cottage. Then I try one-two-three-four. No joy.

My head is thumping, a tight band of pressure circling my skull. Trying my best to ignore it, I spend the next hour with my nose pressed against the keypad, pressing random numbers until the muscles in my back and neck are screaming in agony. Frustrated, I climb back down the stairs, sinking into a ball on the bottom step. I'm not giving up, I tell myself. Just taking a breather while I decide my next move, as if this nightmare I find myself in is a game of chess. Pity Marcus is the one holding all the pieces.

* * *

At some point I must nod off, because when I wake up I'm aware of the sound of someone breathing. My eyes spring open.

'My darkroom is ruined and my wife is halfway across the Atlantic, thanks to you.' Marcus's voice is cold. Menacing. 'Which begs the question, how are you going to redress the situation?'

He is sitting in the chair I used to reach the acetic acid, watching me, his hands resting lightly in his lap, his legs crossed at the ankles.

'What are you talking about?'

'You heard me. You destroyed my work and you took my wife. How are you going to fix this?'

'Perhaps you shouldn't have locked me in here,' I reply as calmly as I can. 'And as for Alana, she's not a possession. She left of her own free will.'

'With your help.'

I don't bother to answer, and I can see this irritates him. He is used to being in control. He uncrosses his ankles and taps a foot on the floor. The sound is as maddening as the noise from a dripping tap and I want to yell at him to stop, but I don't because a reaction is exactly what he craves, and I refuse to give him the satisfaction.

'I should thank you, I suppose,' he says eventually. 'I was growing tired of her. She never wanted for anything. Never did a day's work in her life. Yet she always looked so bloody miserable.'

I shift on the step and as I do something sharp stabs my right buttock. I bite back a yelp of surprise. What the hell? Then I remember the nail scissors I grabbed from Alana's manicure set. Surreptitiously, I inch my right hand into my back pocket, fingers closing round the cold metal. The feel of it gives me courage.

'If you untie me I'll tidy up for you,' I say, nodding at the mess. 'I won't try any funny business, I promise.'

Marcus laughs.

'At least give me a glass of water. Please? I'm so thirsty.'

When he doesn't reply, my hopes fade, but then he shoves the chair back and climbs the stairs, his footsteps slow and deliberate. As soon as the door clicks shut, I spring into action, sawing at the ties with the scissors, twisting and contorting as I try to gain traction. But it's no good. The ties are too thick, the scissors too small. That's when it finally sinks in that my bravado is misplaced.

The moment I realise I'm no match for a man like Marcus.

60

LAURA

When Marcus returns, he is carrying a small plastic bottle of water and his Nikon. My stomach tightens. There's only one reason he'd bring that. Is this how Alana felt when he took out his camera to document the abuse?

I nod when he offers me the water, pathetically grateful when he unscrews the cap and holds it to my mouth. My throat's as dry as sandpaper, and I drink deeply, not caring when it dribbles down my chin, because I don't know when I'll get another chance. I should be hungry – I can't even remember when I last ate – but my appetite deserted me hours ago.

'Thank you,' I say meekly, once I'm done.

Marcus reaches into his pocket, pulls something out and inspects it. It has a yellow handle and looks like a small pizza slicer.

'What's that?'

He glances at me. 'A rotary cutter. I use it to trim the edges of my prints. Among other things.' He runs the tip of his index finger across the blade and I give an involuntary shiver. His pupils are black pebbles and a muscle jumps in his jaw.

He reminds me of a Rottweiler the RSPCA brought into the surgery last spring. The poor dog had been kept in a filthy crate for most of his miserable life, beaten by the bastard who owned him. Some dogs would've been cowed. Not him. He was a pent-up ball of rage just waiting to blow. In the end, they had no choice but to put him to sleep.

Like the Rottweiler, Marcus has been shaped by violence, but that's no excuse. He could have broken the cycle if he'd wanted it badly enough. All this filters through my mind as he leans forwards and runs the rotary cutter lightly over my cheek and down my neck.

The cold kiss of metal on my skin has an instant effect. Liquid fear races through me, shooting down every nerve ending in my body, turning my legs to jelly and my insides to water. I want to scream but I can't let him know how terrified I am. So I focus on keeping him talking. Because while he is talking, he's not cutting me.

I say the first thing that comes into my head. 'I came to Porthmerryn on holiday when I was eleven. I remember what this place used to look like. Before the fire, I mean. I used to picture myself in the turret, like I was some modern-day Rapunzel. It was such a beautiful house. You must have been devastated when it burned down.'

He looks at me sideways, one eyebrow raised.

'I mean, to lose such an important piece of architecture, not to mention the fact that your dad created some of his best work here,' I babble.

'Best work? Don't make me laugh. My father painted the kind of sentimental crap you'd find on a box of fudge. He may have thought he was the next Constable, but he shouldn't have believed his own hype. And, for your information, I hated the place. I always hoped it would go up in flames.'

'And then one day it did.'

'One day it did,' he agrees after a beat.

'You were in London when it happened.'

His eyes narrow. 'Who told you that? Alana, I suppose. Yes, I was in London.'

'It was an electrical fault, right?'

'And your point?'

I remember the article I read about the fire in the local paper. 'Funny that the house you hated was razed to the ground after you were refused planning permission to demolish it.'

'As I said, I was in London.'

'I get it. You weren't here, but Rory was, wasn't he?' It's a stab in the dark but I can tell by the way Marcus's grip on the yellow handle of the rotary cutter tightens that I've hit the mark.

He shifts forwards in his chair, his face a mask.

Keep him talking.

'Alana didn't believe Rory killed himself. She said he'd never have left Mairead to cope on her own when she was so ill.'

'Who gives a flying fuck what Alana said? What's important is what the police think, and they think he topped himself.'

'But there was no note, no record of mental illness, no evidence to suggest he died by suicide.'

'As you say, there was no evidence at all. Shame, that.' Marcus meets my eye and the corner of his mouth twitches in... in *amusement*. I think back to yesterday morning when I'd stood outside Mairead and Rory's shabby bungalow and felt as though I was being watched.

Marcus admitted he never went to London. He was here in Porthmerryn all the time, watching me and Alana. Before I have a chance to consider what this could mean, he starts speaking.

'I don't know why you set such store by what Alana did or didn't say. The bitch betrayed us both, remember?'

Hating myself for it, I latch onto the sliver of common ground. Anything to forge a connection and make him forget about the rotary cutter in his hand.

'You're right. She did.'

'Anyway, I don't need her now I have a new toy to play with.'

Before I can react, he lifts my chin and runs the cutter down my cheek so casually I don't realise he's cut me until a searing pain sets my nerve endings on fire. I scream, shock mingled with fury. The harsh sound reverberates around the enclosed space but Marcus simply tips his head back and laughs.

All Alana's injuries were in places no one could see, I remember with growing horror. The fact that he's just cut my cheek can only mean one thing. I'm not getting out of here alive.

Regret consumes me. I'm not ready to die. I think of my job, the animals I've come to consider my surrogate pets. What will happen to Tallulah if I'm not around to monitor her weight? Who will give Kiara pep talks about the Pomeranian's diet and exercise regime if I'm not there to do it?

And what about Vinnie? We need to sit down and talk about what happens next. Because what we had together was good. Better than good. It was pretty bloody perfect, especially compared to Marcus and Alana's sick excuse for a marriage.

Hell, I'd even agree to sit down with Sam if I make it out of here in one piece.

Marcus leans forwards, his eyes trained on the other side of my face, the bloodied blade of the rotary cutter inches from my nose.

'Come now, be still,' he murmurs.

I jerk away and as my body turns something behind me snaps and suddenly my hands are free. I must have hacked through enough of the duct tape with the nail scissors. With one sweeping movement I whip the scissors from my back pocket and drive them into Marcus's thigh, just above the knee.

'You bitch!' he cries, leaping to his feet, his expression murderous.

I know I have seconds before he comes at me again. I look

around desperately, my panicked gaze falling on the white plastic bottle next to his chair. I grab it, scrabble open the lid and squirt the contents straight into his face.

61

LAURA

Marcus lets out a great bellow and clutches his face, his head moving from side to side as if he can shake off the drops of acetic acid already eating into his skin.

He stumbles across the room towards the far wall, crashing into a filing cabinet and tripping over a plastic tray.

'The sink!' he gasps. 'Water.'

I watch dispassionately from the bottom of the stairs as he feels his way along the one remaining worktop looking for the tap.

'Phone for a fucking ambulance, you bitch!' he howls.

'You took my phone. You'll need to give me yours.' He doesn't seem to hear. 'Give me your phone,' I bark.

This time it registers, and he takes a hand away from his face to reach into his back pocket. His skin is mottled red and white, and his half-closed eyes are weeping. I take the phone and hold it up to his face, but it's already so disfigured it doesn't recognise his features.

'What's the passcode?'

'Zero-one-zero-three.'

My eyes widen. I didn't think Marcus had a sentimental

bone in his body, but it's the date of Alana's birthday. The mirror of mine. I'd thought it meant something, that it was a sign. Kismet or fate or whatever. I'd even been a little hurt that Alana had been so offhand about it. Now I know why. Where I was sentimental, she'd seen everything in cold, pragmatic terms.

'There's no signal down here,' he gasps. 'You'll have to go into the house.'

'What's the code for the door?'

'Six-six-six-six. For Christ's sake, just do it, will you?'

I'm halfway up the stairs when I hear another almighty crash followed by a dull thud. Even though every sinew in my body is straining to get away, I turn and look. Marcus has fallen over the filing cabinet containing the photos of Alana, and is sprawled face down on the floor, his head thrown back at an unnatural angle. I hesitate, my heart telling me to check on him, my head pleading with me to get the hell out of there.

Heart wins, and I sprint back down the steps and kneel beside him. Instinct takes over. I place two fingers on the inside of his wrist and hold my breath.

Nothing.

I stagger to my feet. The darkroom swims and I grip the wall to stop myself from keeling over. I need to get out because there's no way I'm going down for killing that bastard. No bloody way.

I punch four sixes into the keypad and shoulder open the door. The house is in darkness and I fumble for a light switch, eventually finding one on the wall behind me. Once my eyes have adjusted, I stare at Marcus's phone, my thoughts racing.

If I call the police, there's a danger I'll be arrested. Even though I know I was acting in self-defence when I threw the acid in Marcus's face, there's no guarantee they'll believe me. My fingerprints will be all over the house. It's only a matter of time before they realise I'm Alana's double and I was complicit in switching identities. What if they think it was part of a premeditated plan to kill him?

Before I reach a decision, a notification appears on the screen. The doorbell camera has picked up movement. I click onto it, giving a start when I see Mairead's pale face staring back at me in the pitch-dark. Tears stream down her face.

'Let me in, you bastard! I know what you did to Rory. You killed him. You killed my boy. Don't think you're going to get away with it. I have proof, and the police are already on their way. D'you hear me? The police are coming and they're going to lock you up and throw away the key, you murdering shite!'

Once again, I don't have a choice. Slowly, hesitantly, I make my way to the front door, leaving my fate in Mairead's hands.

62

LAURA

Mairead starts when she sees me but quickly regains her composure and pushes past.

'Where is he?' she yells, barrelling into the house with the energy of a whirling dervish.

'Mairead, wait!' I trot after her awkwardly. 'Please. You need to listen to me.'

She stops and turns round. Her eyes are puffy in her thin face and there's a blob of mascara in the corner of one eye.

'Marcus is in the darkroom. He's... he's dead.'

Her brow concertinas. 'Dead?'

'He locked me down there. He fell after I... after I threw acid in his face.'

Her mouth drops open.

'He was coming for me, Mairead! I had no choice. And then he tripped over a filing cabinet. I think he broke his neck.'

'Are you sure?' She's already heading towards the darkroom.

'I checked his pulse. There wasn't one.'

Mairead mutters under her breath and slams a fist against the light switch. She hauls the darkroom door open with surprising strength for someone so slight, then disappears down the stairs like the White Rabbit in *Alice in Wonderland*.

I have no choice but to follow.

Marcus is prone on the concrete exactly where I left him. Mairead bends over him, still muttering to herself as she picks up his hand and feels for a pulse. She shakes her head and tries his carotid artery. His face has started to blister and I turn away, repulsed.

'You're right, he's gone.'

She pushes herself to her feet, one hand massaging the small of her back. She nods at my face. 'He did that to you, did he?'

I touch my cheek, gasping when I'm met with a sticky, congealing mess.

'Let me take a look.' She turns my face gently towards her and peers at the cut. 'Looks worse than it is. You might need a stitch or two, but you'll be grand. Is that water?' She points to the water bottle Marcus brought down for me. I nod and she unscrews the cap and dribbles it down my cheek, cleaning the wound. It stings like mad, and I clench my fists tightly at my sides to stop myself from crying out. When she's done, she rocks back on her heels.

'Why does he have a pair of nail scissors sticking out of his leg?'

'That was me. I stabbed him when he came at me with a rotary cutter.'

'That's what he used on your face?'

I nod and she gives a low whistle.

'Where was Alana while all this was happening?'

'She's gone. She'll be halfway to the States by now. She and I... well, we—'

'Swapped places,' Mairead fills in. 'I know. It was the last thing Rory told me before that bastard murdered him, if you don't count the recording he left.'

'Recording?'

'He called me the night he died and left his phone running so I'd hear what Marcus did. I've been so groggy from all the meds I've only just heard the voicemail.' Mairead fishes an old Nokia from her coat pocket, taps a couple of buttons and holds it out. The recording is faint but audible and I can make out Rory's voice.

'—thought you were in London?'

He sounds agitated and my gaze slides to Mairead. She nods at the phone, telling me to keep listening.

Another voice, faint but growing stronger. The plummy tone is instantly recognisable. Marcus.

'—know you've been helping her. You thought I wouldn't find out?'

A gasp. Rory again. 'I d-didn't mean anything by it, Mr A-Adams. Mrs Adams, she—'

A thud. The scrape of something. A chair? I picture the hallway of Mairead's chalet bungalow. A shallow flight of stairs. Wooden banisters. Wooden floors.

'W-what are you doing?'

'I would have thought that was patently obvious.'

'But Mrs Adams gave me that for Christmas.'

'She did, didn't she? Don't you just love the poetic justice of it all? The perfect symmetry. Now, come here.' Marcus's voice sharpens. 'I said, come here, you little prick.'

'Wait, I—'

More scuffling. Then a dull thump, and silence.

I stare at Mairead in horror. 'Rory didn't kill himself. Marcus murdered him and made it look like suicide.'

'That's the long and the short of it. Bastard,' she spits, glaring at the body on the floor.

'You said the police were on their way?'

'I was lying.'

'They haven't heard this?' I nod towards the Nokia.

'Not yet. I came to have it out with him first.' She prods Marcus with her foot. 'I wanted to look him in the eye and see him squirm. I wanted...' She trails off, her gaze dropping to the floor.

'Revenge?'

She looks stricken. 'Jesus said to turn the other cheek, but how can I when my boy is dead?'

There's no answer to that. Tentatively, I lay a hand on her bony shoulder and pull her towards me. After a moment's hesitation, she surrenders, and I wrap my arms around her frail body as she weeps. We stand like that, two survivors of a storm, until eventually she breaks away and blows her nose on a tatty white handkerchief.

I finger Marcus's phone. 'I should probably call the police.'

'You probably should.'

Before we tramp back upstairs, she bends over the body again.

'What are you doing?'

'Wiping your prints off the scissors.'

'What's the point? I'll explain what happened, that he was holding me hostage in his darkroom and came at me with the cutter. They'll understand.'

Mairead raises an eyebrow but doesn't say anything, and doubt clouds my certainty. Surely the police will realise I am the victim here, and it'd be my body lying prone on the floor if I hadn't fought back?

I hold onto this thought as I dial. When the call handler picks up, I tell her there's been an accident and she needs to send an ambulance and the police. In turn, she informs me they're dealing with a high volume of calls but they'll have someone with us as soon as they can. Once I've given her the address, I hang up. There's no point going into details on the phone.

If only I'd talked Alana into going to the police in the first place. I could have driven her to the local station and held her hand as she reported Marcus's years of abuse. But she'd been adamant they wouldn't believe her. Not when he had half the force in his pocket.

The extent of my naivety hits me again. Marcus may have known a handful of senior officers socially, but there's no way even he could wield that much power. But her paranoia had been contagious and I'd been quick to believe her because I wanted it to be true. It was another reason to hate him, and I ended up as convinced as she was that the police would never help.

If only I could turn back the clock.

Mairead and I settle on either end of the Adamses' vast corner sofa to wait for the police to arrive. Her eyes bore into mine. 'Why did the two of you swap places?'

I shrug. 'Because I felt sorry for Alana. I thought I was doing the right thing. And I thought I could handle myself. Handle him.' My eyes dart to the darkroom door. I'd been wrong about that, too.

Mairead smiles for the first time. 'Rory told me how you manhandled him to the ground the other night. He didn't take much of a shine to you, but then why would he? Alana owned his heart.'

I run my hands through my tangled hair. 'None of it would have happened if I hadn't been so fixated about meeting her. Rory and Marcus would still be alive. Alana would still be here. But I was obsessed.' I look sidelong at Mairead. 'Maybe your fetch superstition was right. I was the catalyst, wasn't I? It's all my fault.'

She shakes her head. 'Rory and I both knew exactly what went on in this house and we stood by and let it happen for years. If anyone's to blame, it's us. And Marcus, he was... broken, thanks to that feckless father of his. Doesn't excuse him, mind. You might feel pity for the boy, but not for the man he became. His death is no loss. And Alana is safe now. So maybe it was meant to happen. You were meant to find her.'

'Even though Rory paid the price?'

She doesn't answer that, and we sit in silence until the faint wail of sirens pierces the air.

'Time to face the music.' I push myself to my feet and dawdle to the front door, my nerves jangling, images of soulless police interview rooms and sloppy prison food playing on a loop in my head.

'Wait,' Mairead says loudly.

I stop and turn, one hand on the latch.

'Tell them it was me.'

'What?'

'Tell them I threw the acid in his face.'

'I can't, I—'

'Just listen for a minute, will you, girl? I came to the house to have it out with Marcus because I knew he killed Rory, only to find he was keeping you prisoner in his darkroom. We argued. He attacked me. I stabbed him in the leg and threw the acid at him in self-defence. You said yourself the fall was an accident.'

'No, Mairead—'

'I'm seventy. I have advanced lung cancer and I've just lost my only child. If I hold my hands up to assault no judge in their right mind is going to jail me for long. I'll probably get off with a suspended sentence.'

Hope flares, then dies just as quickly. I can't let Mairead take the fall for something I did. It wouldn't be right.

'No, Mairead, it's kind of you but I couldn't possibly—'

'Sweet Jesus, child, will you hush for one minute? I'm doing this, and that's that. You were caught up in a mess that was not of your making. You don't deserve to be punished. You were trying to do the right thing.'

A sharp knock at the door makes us both jump.

'Police,' says a gruff voice.

I take a breath, then another. Mairead stands by my side, gaunt, hollow-eyed but resolute.

I open the door.

63

ALANA

Justin has managed to get me upgraded from coach to first class. I realised when I stepped onto the plane and the pretty, raven-haired cabin manager told me with a wide smile to turn left, not right, after checking my boarding pass.

I thought she'd made a mistake, but I wasn't going to argue. When one of her colleagues showed me to the seat across the aisle from Justin, everything fell into place.

'Fancy seeing you here,' he said, looking very pleased with himself.

'How on earth did you manage that? I only paid coach.'

He tapped his nose. 'There are ways and means when you fly transatlantic as often as I do. I had a guy I know in the departure lounge put the upgrade through.'

'I don't know what to say. It's so generous of you, especially when we've only just met.'

He waved a hand. 'It's nothing. Anyway, I just sold my company for a fucking fortune, remember. I can afford it.'

Now, a member of the cabin crew stops by to refill my glass. According to the tracker app on the in-flight screen, we're almost halfway across the Atlantic. Justin and I have just finished a delicious à la carte meal, a world away from the plastic tray and reheated stodge I'd have been given in coach, and I have changed into my complimentary pyjamas.

'So, tell me, Laura,' Justin says, the Rolex on his tanned wrist glittering under the cabin lights. 'Will you have time once you're back home with your mom to come to dinner with me? I can send my driver to pick you up. Or the chopper if it's easier.'

'I'd love to,' I gush. Perhaps I should be playing it cool, but I never was very good at hiding my emotions. Besides, I know in my gut the feeling's mutual.

The lights in the cabin dim and I slip under the crisp cotton duvet, grateful all over again that I'm not cricking my neck in coach. I can't believe my luck. Who would have thought I'd meet a man like this so soon after leaving Marcus? Justin is thoughtful and attentive. Generous and funny. Not to mention successful and pretty damn easy on the eye. He ticks all the boxes and then some. Marcus's constant belittling and abuse left me a shadow of the woman I used to be, but I can feel myself unfurling in the warmth of Justin's gaze like a hothouse flower in a greenhouse.

I pull on the silk eye mask that came with the cute little amenity kit I was given when I boarded, and wriggle into a comfy position. I barely slept last night and grabbing even a couple of hours now will help. But my mind has other ideas. Even though we're 36,000 feet above the Atlantic Ocean, my thoughts keep drifting back to Cornwall and Merryn's Reach.

Marcus must know what I've done by now. He is a lot of things, but stupid isn't one of them. Laura and I might look identical, but we walk differently, talk differently, think differently. There's no way she could've picked up all my mannerisms and quirks in a few short days.

And there's something else. I can't quite shake the feeling that I'd sensed his presence at home when he was supposed to be in London. I'm an expert in reading him, his mood swings, the subtle signs that his irritation is about to tip into violence. I've had to be. It's lesson 101 in self-preservation for victims of domestic abuse.

And if he was still in Porthmerryn, could he have played a part in Rory's death?

We hit a patch of turbulence and the plane jumps and judders. Knowing sleep is impossible now, I pull my eye mask off just as the seat belt lights flash on.

Justin's coffee cup wobbles precariously on his tray and he goes to grab it, but it topples over, spilling onto his chinos. He swears roundly, then jabs at the assistance button above his seat. No one comes.

'Can I get some help here?' he snaps at the nearest member of the cabin crew, a woman about my mom's age with her hair pulled back in a severe chignon.

'I'm sorry, sir, but the captain has told us to stay seated,' she calls from one of the jump seats a few rows ahead of us.

'I don't care what the captain has told you. I need a cloth. Now.'

I sit up and scrabble around in my bag looking for a pack of tissues. 'Take these,' I say, handing them to him. He dabs at the stain, his lips pursed. I touch his arm. 'I'll help you clean up when we're through this, OK?'

A look of irritation flashes across his face and I find I'm holding my breath. Eventually, he nods and smiles.

'You're right. No point crying over spilled milk – or coffee. They're only Ralph Lauren. I'll have my assistant buy a new pair.'

I nod, but something inside me shifts. Suddenly, I'm back on our honeymoon, watching Marcus snap at the hotel staff every time the service fell even a whisker short of his exacting standards. The way he spoke to the window cleaner, the postman, the waiters at Harbour Lights. Anyone he deemed unimportant.

The way he spoke to me.

I feign a yawn and pull my eye mask back on to give myself time to think. I've spent too long in the company of a narcissist not to recognise the signs. No one does charm better. No one is more attentive, more flattering... until they aren't.

Justin is clearly a rich, successful, powerful man. I might kid myself his laser-focused attention comes from a genuine place but, goddammit, I'm better than that.

What's the point of jumping out of the frying pan straight into the fire?

I cannot, I *will* not, make the same mistake again.

When Justin asks if I'd like another glass of champagne, I pretend to be asleep.

64

LAURA

The interview room at Exeter Police Station is just as I'd imagined: small, beige and functional. A table. Three chairs. Some kind of recording device. Opposite me sit a detective inspector and a detective sergeant from the Devon and Cornwall Police major crime investigation team. DI Rosie Harper is tall and slender with long, ash-blonde hair and clear grey eyes that seem to stare right into my soul. DS Gary Chidwell is short and stocky and brusque to the point of rudeness. An Afghan hound and a pit bull.

'If you could just read through the statement you gave my colleague earlier and sign it, if you're happy,' DI Harper says, pushing four printed sheets of A4 paper and a pen across the table to me.

I scan the statement I gave under caution after arriving at the police station in the early hours of this morning. Mairead and I were brought here after the first two officers to arrive at Merryn's Reach found Marcus's body in the darkroom. Before they came back up the stairs, Mairead had gripped my arm.

'I did it, remember? I came over to confront that bastard about Rory, but when I knocked at the front door there was no answer. I tried the handle and the door was open, so I let myself in. I heard screaming from the darkroom and found him attacking you.' She reached out to touch my cheek gently. 'He came for me, so I stabbed him in the leg with the scissors and squirted the bottle at him. We didn't know it was acid until we saw it chewing away his face. Everything else happened as you described it. He tripped over the filing cabinet and landed awkwardly. We tried to help him, but it was too late, so you called the police.'

'What about Alana? Do I tell them we switched places?' I whispered, one eye on the darkroom door. The buzz of a police radio was just discernible as the officers called for urgent back-up.

Mairead thought for a long moment, her brow furrowed. Finally, she nodded. 'I don't see why not. I doubt you'll be in trouble once the police realise Marcus had been abusing her for years and you were just trying to help her leave.'

So I told the duty DS who interviewed me earlier that I'd come to Porthmerryn on my own after splitting up with my fiancé. How, after seeing a photo of a woman who looked just like me, I'd tracked her down and introduced myself, discovering she was the wife of the photographer Marcus Adams. I described our burgeoning friendship and how Alana had confided in me that she was not just a victim of domestic abuse but was a virtual prisoner in her own home.

The detective, a careworn guy in his late forties, had nodded solemnly.

'Forensics have found a stack of photos of her injuries in Adams's darkroom. I don't like to speak ill of the dead, but the guy was a nasty piece of work. Yet I've checked our records. Mrs Adams didn't report a single instance of domestic abuse in all the years of their marriage.'

I looked him square in the eye. 'To the outside world, Marcus was charming and charismatic, but at home he was a controlling bully who twisted the truth to suit his narrative. He convinced Alana he had half the force in his pocket.' The detective frowned and I sighed. 'You know and I know that wasn't the case, but Marcus had spent years chipping away at Alana's confidence and self-esteem until there was nothing left. She believed every lie that came out of his mouth. Never mind the fact that he tracked her every move. Even if she had managed to call the police, she didn't think anyone would believe her.'

He rubbed the back of his neck. 'I had a horrible feeling you were going to say that.'

I explained how it had been my idea to give Alana my passport and book her a flight to the US.

He'd looked up from his notebook. 'Why swap places and put yourself in danger when you could have driven her to Heathrow yourself?'

'Because Marcus had to believe she was still here, otherwise he might have found a way to stop her leaving. I know it sounds crazy, but it seemed the only solution. She'd tried to escape twice before. Both times, he found her. The first time he poured acetic acid over her. The second time he stubbed a cigar out on the inside of her thigh. No doubt you've seen the pictures.'

'I have,' he said, his voice grave. 'So you decided to switch places. Then what happened?'

'When Marcus realised I wasn't Alana, he dragged me down into his darkroom and locked me in there. I tried to get out but I didn't know the code for the door and my hands were tied and...' I broke off, tears pricking the corners of my eyes.

'Take your time,' the DS said kindly.

'I have no idea how long I was down there. Hours, anyway. Eventually, he came back down.' I bit my lip. 'He flew into a rage when I wouldn't tell him where Alana was and trashed the place.' I'd decided that blaming Marcus for wrecking his darkroom made sense because telling the police I'd done it after seeing red wouldn't help my case. After all, the only other person who knew what really happened was dead.

'Then he... he threatened me with the rotary cutter.' I shuddered.

The DS looked up from his pocket notebook, nodding at my cheek. 'That's when he did that?'

'Yes.' The moment the blade sliced my skin will live with me for the rest of my life. The paramedic who cleaned and dressed the wound told me I was lucky I didn't need stitches. 'Then the doorbell rang. I couldn't answer it, obviously. The next thing I heard was Mairead calling for Marcus.'

He frowned. 'You know Mrs O'Cleary?'

'I met her the first time I came to Merryn's Reach to see Alana, and I saw her son Rory at the house a couple of times.' I didn't mention Rory's part in engineering our meeting. The poor guy had already paid the ultimate price for getting caught up in our mess.

'What happened next?'

'It's all a bit of a blur.' I lowered my gaze and forced my voice to remain steady, conscious that if even the smallest part of my account didn't match Mairead's we were both screwed. 'Marcus was yelling at Mairead, then he went for her. He was so mad I thought he was going to kill her. She stabbed him in the leg with something, I don't know what. But he kept coming.' I lifted my chin and met the detective's eye, holding his gaze. 'She squirted this bottle of stuff in his face. I don't think either of us knew it was acid until we saw what it was doing to his skin. He was stumbling around the room screaming and clutching his head, then he tripped over the filing cabinet and fell. We tried to help but it was obvious he was dead. That's when I called you.'

After I took the duty detective through what happened one more time, he closed his notebook with a snap.

'Are we done?' I asked him.

'Major crime will want to talk to you. They're interviewing Mrs O'Cleary as we speak. Depending on how things develop, we may be able to put you in touch with someone from Victim Support. First, we need to get a clearer picture of what happened.'

I nodded and told him that was fine by me, even though my stomach was flipping somersaults. Major crime sounded so *serious*.

The hours dragged by and I was giving up hope of ever being allowed to leave when DI Harper and DS Chidwell appeared. Markedly less friendly than the duty detective sergeant I'd spoken to earlier, they took me through the events of the night one final time.

I sign my statement and give the two detectives a wan smile, hoping the ordeal is almost over.

'What happens now? Can I go?'

Chidwell the Pit Bull regards me suspiciously. 'You do realise that giving someone your passport is a criminal offence under the Identity Documents Act 2010, and can carry a sentence of up to ten years?'

I gape. 'You're sending me to prison?'

DI Harper takes my statement and slides it into a folder. 'We don't send anyone to prison. A magistrate or judge does that. As I explained earlier, you've been interviewed under caution. Right now, we're going to release you pending further investigation. Once our investigation is complete, the Crown Prosecution Service will decide whether or not you are charged with an offence.'

'Oh.' I shift on the hard plastic chair. 'What about Mairead? Will she be charged?'

'That's not for me to say,' DI Harper says. 'Though we treat acid attacks extremely seriously, even if committed in self-defence.'

'Neither of us knew it was acid. Mairead just grabbed what

was to hand. Marcus would have killed her otherwise. He'd have killed us both!' My voice is rising, and I tell myself to shut up. The less I say, the fewer opportunities I'm giving myself to slip up. To change the subject, I blurt, 'And what about Alana? She's not in any trouble, is she?'

'We'll be contacting our colleagues in America to discuss next steps with regards to Mrs Adams.'

'Right.' I slump in the seat, exhausted.

The DI gathers the folder and her phone and tells me I'm free to leave.

'For now, maybe. But I'm not off the hook yet, am I?'

She eyes me keenly. 'If you're telling the truth, you have nothing to worry about, do you?'

65

LAURA

'You're being released under investigation,' the custody sergeant reminds me, handing over my purse, coat and the pay-as-you-go phone. 'Don't make any plans to leave the country.'

'Chance'd be a fine thing,' I mutter under my breath, joining DI Harper at the entrance to the custody suite.

As she shows me out of the police station, she tells me Beatrice has been located in one of the short-stay car parks at Heathrow's Terminal 5.

'I'm afraid you'll have racked up a hefty parking charge.'

That, I want to tell her, is the least of my worries. My main concern is what happens now. All my stuff's back at the holiday cottage. I'll have to go back for it sooner or later, even though the thought of setting foot in Porthmerryn fills me with dread. I could catch the train to Mum's, but I'm not sure I can face the inevitable inquisition and subsequent assertion that I must have taken leave of my senses. What I want more than anything is to go home to my little flat in Margate, but I can't because I don't live there any more.

I do the only thing I can: head to Gull Cottage. I have

another week before I'm due to check out, which at least gives me some breathing space before I work out what happens next.

Before she disappears back into the bowels of the building, DI Harper gives me the number for a local cab firm, and I spend the twenty-minute journey to Exeter St David's train station staring mindlessly out of the window while marvelling at how my life has managed to unravel so spectacularly in a little over a week.

As we near the station, I lean forwards in my seat.

'How much would it cost to Porthmerryn?'

The taxi driver sucks his teeth. 'You're not going to get much change from two hundred quid.'

I know I should be saving my money for a deposit on a flat but I can't face the train, not today.

'Can you take me?'

'Course I can, love.'

I flash him a grateful smile in the rear-view mirror and settle back in the seat, my eyelids growing heavy. When I wake up, we've reached Camborne and the pips for the five o'clock news are sounding. The pay-as-you-go phone has run out of juice and I'm about to ask the cabbie if he has a lead I can borrow when my ears prick up.

'The body of Cornish photographer Marcus Adams has been found at his clifftop home in Porthmerryn...'

'Can you turn it up?' I say instead, my back ramrod straight.

He stabs the volume control with a stubby middle finger and the newsreader's perfectly modulated voice fills the taxi.

'Police, who've been at the scene since the body was discovered last night, say they are treating the death as unexplained. DI Rosie Harper from Devon and Cornwall Police's major crime investigation team has confirmed that two people are helping police with their enquiries and that as yet no arrests have been made. She urges anyone with information to contact officers.

'Adams was one of the county's finest photographers, and close friend Jasper Trelawney, owner of The Seaforth Gallery in St Ives, described his death as a huge loss to the art world...'

'Know 'im, do you?' The taxi driver is watching me in the mirror. 'A mate used to pick him up from Penzance Station sometimes. Said he was a knob.'

'I did,' I say, giving him a glimmer of a smile. 'And he was.'

* * *

Before long, the taxi is pulling into the car park on the outskirts of Porthmerryn. I settle up with the cabbie, filing my money worries at the back of my mind, and set off down the hill towards Gull Cottage.

This time, I barely register the cobbled streets and pretty terraces, the colourful front doors and occasional glimpses of the sea. My mind is on Mairead and whether she too has been released. She gave me her number before we left Merryn's Reach. I'll phone her once I'm back at the cottage. But as soon as I think this, doubts creep in. What if DI Harper and her pit bull sidekick are monitoring our calls? Would it look suspicious if we talked? Is this what my life will be like from now on: worrying that the police could turn up at any moment and arrest me for killing Marcus?

My plummeting mood sinks further as I pass the gift shops and café. What were Mairead and I thinking? We should never have lied. So what if I was arrested and charged? At least on remand I wouldn't have to worry about not having anywhere to live. And there'd be a trial, an opportunity to convince judge and jury I was trying to do right by Alana, and that although I did throw acid at Marcus, his death was an accident. I deserve a chance to prove my innocence.

I can see Gull Cottage from here, and my heart misses a

beat when I notice a man in dark clothing loitering outside the blue front door.

A plain-clothes detective come to arrest me?

I slow my pace, feet dragging over the cobbles. It'll be a relief, I tell myself. Like pulling out a splinter or a rotten tooth. No pain, no gain. Come on, Laura. You've got this. You've *got* this.

I reach Gull Cottage, the tang of the briny harbour breeze on my lips. Taking a deep breath, I address the man who holds my fate in his hands.

'I think you might be looking for me?' He spins round, and my stomach turns in on itself.

'Vinnie!' I cry. 'What the hell are you doing here?'

66

LAURA

Vinnie and I lock eyes. He drops his gaze first.

'Can I come in?'

I hesitate. After the week I've had, the last thing I need is more drama. But he's come all this way. It would be churlish to send him packing. Besides, I don't have the energy to argue with him.

'Fine,' I say, unlocking the door and shouldering it open. Questions buzz in my head as I trail upstairs. The first spills out before we've reached the living room. It's the same one I asked him outside.

'What are you doing here, Vinnie?'

'I was out of my mind with worry. You call me using some random's phone, sounding weird. Frightened. Going on about telling the police you were at this place called Merryn's Reach if something happened to you. I didn't know what to think. First, your phone's pinging at Heathrow. The next time I look, it's in Boston. Not Boston, Lincolnshire, mind you. Boston, America! What's going on?'

I perch on the edge of the sofa, my arms crossed. Vinnie drops into the armchair opposite me. Dark shadows bruise his eyes and his face is peppered with stubble. He looks shattered. But any compassion I feel is eclipsed by sadness. We were so good together. Why risk what we had for a blonde bimbo like Tammy?

'If I told you, you'd never believe me,' I say finally, sidestepping the question.

He looks as if he's about to say something, then shakes his head. In the awkward silence that follows, I think about Mum, who was left in the dark for most of her marriage, completely clueless that Dad had another family. And I think about Alana, who didn't realise her charming husband was a monster until it was too late. I don't want to be like them. I want to know what Vinnie has done. Pull the splinter out, no matter how much it hurts. At least then I can start to heal.

But it isn't just that. Vinnie deserves a fair trial too. I decided he was guilty without hearing his side of the story. It's only fair I give him a chance to explain himself.

I take a deep breath. 'You need to tell me what happened with Tammy, Vinnie. I deserve the truth.'

He clasps his hands together and nods. 'Of course.' His chest rises as he takes a deep breath. 'She started popping into my office for a catch-up every time she stopped by the surgery. I didn't think anything of it at first, because we were only chatting, and anyway, she knew you and I were engaged.

'Then, about a month ago, she began texting me. Just a few memes to start with, a bit of harmless banter. When they started getting a bit flirty, I ignored them, but that just seemed to make her keener than ever.'

'I don't understand. If you were ignoring her texts, how did you end up having lunch with her?'

'I thought it was a work thing. She said her boss would be joining us, and they had some news on the latest drugs they were trialling. I thought it would be fine. But when I got there, her boss was a no-show and it was just me and her.'

'You could have made your excuses and left.'

'I know. But it was a free lunch. And I guess my fragile male ego was flattered.' He gives me a sheepish look but I'm not ready to forgive him quite yet.

'She kissed your hand!'

'I was as surprised as you, I promise. I've been thinking about it since. Haven't thought about much else, to be honest. I reckon she saw you outside and did it on purpose to make you think something was going on between us.'

I force myself to replay the moment I saw them in the restaurant together, picturing the proprietorial way Tammy picked up Vinnie's hand and kissed it. The challenge in her eyes when she saw me watching. I examine the scene like it's a movie clip, still by still. I have to admit, at no point had Vinnie reciprocated or taken the lead.

'When I saw you outside the restaurant, I knew how stupid I'd been to put myself in that situation. I should have realised she had an ulterior motive. Please believe me when I say I don't care about her, or anyone else for that matter. All I care about is you. But you were gone before I could explain. And at the flat, you were so angry. Understandably,' he adds quickly. 'I knew what you were thinking, that I was no better than your dad, and who could blame you? Then you disappeared to Cornwall without me, and I was worried I'd blown everything. This last week has been the worst week of my life.'

'It hasn't exactly been a walk in the park for me either.' I fiddle with my sleeve, mulling over everything he's said. Vinnie's never lied to me before. He's someone who prides himself on his honesty. He once drove almost twenty miles from our flat back to Canterbury when he realised he hadn't paid for a pair of socks in Sports Direct. 'Suppose I was to believe you, what happens then? We can't just go back to how we were.'

His head jerks back like I've slapped him. 'Why not? I love

you, Laura. I have loved you from the moment we met. And I hope you still love me. Please don't let this be the end of us.'

I chew my lip. God knows I want to believe him. I've met girls like Tammy, who fixate on what they can't have and don't care who they hurt to get it.

'I'll think about it,' I say finally.

He nods briefly. 'Thank you. It's all I ask.'

Over on the kitchen countertop the screen of the pay-as-you-go phone lights up with a message. I jump up and grab it. My eyes widen. It's a text from Alana.

Heard on the news Marcus is dead. Are you OK, Laura? Please tell me you're OK.

Vinnie is watching me expectantly, those clear green eyes of his compassionate. Steady.

'Everything all right?' he checks.

'Depends on your definition of all right.'

He opens his mouth to speak, and I know he's going to ask me what the hell's been going on, so I deflect it with a question of my own.

'When did you drive down?'

'Last night. Grabbed a couple of hours' kip in the car this morning.' He grimaces. 'Sorry, I probably reek to high heaven.'

'You don't.' He smells faintly of his favourite citrussy antiperspirant and his worn leather jacket. He smells of home. 'Have you eaten?'

'Not since yesterday.'

'Want some cheese on toast and a cuppa?'

'Got anything stronger?'

I pull a face. 'I drank all the wine drowning my sorrows. But the corner shop should still be open. It's down on the harbour.'

When Vinnie's gone, I light the wood-burner and busy myself in the kitchen, cutting bread and slicing cheese. I take two wine glasses from the cupboard and set them and a towering plate of cheese on toast on the coffee table with a couple of squares of kitchen roll. It's a far cry from the night Alana came over, when I thought I could win her round with linen napkins and candles, but it feels much more real.

Vinnie appears in the doorway, shrugging off his coat. He pours us each a glass of wine and we tuck into the makeshift dinner, chewing in silence, our eyes on the flames dancing in the fire.

After a while, he sets his empty plate on the table.

'Thank you.' His gaze meets mine and my pulse quickens because I'm pretty sure I know what's coming next. I take no pleasure in being proved right.

'Babe, I think it's time you told me what's been going on, don't you?'

* * *

Even though I'm longing to offload, I hesitate. If I tell Vinnie everything, I'll make him complicit, and that doesn't seem fair. But I demanded honesty from him. It's only right I offer him the same. I reach a decision.

'D'you want the edited or the warts-and-all version?' I ask.

He holds my gaze. 'What d'you think?'

I sigh. 'OK, warts and all it is.'

He listens open-mouthed as I recount everything that's happened in the last week, from seeing Alana's photo to waving her off as she headed for Heathrow.

'You let her take Beatrice?'

'Yup.'

'Blimey.'

His eyes grow rounder as I describe how Marcus came home early and how I thought I'd tricked him, only to discover the joke was on me. Not a joke at all. Bloody terrifying, actually.

'You stabbed him in the leg with a pair of nail scissors and squirted acid in his face?' Vinnie shakes his head and gives a low whistle.

'I didn't mean to kill him. I just wanted to stop him. It wasn't my fault he fell. If I hadn't fought back, he would've—' My voice breaks and Vinnie scoots over and plonks himself on the sofa next to me.

'Hey, it's all right,' he soothes, squeezing my hand. 'You did what you had to do.' His fingers twitch. 'If I were in your shoes I'd have strangled the bastard. So this Irishwoman, Mary—'

'Mairead.'

'Mairead has told the police it was her?'

'I didn't want her to, but she said it wasn't my fault I was caught up in it all. She insisted.'

We are both quiet for a moment, then Vinnie says, 'Who was the text from?'

I show him the phone.

'Block it. Block her.'

'But—'

'She left you at that bastard's mercy and now has the cheek to pretend she's concerned? She can go screw herself. Block her,' he repeats.

On an intellectual level I know he's right. Alana is claiming she's worried about me, yet she was happy for me to risk my life so she could flee from hers. I think back to the morning we met, that instant connection I'd felt with this stranger who looked like me. It hadn't just been our likeness. It had been deeper than that. But where I'd seen her as the other half of me, she'd seen me as nothing more than an opportunity, a means to an end.

My finger hovers over the screen, but at the last minute I shake my head and fling the phone onto the coffee table.

I can't bring myself to cut ties with her. Not yet.

Not when there's still unfinished business between us.

67

LAURA

TWO WEEKS LATER

Margate has never looked more beautiful as Vinnie and I walk hand in hand along the seafront towards our favourite café. I'd craved Cornwall's wild cliffs and craggy shorelines, but the familiar views of my home town – the big skies that once inspired Turner, the curve of sandy beach dotted with dog walkers and anglers, the Edwardian elegance of the Old Town – are a balm to my soul after everything that happened in Porthmerryn.

I have forgiven Vinnie for the thing with Tammy. Was it even a thing? It certainly seems insignificant in the grand scheme of things. A minor wobble that he's promised will never happen again. And I believe him. He's not perfect, but he's not my father.

We drove back from the West Country a week ago. We spent the journey talking – properly talking – about what happens next.

The police investigation into Marcus's death is still in its infancy, but his inquest has been opened and the post-mortem results have revealed he died from a broken neck consistent with a fall.

Mairead rang yesterday to update me.

'Good news. DI Harper says the Crown Prosecution Service feels it isn't in the public interest to press charges, given the extent of Marcus's domestic abuse and our matching accounts of what happened. If they're not going to charge me, they sure as hell won't charge you. So stop worrying, Laura. You and Vinnie need to put all this behind you and get on with your lives.'

Which is why we have decided that we're going to start looking for a house the minute the police investigation is over, and once we're homeowners we'll try for a baby.

'Storm clouds ahead.' Vinnie points to a gathering mass of carbon-grey clouds out to sea.

'Just what I need,' I groan.

As we watch, a shaft of sunlight breaks through. 'An omen,' he says, nudging me with his elbow.

'God, I hope so. I feel sick.'

'There's no need to be nervous. You're going to love her.'

'Easy for you to say.' My mouth is dry, my palms sticky. It's ridiculous to be so anxious. Utterly ridiculous. 'What time did you say I'd meet her?' I ask.

'Ten.'

'So we have time to sit for a bit?'

'Of course.'

We find an empty bench overlooking the choppy North Sea. Vinnie holds open an arm and I snuggle up against him. Margate may be looking her best, but the wind is biting and my cheeks are pink with cold. I finger my scar, a legacy of my week in Porthmerryn. I'm getting used to seeing it when I catch my reflection in the mirror and I suspect that one day I might even like it. One thing's for sure, I'll never be mistaken for Alana again.

I haven't heard from her since that last text. I assume she's back with her mum in sleepy Camden, her marriage to Marcus fading like a nightmare at dawn. Sometimes I find myself wondering if she'll be charged with using false documents or entering the US illegally. Once or twice, I've been a breath away from dialling my old number, just to hear her voice. There's so much I want to say. So much I need to get off my chest. But something always stops me. And, deep down, I know what it is: the fear that I meant nothing to someone who, for a few crazy days, meant everything to me.

Vinnie has offered to buy me a new phone but I'm going to stick with the pay-as-you-go for now. Just in case Alana calls.

In the meantime, I have more pressing matters on my mind. I'm about to meet the woman whose place in my life should never have been in question.

Sam.

I'd made a pact with myself while I was locked in Marcus's darkroom that if I got out alive, I would agree to see my half-sister.

Mum was so overjoyed by this unexpected turn of events that she hadn't thought to quiz me too closely on what exactly had happened in Cornwall, which suited me just fine. All she knew were the barest details: that I'd befriended a woman in an abusive relationship, and things had turned nasty when I'd tried to intervene.

'Dad would have been so proud of you,' she'd said tearfully when I told her.

I'd been about to scoff that I couldn't care less what Dad thought when I realised I couldn't force the words past the lump in my throat.

And now I'm moments away from meeting my sister.

'Come on, else you'll be late.' Vinnie jumps to his feet and holds out a hand to pull me up.

The butterflies are back, worse than ever.

'What if she won't forgive me for shutting her out all these years? What if she hates me?' I wail.

Vinnie wraps me in a bear hug and whispers in my ear. 'She's your *sister*. Of course she'll hate you.' He laughs, and my own mouth twitches. 'But she'll love you too. It's how siblings roll. Everyone knows blood's thicker than water. You might only share genes now, but you'll share memories and experiences too, in time.'

'You're right, Mr Know-It-All.' I break away and set off towards the café, feeling the first stirrings of excitement. Still laughing, Vinnie lopes after me.

'Don't you remember me telling you on our first date that where love is concerned, I'm *always* right?'

* * *

Outside the café, he kisses me.

'Ready?'

I pull a face. 'As I'll ever be.'

'You'll be fine.' He smiles. 'See you in an hour. If you love me you'll get me a pecan brownie.'

I grin back. 'If you loved me you wouldn't ask.'

I'm still smiling as I push open the café door. A pretty, dark-haired woman is sitting at one of the tables facing me. She has Dad's eyes. My breath catches in my throat. She scrambles to her feet when she sees me, knocking the table, and a teaspoon clatters to the floor. She's clearly as nervous as I am, and that steadies me.

'Laura!' she cries, rushing over. There's an awkward moment when I hold out a hand to shake and she comes in for a hug, but I surrender stiffly to her embrace. When she finally lets me go, I follow her to the table.

'Thank you for coming—'

'I'm sorry I—'

We both speak at once and Sam claps her hand over her mouth.

'Sorry. I'm so nervous!'

'Me too.'

'How are you? Your mum told me what happened down in Cornwall. It sounds awful.'

'It was, but I'm fine.'

'Good,' she says. 'I'm glad.'

We fall silent as the waitress appears at the table.

'Another latte for me, please,' Sam says. 'And a slice of that lush-looking carrot cake.'

It's exactly what I'd have ordered. For a moment I consider asking for something else just to be bloody-minded, but I give myself a talking-to, then smile at the waitress. 'I'll have the same, thanks.'

Sam is fishing around in a voluminous handbag. 'I brought something to show you,' she says, pulling her hand out. She turns her fist and opens it to reveal a white shell necklace. It's identical to the one Dad bought me in Porthmerryn all those years ago.

I take it from her and examine the shells and the delicate silver clasp. 'Dad gave you this, didn't he?'

She nods.

'I had one too. Still got it somewhere.'

'He told me you had one. I used to think of it as a link between us. Like a secret badge or something. Silly, right?' She is blushing, colour creeping up her neck to the tips of her ears, just as it does when I'm embarrassed.

'I'm the silly one.' I run a hand around the neck of my sweater, suddenly too hot.

She reaches across the table, though stops short of touching my arm. 'It's OK, Laura. I get it, I really do. Dad let us both down. The way I see it, we can spend the rest of our lives looking back, or we can put the past behind us and start over. And I know which I'd rather do.'

I fiddle with the corner of the laminated menu, flicking it with my thumb.

'You're right,' I say finally.

The waitress brings our coffees. She sets them on the table and tilts her head quizzically.

'Sisters, right?'

I stare at her in surprise but Sam smiles. 'How could you tell?'

'You have the same eyes.' She tucks the menu behind the cruet set. 'I'll be right back with your carrot cake.'

Once she's gone, Sam clears her throat. 'So, are we good?'

If the last couple of weeks have taught me anything, it's that while I was busy chasing a fantasy, the person I really needed was right here all along.

I smile at Sam. My sister. 'We're good,' I say.

68

ALANA

Mom layers sheets of lasagne, bolognese and bechamel sauce with the precision of a surgeon. She never cooked from scratch when I was a child. She was too busy preparing for her next big case to spend time preparing meals for the two of us.

While I might have grown up on a diet of plastic-ham sub rolls and microwave meals, since I've been home she's been treating me like I'm convalescing from some life-threatening disease. Something the heroine in a historic novel might get, like consumption or scarlet fever.

The kid glove treatment started the moment I sat her down and told her the truth about my marriage. How Marcus controlled every aspect of my life. The punishments. The rules. The isolation. The fear.

For a while, she sat slumped in silence, her hands trembling in her lap, her eyes glassy. Then she dragged her hands down her face, ageing ten years in as many minutes.

'Oh, honey, why didn't you tell me?'

I answered as best I could. Explained how Marcus never let me speak to her unless he was there, how I didn't have a cell phone or the WiFi code. How I wasn't sure she'd believe me even if I had.

'Of *course* I would have believed you.'

'Sometimes I didn't even believe myself, Mom. Besides, you were on the other side of the Atlantic. There was nothing you could have done.'

'But you're my daughter. I should have seen what he was really like. The misery he was putting you through.'

Her distress cut me to the quick and I scooted over and drew her close. 'Please don't blame yourself. Marcus was clever. No one knew what he was really like.'

She rubbed her eyes and sat straighter.

'Well, I hope the bastard rots in hell.'

The fact that Marcus is dead is still sinking in. That, after years of physical and emotional abuse, of domination and manipulation, I'm safe.

I finger the scar on the back of my hand, still so pronounced after all this time. I know the emotional scars will be just as stubborn to fade. Marcus spent too long telling me I'm worthless, that I would never survive without him. A part of me will always believe he was right.

Sometimes, I catch myself flinching when I spill a drop of tea or shut a door a little too loudly, bracing myself for an outburst of anger. The response is Pavlovian. Pure muscle memory. The relief he's someplace he can't hurt me any more is tempered by the knowledge that he's in my head and probably always will be.

That's something I'm just going to have to learn to live with.

When I first heard he'd died, I felt like the pretty Hamptons rug in Mom's living room had been whipped from right under my feet. It didn't seem possible. Marcus was like a riptide. Deadly but unstoppable. The idea he could be gone was incomprehensible.

I scoured the internet trying to find out what happened,

gleaning what little I could from UK news reports. His death, the police said, was 'unexplained'. What the hell did that even mean? Died of a heart attack or in an accident? Was he *murdered*? What about Laura? Was she OK? The fear that Marcus might have hurt her consumed me. Sleep was impossible. I was on a constant knife-edge.

Eventually, I found a report that said two people were helping police with their enquiries, though no arrests had been made. I assumed Laura was one of them, but who was the other? I wanted so desperately to call her to ask, but how could I, after what I'd done? I'd left her at the mercy of a madman, knowing full well what he was capable of. There was no way she was ever going to pick up and I couldn't say I blamed her.

In the end, I sent a single text asking if she was OK. When she didn't answer, I took it as a sign that she wanted nothing more to do with me. Instead, I summoned the courage to call Jasper at the gallery.

'Darling, where are you?' he cried. 'Are you all right?'

'I'm back in the States. I'm fine.' I rested my forehead against the kitchen window. Outside, the scarlet, orange and gold leaves of Mom's sugar maple looked like they were on fire. 'What happened to Marcus, Jasper?'

'The police haven't been in touch?'

'No one's been in touch.' I didn't bother to hide my frustration.

'I'm sure they will be. As for what's happened, I'm still trying to get my poor old head round it. Seems Mairead suspected Marcus of being involved in Rory's death and went to the house to have it out with him. There was some kind of tussle in the darkroom and Marcus fell and broke his neck. Your doppelgänger was there. That girl from Kent?'

'Laura,' I said weakly.

'That's the one. Heaven knows how she got caught up in it all, but neither she nor Mairead have been charged, so—'

'Are they both OK?' I blurted.

'Laura and Mairead? Absolutely fine, as far as I know. It's just poor old Marcus...' He trailed off, then uttered a long sigh. 'I'm sorry if I wasn't more help to you, my dear. I know he could be tricky at times.'

Tricky? I wanted to say. Don't make me laugh. The man was an out-and-out psychopath. But I didn't, because Jasper was always kind to me. There was no point sullying his memories of Marcus just to make me feel better.

'It's OK,' I told him. 'Like they say, you make your bed, you lie in it. And I'm sorry, too. I know how fond you were of Marcus. His death must have hit you hard. You were the closest thing to a father he had.'

'Obviously I'm absolutely stricken...' He paused.

'But his work has shot up in value now he's dead?' I guessed.

'Every cloud, Alana, old love. Every cloud.'

We said goodbye with promises to keep in touch. It might be a chapter in my life I'd rather forget, but I know I need to remember, if only to stop myself falling for a man like Marcus again.

The next day, two burly guys in dark jeans and padded jackets showed up at the door, flashing their IDs before I had a chance to unlatch the chain. They were, they told me, federal agents from Homeland Security, and they were here concerning my recent re-entry to the US.

I took Mom's advice and told them everything.

When the two agents finished with their questions, I asked them one of my own.

'What happens now?'

'Our investigation is ongoing. You'll be hearing from us soon, ma'am.'

I have no choice but to wait it out. I console myself with the fact that at least I know a great lawyer.

Mom pours us each a large glass of California Syrah and settles on a stool at the kitchen island. Something's on her mind, I can tell. She won't meet my gaze and her hand trembles slightly as she brings the wine glass to her lips.

'What's up, Mom?'

She looks pained as she runs a hand through her immaculate blonde bob and I feel a flicker of disquiet. Is she about to tell me she's ill? Please, no. I can't lose her too. I take a slug of my own wine, hoping it'll ease my anxiety. It doesn't.

'Mom? What's wrong?'

She finally meets my gaze. 'There's something I need to tell you. Something I should have told you years ago, but the time was never right.' She plays with the stem of her glass. 'It's about your father.'

'What about him?' Dad and I haven't spoken in years. I only know he's in a nursing home because Mom swaps Christmas cards with my stepsister Hannah. 'Is he ill?'

She slides down from her stool to peer into the oven to check on our dinner, a distraction technique if ever I saw one.

'Mom! Is Dad sick?'

'Derek's fine. I'm not talking about him.'

'Then who the hell are you talking about?'

She puffs out her cheeks, exhales. 'Your real father.'

Icy fingertips skitter down my spine as her words sink in. I open my mouth to speak but she holds up a hand to silence me.

'I did meet Derek at that law conference in London all those years ago. But I also met a guy the previous week at a pub in Whitechapel. A lovely guy, actually. Salt of the earth, as the Brits would say.'

My mother is playing with the plain gold chain around her neck. 'We, um, well, we hit it off.' She clears her throat. 'One thing led to another and, oh God, this is difficult. We spent the night together.'

'Where?' I demand.

Mom frowns. 'Does it matter? At my rental, if you must know. The next morning, I asked if he wanted to hook up again. That's when he told me he was married. He wasn't wearing a ring, otherwise I'd have stayed well away. Anyway.' She shakes her head as if chasing the memory away. 'A week later I met Derek at the conference. I guess I was still smarting from my brush-off the week before. Besides, there's something so sexy about an older guy. He was upfront about Carol from the start and I admired him for it. Two weeks after that I found out I was pregnant.'

'Are you telling me either one of them could have been my dad?'

She doesn't answer directly. 'I had a choice to make, Alana. Who did I want to be a father to my child? A guy who worked for a trucking company or a partner in one of the biggest corporate law firms in London? I chose Derek.'

I jump off my stool and stride to the window by the sink. The maple is almost stripped of its fiery orange coat now, its leaves clumping in the gutter in a decaying wet mass. In the space of one conversation my mother has reframed my entire childhood, upending everything I thought I knew. Questions collide in my head like bumper cars on a track, each jostling to be heard, but before I can form a single one, Mom starts speaking.

'Your father – Derek – was the perfect gentleman, as I knew he would be. Financially generous and happy to be involved, however much or as little as I wanted. It was the perfect arrangement. But as you got older, I started noticing things about you. Your eyes. Your smile. That auburn hint to your hair. And I knew you weren't Derek's biological child.'

I stiffen.

'Perhaps I should have done a paternity test, but sometimes it's better not to know. The world is coloured in shades of grey, Alana, honey.'

I shiver. She doesn't know it, but the world she's describing couldn't be further from how Marcus saw things, a man who only ever dealt in black and white.

'If what you say is true, and Derek isn't my dad, what about this other man? The trucker? Does he know he has a daughter? That's if you didn't sleep with any other random men that week?'

Mom flinches but I harden my heart. How did she expect me to react to the news that the man I'd thought of as my father all my life wasn't even related to me?

'I told you,' she says. 'He was married. Anyway, I knew nothing about him. Where he worked, where he lived. I didn't even know his last name.'

'What *did* you know?'

She closes her eyes briefly, then looks at me.

'That he was called Pete, and that he had a wife and a three-year-old daughter. Laura.'

EPILOGUE

ALANA

Dearest Laura,

Nothing I can do will ever truly make up for what I asked of you, or the danger I left you to face. But I hope I can try at least to make things right.

Merryn's Reach is yours now. Do whatever you want with it. Sell it. Burn it. Live in it. Turn it into an animal rescue centre for Cornwall's waifs and strays, if you like.

You gave me a way out when I didn't deserve one. This is my way of saying thank you, no strings attached.

There is one more thing.

When I got back home, my mom told me Derek isn't my biological father. She said there was someone else. A guy she met in London. She never saw him again.

His name was Pete. He worked in haulage. He was married, with a wife and young daughter.

A daughter called Laura.

I thought you should know.

Alana x

I put down the fountain pen, fold the single sheet of paper and slide it into an envelope, then pick up the deed transfer documents I had my solicitor FedEx over from the UK a few days ago.

It's been a couple of weeks since the reading of Marcus's will. He left me everything: Merryn's Reach, a property in the south of France, his body of work and his sizeable investment portfolio. I'm a wealthy woman.

At first, I wanted nothing to do with his money, but Mom put me straight.

'See it as reparation for the years you lost to that bastard, honey. Accept it as your due.'

So I will keep the house in France, his photographic estate and the investments, but there's no way I'm keeping Merryn's Reach. It's too full of bad memories. In fact, I hope I never set eyes on the place again.

Gifting the house to Laura was the obvious solution. Reparation for her, too. Maybe it will help make up for the hell I put her through.

If I'd known what would happen when I first glimpsed her through the window all those weeks ago, would I still have done what I did?

Maybe.

Probably.

I told myself I just wanted to meet her. To see if the resemblance was real. But I was lying to myself, to us both. I wanted her life. I sure as hell wanted out of mine.

Throw a stone in a pond and the ripples will reach far and wide. Who could have predicted that our meeting would have such far-reaching consequences?

Such deadly consequences.

And now, I've done the only thing I can. I've tried to make things right.

I don't know if I'll ever hear from her again.

But I hope, more than anything, that I do.

A LETTER FROM A J MCDINE

Dear Reader

Thank you so much for reading *The Girl in the Window*. I hope you enjoyed it! Maybe this is the first of my books you've read. If so, thank you for choosing it. If you've been around since the beginning, a heartfelt thank you for sticking with me. You are the reason I get to spend my days making up stories!

If you'd like to be the first to hear about my new releases, you can sign up to my newsletter using the link below. Your email address will never be shared, and you can unsubscribe at any time.

www.bookouture.com/a-j-mcdine

People often ask where I get the ideas for my books. Sometimes it's hard to pin down exactly when a premise pops into my head, but with *The Girl in the Window* I remember the precise moment.

We were staying with my mother-in-law in Plymouth when, one afternoon, I was scrolling through Facebook and came across a post about the Canadian photographer François Brunelle.

Brunelle has been photographing doppelgängers from all over the world since 1999 and I was struck by how alike his subjects were, even though they weren't related.

Idly, I read through the comments. Dozens of people had

shared anecdotes about meeting their doubles, but one story in particular caught my eye. A woman was in a bar in Tenerife when she spotted a board plastered with holiday snaps of people who'd visited over the years. Imagine her surprise when she noticed a woman in one of the photos who looked exactly like her. Not only that, the woman was wearing the same outfit she had on that night. She even had the same haircut!

Even though the photo was clearly a few years old, her friends refused to believe she hadn't been to the bar before.

My imagination immediately went into overdrive, because it was the perfect premise for a psychological thriller.

What if a woman walked into a bar and saw a photo of someone who looked exactly like her? What if she sought this woman out – and got more than she bargained for in the process?

Once I had the bones of a plot, I needed to decide where to set it. When my editor, Natasha Harding, suggested Cornwall I was only too happy to oblige. We used to take our boys on holiday to Praa Sands every year when they were little, and I have nothing but happy memories of the place.

Porthmerryn is a fictional village, based (very loosely) on Porthleven, just along the coast from the cottage we used to stay in. Merryn's Reach is also a figment of my imagination, though I can picture it so clearly in my mind's eye, it feels almost real.

Unusually for me, I planned this book in detail before I started writing. Normally, I have a vague idea of how a story starts and ends and dive straight in, hoping the plot will reveal itself to me along the way. Which it always does... eventually!

Having a beat-by-beat outline really helped keep me on course and I finished the first draft in under three months. That's when the hard graft really starts, of course, with rounds of structural, line and copy edits to wade through. But I got there in the end!

If you enjoyed *The Girl in the Window*, I'd be so grateful if you could leave a review on Amazon or Goodreads. I always love to hear what you think, and reviews really do help readers discover new books.

But, please, no spoilers!

I also love to hear from readers, so please feel free to drop me a line at amanda@ajmcdine.com, visit my website or come and say hello over on Facebook or Instagram.

All the best,

Amanda x

www.ajmcdine.com

facebook.com/ajmcdineauthor

instagram.com/ajmcdineauthor

ACKNOWLEDGEMENTS

They say it takes a village to raise a child, and it certainly takes a whole team to publish a book.

I count myself extremely lucky to have the fabulous and talented team at Bookouture helping me get my stories into the hands of readers around the world.

Biggest thanks, as always, goes to my editor, Natasha Harding, not just for her faith in me and my writing, but for her on-the-money editorial insights that make my books the best they can be. Every. Single. Time.

I am so grateful to my copyeditor, Jane Eastgate, and proofreader, Jenny Page, for the care and attention they gave this book, and to publicity queen, Noelle Holten, for spreading the word about *The Girl in the Window*.

A massive shout-out to the rest of the Bookouture family for everything they do for me and my books.

Special thanks to my friend and neighbour, Holleen Wager, one of my very first readers, for generously checking the aviation details. Holleen flies for a living, but any errors here are mine alone – and I may have bent a rule or two to serve the story (like Justin being able to swing Alana that cheeky upgrade!).

Thank you to Harriet Monday for so graciously agreeing to yet another final, final read-through – you're a complete star! I'm also eternally grateful to the bloggers, reviewers and book lovers who take the time to read, review and share my books.

Where would we be without you?

Big thanks to my own family – my husband Adrian and our sons Oliver and Thomas – for all their help and moral support. Not forgetting the cats, Minstrel, Amber and Charlie, who keep me company while I write.

But most of all, thank *you* for picking this book from the millions of others you could have chosen. I hope you enjoyed it!

PUBLISHING TEAM

Turning a manuscript into a book requires the efforts of many people. The publishing team at Bookouture would like to acknowledge everyone who contributed to this publication.

Audio
Alba Proko
Sinead O'Connor
Melissa Tran

Commercial
Lauren Morrissette
Hannah Richmond
Imogen Allport

Cover design
Emma Graves

Data and analysis
Mark Alder
Mohamed Bussuri

Editorial
Natasha Harding
Charlotte Hegley

RAISING READERS
Books Build Bright Futures

Dear Reader,

We'd love your attention for one more page to tell you about the crisis in children's reading, and what we can all do.

Studies have shown that reading for fun is the **single biggest predictor of a child's future life chances** – more than family circumstance, parents' educational background or income. It improves academic results, mental health, wealth, communication skills, ambition and happiness.

The number of children reading for fun is in rapid decline. Young people have a lot of competition for their time, and a worryingly high number do not have a single book at home.

Hachette works extensively with schools, libraries and literacy charities, but here are some ways we can all raise more readers:

- Reading to children for just 10 minutes a day makes a difference
- Don't give up if children aren't regular readers – there will be books for them!

- Visit bookshops and libraries to get recommendations
- Encourage them to listen to audiobooks
- Support school libraries
- Give books as gifts

There's a lot more information about how to encourage children to read on our websites: **www.RaisingReaders.co.uk** and **www.JoinRaisingReaders.com**.

Thank you for reading.

www.ingramcontent.com/pod-product-compliance
Ingram Content Group UK Ltd.
Pitfield, Milton Keynes, MK11 3LW, UK
UKHW011816011225
9290UKWH00031B/208

9 781805 502944